No Longer a Captive

Carol James

T0155356

No Longer a Captive
COPYRIGHT 2021 by Carol James

Cover Art by *Nicola Martinez*
White Rose Publishing, a division of Pelican Ventures, LLC
www.pelicanbookgroup.com PO Box 1738 *Aztec, NM * 87410
White Rose Publishing Circle and Rosebud logo is a trademark of Pelican Ventures, LLC

Publishing History
First White Rose Edition, 2021
Electronic Edition ISBN 9781522303442
T.P Edition ISBN 9781522304173
Published in the United States of America

Dedication

For Mom and Dad, Jimmy, Lauren, and Jordan. Thank you for living out unconditional love and for loving me and each other well.

Acknowledgements

To the patient and perceptive Fay Lamb, thank you for working so hard with me over the years to make my writing the best it can be.

To the talented and creative Nicola Martinez, thank you for your encouragement and your beautiful cover designs. I have been blessed to serve together with you as a part of the Pelican family.

What People are Saying

"Carol James tells beautiful stories that will capture your heart. She has quickly become a go-to author for me, reliable and consistent with a clear message of hope."

~Stacey Weeks, award-winning author of
In Too Deep and *The Builder's Reluctant Bride*

Praise for *The Waiting*: "I was captured from the beginning. I couldn't put it down... I love the characters, the mixture of serious and humorous moments. Carol James did a great job of showing that God loves us where we are."

~Cynthia M.

Other books by Carol James

The Waiting
Season of Hope
Mary's Christmas Surprise
The Unexpected Christmas Gift

1

"So if the Son sets you free, you will be free indeed."
John 8:36

The gravel crunched beneath the tires as Ethne O'Connor steered the box truck onto the shoulder of the narrow country road. Today would be a scorcher. The clock hadn't yet reached nine in the morning, and already the numbers on her dashboard read ninety-two. The birth of another lovely summer day in Central Texas.

The heat waves rising from the pavement in front of her mirrored the waves of nausea that had steadily intensified since she'd left Fort Worth. She shifted the truck into park, flipped on the emergency flashers, and turned the air conditioning on high. Closing her eyes, she pushed her head back against the seat and begged the cold air to rush across her face and relieve her churning stomach.

She couldn't believe she was doing this. One May evening ten years ago, with her suitcase already packed in the trunk of her car, she walked across the stage in the high school auditorium, received her diploma, and made a promise to herself, a vow that had never been broken...until today. Sean's pleading phone call on Monday had changed everything. She was returning home.

The nausea somewhat under control, she shifted the truck into drive, pulled back onto the roadway, and turned off the emergency flashers. One last mile to go. Anticipation was a funny thing. When she wanted something to happen, it took forever to come. If she dreaded an event, it arrived before she knew it. These last several days had gone by way too fast.

Slowing the truck, she turned left and began the journey down a meandering river of asphalt. As she rounded the final curve and her

1

childhood home came into view, she gasped. In the ten years she'd been gone, absolutely nothing had changed. The two-story farm house was still painted white with black shutters. Large Boston ferns hung from under the edges of the front porch and swayed in the ever-present Texas wind. Even the flowers waving in the pots beneath them were the same—purple petunias.

Nine o'clock and no Sean, but she wasn't surprised. Punctuality had never been expected of him. On the other hand, Vaughn had always demanded she be on time. Even early. That requirement had served her well over the years, birthing in her the organizational skills that helped her successfully start and run her business.

She parked the truck at the top of the circular drive, and despite the heat, slipped on her sweater, and inched across the pavement and up onto the porch. She grasped the doorknob. As she expected, it was locked, and she didn't have a key. Years ago, she'd thrown hers away because she would never need it again. If she'd kept it, she could have at least gone inside and escaped the heat.

She turned and walked toward one of the rocking chairs. A forgotten green turtle with a chipped front leg smiled at her from underneath one of the pots of flowers. She picked it up and slid back the door on its belly. A key fell out into her hand. When she was a little girl, she always believed the key was there for Sean and her—in case they got locked out and Vaughn was still at the office. That was certainly one of the reasons, but when she was eleven, she'd discovered another.

She returned the oblivious little turtle to his home and then inserted the key into the lock. Taking a deep breath, she turned the key and pushed the door open. Cool, silent darkness greeted her as she stepped into the spotless—Vaughn would have it no other way—foyer.

She set the key on the console table beside the door and then tiptoed, for some unexplainable reason, further in. She paused and glanced first toward the living room to her right and then toward Vaughn's home office to her left. There was only one choice to make. She headed right and walked to the wingback chair next to the fireplace. Sitting, she nestled into the cushions. She pressed her nose against the fabric. Even after all these years, she could imagine the soft fragrance of Mother's perfume lingering in the ivory brocade.

Heavy draperies hung closed over the living room windows. A shaft of light shot out from the middle space where the panels failed to meet completely and illuminated a flock of dust motes as they floated in the bright morning sun. When she was five, Mother told her the particles were tiny fairies dancing in the sunshine, but they were usually invisible. Only the magic of the sun unveiled them.

One day, Ethne had asked Vaughn if she could borrow his magnifying glass to see the fairies, but he'd refused, saying Mother had filled her head with nonsense. Fairies weren't real.

Turns out, that was one of the few truthful statements he'd ever made to her. She now knew the "fairies" were nothing more than a combination of dead skin cells, fabric fibers, pollen, and dirt. He was right. Nothing magical about that.

As she walked over to the window and threw open the curtains, the fairies disappeared.

"So, the prodigal sister hath returned."

She jumped and spun to face the foyer. Her little brother spanned the doorway. He had grown up. The last time she'd seen him at his college graduation three years ago, he was at that stage where the calendar said he was a man, but his body was trying to catch up. He had certainly filled out, and he now sported a short, precisely-trimmed, chestnut beard. His hair, unlike hers, had deepened from bright copper to rich auburn.

"Sean. You're late," she snipped. This was not the way she'd envisioned their first meeting after all this time. She took a deep breath, reined in her emotions, and smiled. "Or maybe I'm a little early. I have a reputation for that." She pulled him into a sisterly hug.

His grin answered hers. "Early, late, whatever. I'm just glad you came. I was beginning to wonder if I'd ever see you again."

"The road runs both ways, you know."

"Yeah. Sorry." He held up the key she'd placed on the console table. "I see you remembered the turtle. I figured I'd find you sitting on the porch in one of the rockers."

He set a small, black gym bag on the floor. "Where's your

suitcase? Need me to get it out of the truck?"

"I'm not staying here. I've got a room in town."

"Eth, I can see how hard this must be for you." Tears filled his eyes. "Believe me. I know."

He really had no idea. The man he knew as Dad was not the same one she knew as Vaughn.

The doorbell rang.

"Are you expecting someone?"

"Jackson Williams," Sean replied. He swiped away the tears with the back of his hand.

"What's he doing here?"

"He was the one who wanted us to meet today. Just a formality, I'm sure."

Sean opened the door to reveal a distinguished gray-haired man dressed in a blue seersucker suit with a white shirt and butter-yellow tie. No Stetson, no boots. He looked more like an attorney from the deep South rather than one from Central Texas. A brown leather valise hung over his shoulder.

Vaughn's best friend shook her brother's hand and then turned toward her. "Ethne, it's so good to see you again. What an accomplished young woman you've grown to be! I know your daddy would be proud."

Vaughn, proud of her? Definitely not. She offered her hand. "Hello, Mr. Williams. It's good to see you again, too."

"Please let me say how sorry Mrs. Williams and I are about your daddy. Our town has lost a great man. And I've lost a good friend."

No appropriate response would come. She'd lost Vaughn—no, Vaughn had lost her—long before she moved away from home.

Breaking the silence before it became awkward, Sean answered for both of them. "Thank you, Mr. Williams. We appreciate your kind words."

"Well, what y'all say we go into your daddy's office? There's a little chunk o' business we need to attend to." Without waiting for a response, he stepped across the threshold into the foyer and turned left.

As she looked up into Sean's eyes, he shrugged his shoulders. He was apparently as clueless as she was.

Although she hadn't been in this office for years, something was different. She couldn't quite put her finger on what it was, though. The large antique wooden desk and desk chair still faced the doorway. On the wall behind the desk sat Grandma O'Connor's buffet, converted into a credenza by Vaughn years ago. This would make a great piece for the store if Sean didn't want it. The framed originals of all Vaughn's diplomas and certificates and the Hippocratic oath hung on the wall above it.

To her right, floor to ceiling bookshelves lined the wall. Those on the left held his medical and scientific volumes arranged by topic. The ones on the right displayed literary classics arranged in alphabetical order. Despite the warmth of all the wood furnishings, the room was sterile, cold, impersonal. No family photos and none of the trinkets she and Sean had made in grade school as gifts for him were displayed.

Mr. Williams drew back the drapes and opened the louvers of the plantation shutters to brighten the room and, dropping his valise on the top of the desk, made himself at home in Vaughn's chair. He motioned to the chairs facing the desk. "Have a seat. We'll begin in a few minutes."

She followed Sean's lead and sat down. That's what was different. Three chairs faced the desk instead of two. The one from the back corner had been moved up.

The grandfather clock on the wall behind them gonged once for the half hour, and then the doorbell rang. The attorney smiled. "Right on time. Excuse me a minute while I answer that." He stood and walked back into the foyer.

As Ethne looked at her brother, this morning's earlier nausea returned. At least she wasn't alone. "Sean, what's going on here?"

"You got me. Your guess is as good as mine. All he told me when he called was that we needed to meet here today at nine thirty."

As voices from the foyer increased in volume, Ethne stood and turned toward the office door. Mr. Williams was back, bringing with him a tall man with dark hair cut short on the top and even shorter on the sides. Although he was clean-shaven, a heavy beard shadowed his face. He wore a navy European cut suit with a tieless white dress shirt and a pair of tapered brown oxford shoes. Nothing about him was familiar.

"Daniel, I'd like you to meet Ethne and Sean O'Connor."

The tall man held out his hand to her and smiled. His dark chocolate eyes sparkled with life. Heat radiated from his hand as he grasped hers. "Daniel Spenser."

He released her hand, leaned across her toward Sean, and repeated the same scene. "Daniel Spenser."

"Well, now that all three of you are here, we can begin. Please, sit down."

Sean dropped onto his chair, but Daniel stood until Ethne sat, and then he unbuttoned his suit coat and sat in the one empty chair left. The chair next to hers. Whoever he was, he had nice manners. She grasped the edge of the left sleeve of her sweater and eased it back down to her wrist.

Mr. Williams opened the valise, pulled out two file folders, and crossed his arms on top of them. "Thank you all for coming today. I know it's not always easy to rearrange your schedules on such short notice." As he paused, his face reddened. "I'm deeply saddened by the cause of our meeting. Vaughn O'Connor was a fine man and will be sorely missed in our community."

Ethne glanced left at her brother and then right toward the stranger. The brows of both men were knit in apparent confusion. Obviously, Daniel had no more idea what was going on than she and Sean did.

"I am the executor of your father's"—Mr. Williams' gaze moved toward Daniel—"Dr. O'Connor's will. The will is straightforward, so I don't expect any snags in probate. But before I submit it, I wanted to meet with y'all. So, to honor Dr. O'Connor's wishes, I assembled the three of you—his beneficiaries— as soon as possible after his passing."

Beneficiaries? Sean's face registered the same shock that took her breath away. They were Vaughn's only children. At least the only ones she knew of. Her stomach began to churn again as she turned toward Daniel. Surely not. He looked nothing like an O'Connor.

Nothing at all.

Daniel shot up. "Mr. Williams, sir, I think there must be a mistake. I didn't even know Dr. O'Connor."

Mr. Williams stood in response. "Have a seat, son."

As Daniel eased down into his chair, the attorney smiled. "Now, I can see how this is confusing to all of you, but if you'll give me a few minutes, I think I can set everything straight." He kept a matter-of-fact tone.

She'd made a mistake by coming here today. Sean had begged, and against her better judgment, she'd eventually agreed. But she shouldn't have.

Mr. Williams again sat in Vaughn's chair and opened the first file. Even upside-down, Ethne was able to read the words "Last Will and Testament." Then he removed what was obviously some sort of contract from the other folder.

"Rather than take the time to read all this legal mumbo-jumbo, I'll just summarize for y'all. If that's OK, that is."

~*~

Daniel waited for someone to jump out from behind the curtains and yell, "Gotcha." But that didn't happen. The two beside him, Dr. O'Connor's rightful heirs, were in a state of shock. And who could blame them? He was, too. Something about this just wasn't right.

Mr. Williams continued, "Well, Daniel's father and yours went to college and medical school together, and none of you probably know this, but when they graduated, they came here and opened a practice together. They—"

"Vaughn—uh, my father—was never in practice with anyone else," Ethne interjected.

Ethne...what an unusual name. He'd never heard it before. There must be a story there, but if her body language signaled anything, he'd never find out. At least not from her. Her right hand gripped her left forearm and her legs wound around each other, crossing at the knees and then again at the ankles. How did she even do that?

The attorney laid down the contract. Then he reached into one of the manila folders, produced three documents, and slid one copy toward each of the beneficiaries.

Ethne jerked hers off the table and leafed through it. "What is this?"

"As I said, when your father and Daniel's father graduated from medical school, they decided to open a practice together. Each man invested half of the money required with the understanding that if one of them ever chose to leave the practice, the other could buy him out."

Daniel drew his copy of the contract across the glossy surface of the waxed desktop and glanced over the first page. The language was standard legalese. *Party of the first part, party of the second part. Hitherto, henceforth, herewith.*

But Mr. Williams was right. This was not the time and place to read it line by line. He'd look over it later when he got back to the hotel. There was only one thing he wanted to see right now. He flipped to the last page, and there it was—Dad's signature right next to Vaughn O'Connor's. Whatever the terms of the contract were, Dad had agreed to them.

"Y'all turn to page two and go down to clause nine," the attorney continued.

Papers rustled as all three did what he asked.

"Basically, this says that if either party left the practice, the other would have the option to buy his interest in the partnership."

The attorney paused for effect to let his words sink in as if a jury had been sitting along the side wall gathering information to render a verdict.

"Well, Daniel's dad met this cute little filly, married her, and decided to move to Fort Worth."

Daniel had grown up in Fort Worth.

"And, they hadn't been in practice long enough for your daddy— Ethne and Sean—to have earned enough money to buy out Daniel's dad. So…" He reached into the valise again and produced an envelope. "Your daddy, Daniel, basically let Dr. O'Connor have his half of the practice with the understanding that he would pay him back when he could."

The only sound in the office was the crackle of thirty-something-year-old paper as Daniel accepted the envelope from Mr. Williams, removed the folded page, and read it. Yes, that's exactly what the letter said. He handed it to Ethne. She glanced over it and then passed it to Sean.

"So, long and short of it, Ethne and Sean, your daddy never paid off Daniel's daddy. And, Daniel, to right that wrong, Dr. O'Connor named you as one of his beneficiaries." He held up the will. "His wishes were that you inherit one third of his estate."

2

Ethne hadn't been in The Perks in years. The last time was the week before graduation when she was studying for her final in senior English. But the place hadn't changed a bit. The decor was timeless. Warm wood-paneled walls enclosed intimate seating areas composed of booths, tables, and overstuffed chairs. The soothing aroma of coffee radiated from every inch of the café.

Her favorite spot had always been one of the leather chairs next to the rustic stone fireplace at the far end of the room. In the turmoil that had been her life, this place, with its warm atmosphere and serene classical music, had brought her peace. Today, though, the fireplace was dark and cold. Even with air conditioning, the Texas summer temperatures were too hot for a cozy fire.

"Well, that was a shock." Sean set the tray on their table and then slipped into the seat across the booth from her.

Just another one of Vaughn's little secrets. "Thanks, Sean." She picked up her iced coffee as he grabbed his latte and set a plate of scones onto the table. They looked delicious, but her stomach still churned from the meeting at the house.

Sean's voice pulled her back to reality. "We could contest if you want."

"What?"

"The will. We could contest it." Sean shoved half a scone into his mouth. "These are great! You should try one," he mumbled.

Ethne, take small bites and never speak with your mouth full. Apparently, Vaughn's rules applied only to her. "No, thanks. Why would I want to?"

"Because they're great!"

"No, not the scones. The will. Why would I want to contest the will?"

Sean shrugged. "Simple math. One-half is more than one-third."

"You heard Mr. Williams. Vaughn made sure everything was in good order. The will should sail through probate. And if all you're interested in is money, you'd probably lose any potential gain, or more, to attorneys' fees. Not worth it."

She would never contest the will. She didn't care about his money. The idea of accepting anything in death from a man who gave her nothing in life repulsed her.

Plus, Vaughn was like a local celebrity, and the last thing they needed was some sort of scandal attached to the O'Connor name. If it somehow made the news, it could damage her business. "Besides, right is right, and it isn't Daniel Spenser's fault our father failed to live up to the commitment he'd made." A life-long pattern.

Sean washed down the last bite of scone with his coffee. "Just checking. Glad to see we're on the same page." He stood and waved toward the door. "Dr. Lewis just walked in."

She looked over her shoulder and saw the man who'd been more than a pastor to her. Josh Lewis had been the father Vaughn O'Connor never was. The month after Mother's funeral, he'd invited Ethne to come to the church office to help his secretary for a few weeks by doing some mundane clerical chores. Vaughn agreed, and Ethne was grateful for anything that got her out of the house.

Those weeks grew into months and then into years. Working at the church was the only job she had before she left for college. Even though Josh may not have realized it at the time, he had done more than occupy her time. He'd rescued her.

He'd aged since the last time she'd seen him on the night of her graduation. The hair that had been salt-and-pepper ten years ago was now completely silver. His eyes, though, had not changed one bit. They were still the most piercing shade of blue she'd ever seen—like the Texas sky on a crisp January day.

He waved and began the short walk from the counter to their table. She bolted out of the booth and into the waiting fatherly hug. She missed him more than she'd realized.

"Ethne," her pastor said. "It's been way too long. What a lovely young woman you've become."

The first few months after she left Crescent Bluff, she either called or e-mailed him every week—sometimes both—and many times more often. But as the time passed and the living of life intervened, the communications became fewer and fewer. He'd call and leave a message, but oftentimes she'd be too busy and forget to call him back. He'd understood she was ready to break away, so he'd given her some space.

"Josh." If she said any more, the dam of control might crumble and the tears burst through. Of course, this was an appropriate time for tears. No one would fault her for crying over Vaughn's death. That, although incorrect, would be the assumption. She hugged him and sat back down.

Josh turned toward Sean. "So, Coach, how's that new job going?"

"Great! All predictions say we'll take state. Pre-season practice starts in two weeks, so we'll see."

After the two men shook hands, Josh took a chair from the table across the aisle, pulled it up to the end of the booth, and sat down.

"Really sorry about your father. I'm sure it's a shock to you just like it was to the rest of us. He'll be missed."

"Thanks, Dr. Lewis," Sean answered for them.

"The memorial service is tentatively set for ten o'clock Saturday morning. We scheduled it then so most of the town could attend. I hope that's OK with you, Ethne. I imagine Saturdays are busy days for you."

She nodded. Alicia was more than capable of managing the store for the next few days. Besides, her plan was to turn this time away into a business trip. That's why she'd brought the truck. "It's not a problem. I've got a responsible partner."

"I'd expect nothing less from you." The preacher smiled and patted her hand. "One of these days soon, Hope and I need to come up and pay you a visit. She's remodeling the guest room, and she's looking for an antique chest."

"I'd love that," she replied. And she would. "We could have lunch or dinner together."

"Perfect. We'll do that soon, but right now, we need to talk about the memorial service. Do y'all have any special requests? Anything you'd like to be done? Or not done?"

She and Sean shook their heads in unison.

"Would either of you like to say a few words?"

She grasped her forearm. "No." She wouldn't. Couldn't. The father she knew was not the same man the town loved.

Josh turned toward her brother. "Sean?"

Tears glistened in his eyes. "I don't think I could get through it."

He placed a hand on Sean's shoulder. "No need to even try. Just thought I should offer. But with your permission, I'd like to open it up to the congregation. Your father meant so much to so many people. I'm sure some of his friends and patients would like to speak or share stories."

"That would be great," Sean replied.

"OK with you, Ethne?"

Her immediate reply was a simple shrug of her shoulders. She wouldn't even have agreed to come today except for Mother—for the sake of her memory. What people thought of the family, the O'Connor name, had always been important to her. So, to honor Mother, Ethne had come, and to honor Mother she would play the part.

"You know," Josh continued, "your father was a pillar of our community. He did a tremendous amount of good, and people loved him for that. But, like all of us, he had his flaws. He tried but fell short of the mark and needed forgiveness and a second chance."

Or third, or fourth, or fifth, or… How many was enough?

Seventy times seven. The words rang in her heart.

Yes, seventy times seven. And she had tried to forgive him time and time again. But forgiving him didn't mean she had to continue to place herself in the path of his flaws. What was that verse in the Bible about being as shrewd as a snake and as innocent as a dove? Even snakes would slither out of the way of danger rather than confront it, if at all possible. And that's what she did. She'd gotten out of the way.

She'd left.

~*~

The cry of the mourning dove calling its mate moaned above her head. She usually heard their sad song in the early morning. Never had she heard it this close to noon. But if a mourning dove was singing off schedule, the appropriate place to do so was here…in a place of mourning.

Her family's plot lay on a slight rise under a clump of live oak trees. Sean rejected the invitation to accompany her, and maybe that was good. She could stay however long she wanted. Or didn't want.

A large granite monolith toward the back was inscribed with "O'Connor" at the top and then Grandpa's and Grandma's names — Vaughn Patrick and Ethne Claire. The birth and death dates chiseled below ineffectively sought to describe their lives. Nothing about the cold stone spoke of the warmth of their home, the laughter caused by Grandpa's ridiculous jokes or by Grandma's blanket-warm hugs. Memories. The only souvenirs she had.

In the foreground was another, smaller headstone also chiseled with the O'Connor name. "Mary Elizabeth" was carved on the right side. The span of numbers denoting her life totaled only nine years more than Ethne's present age. According to the death certificate, Mother had died from an aneurysm, but the doctor was wrong. Her life had been stolen by a broken heart long before the burst blood vessel stilled her breathing.

The blank space on the left of the same headstone would soon bear the name "Vaughn Patrick, Jr." — after his medical school returned the cremated remains. Even in death, the world would see only the air-brushed picture of their lives. As Mother had always wished, and would have wished now if she were here, no scandal would be attached to the O'Connor name.

To the right of Mother was the smaller marker of her older brother, Vaughn Patrick O'Connor, III — his life a mere number of days rather than years. This was the first-born son Vaughn had always wanted but then lost. The son she had never been and never could be. The son he had punished her for not being.

She'd moved away from home to gain freedom, but all she really achieved was separation. Even after all the years and all the trying, freedom still eluded her.

The dove moaned again, and then a distinct whistling sound rose from the top of the live oaks as it flapped its wings and soared upward and away. Like her, it had not found what it was looking for in this place. Like it, she, too, would leave.

Maybe another day. Maybe another place. Or maybe never at all.

3

Ethne stood sandwiched between Josh and Sean, insulated on both sides. The three of them were stationed at the main doors of the sanctuary, allowing those who attended the memorial service to express their condolences as they left. She had shaken what felt like thousands of hands, but it was really only a few hundred, and the end of the line was no longer wrapped around the building.

Josh played the role of her "handler." Occasionally, he prompted her with comments like, "You remember the Smiths." She may as well have been the Queen of England or some famous politician.

Transporting Ethne back in time, the distinct flowery fragrance of a particular perfume announced the next mourners. She'd been eleven years old and lying sick in bed the first time she'd smelled the scent.

"You remember the Porters." Josh's left arm encircled Ethne's shoulders, protecting her, supporting her.

Yes, she couldn't possibly have forgotten them. "Of course."

Mr. Porter took her hand and spoke as his wife sobbed silently at his side. "We sure were sorry to hear about your daddy. He was a fine man, and Rebecca and I thought the world of him."

Ethne had known that for a long time. She looked deep into Rebecca's eyes and saw pleading, fear. She could say so much, but she wouldn't—for the sake of Mother's memory. For the family's name. Besides, what good would it accomplish? "Thank you for your kind words, Mr. Porter. My father meant a great deal to many."

Mr. Porter placed his arm around his grieving wife and ushered her away. Did he know? Did he share the secret? And how many others of these who had attended shared a similar secret? The next person needed no reminder from Josh. "Molly…" Suddenly tears that had remained in check washed away any other words she wanted to speak.

"Ethne."

She melted into her friend's embrace as memories flooded her heart. After Mother's death, Ethne spent almost every Friday night at Molly's. Her best friend's house was the safe harbor in the midst of life's storms. An escape. A place where she dared to have hopes and dreams for her future. "I'm so glad you came. I hoped you would."

"And I hoped you would, too." Molly smiled. "I'd love to catch up, but Adam's got the girls, and I promised him I'd be home in time to feed the baby. How long are you going to be in town?"

"For about a week."

"Maybe we can get together for lunch."

As she nodded, Ethne grasped Molly's hands. "Sounds great. I'll call you."

Molly pulled her into another embrace. "I better move on. I'm holding up the line."

That was just fine with Ethne—the holding up, not the moving on. She loved Molly, and leaving her had been the hardest part of moving away. But life had placed them on different roads, and the ten years that passed since they last saw each other felt like an eternity. Their parting was no one's fault, really. Just the unexpected turns of unpredictable lives.

She let go of Molly and turned back toward the doorway. The next visitor came into view. He'd been waiting patiently, quietly. Today he wore a white shirt, gray slacks, and navy blazer, red tie, and black tassel shoes. His shoulders were back, and he was taller than she remembered. *Stop slouching, Ethne. People will think you're weak or ashamed of something. Stand up straight.* He must have gotten the same admonition from his father she'd heard a million times from Vaughn.

She straightened her shoulders and shook down her left sleeve. "Hello, Daniel. Thanks for coming."

His handshake was firm, but his eyes were tender. "I hope you don't mind. My dad would've been here if he could have. So I wanted to come in his place."

"That's very thoughtful of you."

"Daniel, good to see you." Sean said more than the quick "Thank you for coming" he'd given to everyone else. The two men shook hands.

Surprise covered Daniel's face. Or maybe it was relief. "Thanks. I, um, have a favor to ask of you both. I'm going to be in town for a few more days, and I'd like to get together and talk over some stuff. Maybe I could take you both to dinner one night soon?"

"Sounds great. How about tonight?"

What was Sean thinking? This had been an emotionally exhausting day, and it was barely noon. Her agenda included nothing more than sequestering herself in her room all afternoon with a book in hand. And if a nap interrupted her reading, she wouldn't fight it. But now he'd agreed to dinner. And with a complete stranger.

As Daniel grinned, his eyes sparkled. "Tonight's perfect. There's this little Tex-Mex restaurant on the square. We could meet there about seven, if you don't mind."

"Nacho Mama's. Sounds good to us," Sean replied. "Right, Eth?"

She stared back into Daniel's chocolate eyes. They truly were the color of chocolate kisses. When they were warm and creamy and shiny. She could almost smell the rich deliciousness.

"Eth?" Sean's insistence jerked her out of her thoughts.

"No." Her face burned. "I mean, not no, but no, I don't mind. Yes…of course we could do that. The three of us. Have dinner. Tonight, at seven."

Daniel grinned. "See you then."

As Daniel left, she turned back toward Josh. A smirk blanketed his face.

"Why're you laughing?"

"No reason. No reason at all."

~*~

Even though the restaurant sat just across the square from the inn, Daniel left ten minutes early. He'd been lying on the bed and channel-surfing, ready to go since about six thirty. That's one thing his years in the Air Force had done for him. He was never late. Most of the time early, but always, always on time. The directions his GPS gave the other day had been wrong, and he'd barely made it to the

O'Connor house for the meeting with Jackson Williams. But he had made it, and he hadn't been late.

He walked across the green area of the city square beneath a group of live oaks whose branches, spanning from tree to tree, made a canopy. The shade provided protection from the evening summer sun.

The restaurant didn't look busy enough to have a wait, so there was no need to go inside and put his name on a list before the others arrived. He sat on a bench across the street from the entrance. These last few days since the meeting at Dr. O'Connor's house had been spent in prayer, and yet he still had no clear feeling about how to proceed. But he had to do something. Time just to trust.

"Hello."

He knew, or at least was acquainted with, only one woman here in town. As Ethne rounded the bench and came into view, he stood. "Hi. Where's Sean?"

"Oh, he'll be along. He runs on SST—Sean Standard Time."

He chuckled in response, and although she had a smile on her face, her eyes were a lifeless gray. But why shouldn't they be? Her father had just died. "Thanks for coming."

"You're welcome. Sorry for all the babbling earlier. I'm pretty much brain dead."

"That's certainly understandable. I remember when my dad died. Grief really takes its toll. I'm sure you're emotionally and physically exhausted."

She looked at him as if he'd spoken to her in Japanese—as if she heard the sounds of the words but had no clue to their meaning. Better change the subject. "Do you want to go on into the restaurant or wait here for Sean?"

"It's nice out here." As she sat on the other end of the bench, the decision was made.

"Not too bad." He dropped back onto his seat. The evening song of the cicadas filled the conversational void between them. The seconds passed, and the silence grew uncomfortable.

"So, Ethne, what do you—"

"Tell me about your—" She'd spoken over him. She smiled.

"Sorry. Go on."

"Ladies first, as they say."

"OK. So, Daniel, tell me about yourself."

Not a lot to tell. He'd been driving along the path of life, making headway toward his goals, when suddenly he turned a corner and the bridge ahead was out. No way to get over to his dreams on the other side. "I just got out of the service and was on my way back home to Fort Worth when Mr. Williams contacted me. So I took a detour, and here I am."

As her face registered politeness rather than interest, she nodded her head. "And what's in Fort Worth, besides your family?"

"No family. Only an empty house. My dad passed away a couple of years ago, and my mom's working overseas with a mission organization. She'll be out of the country for at least another year." She was looking at something other than his face. Sean? An escape route?

"Where is she?"

"If I tell you, I'll have to kill you."

Her gaze returned to his, and she smiled. "Hmmm, not sure I'm that curious."

At least he'd gotten her attention. "Just kidding. She's teaching English to high school students in China. How about you? What do you do?"

"I own a couple of stores in the Fort Worth area. Resurrections."

Of course. "I just saw an ad on TV. Used furniture, right?"

"Kind of. A little more than just used. We take old furniture pieces people no longer want—items that have often been discarded—and give them new life. Resurrect them, in a way."

"Awesome. I like that. It's kind of anti-establishment. We live in such a throw-away society."

"You're right. Just because something's old or used doesn't mean it's lost its value." Her eyes sparkled to life, and the tone of her voice intensified. "I love setting the true personalities of these old pieces free and making them everything they could have been all along. It's really satisfying. Although, we've gotten so busy, I don't have the chance to put my hands to the sander and paintbrushes much anymore. I mostly do paperwork and go around and find new pieces. In fact, I'm headed out to a flea market near Round Top when I leave here."

"You enjoy your work. I can tell." He smiled.

She looked right in his eyes and smiled back. "Yes, I do. Funny how life takes you places you would have never dreamed of or planned."

"Yes. Funny. Surprising." Very surprising. Her passion brought her whole face to life. Her cheeks flushed pink, and her eyes sparkled like the emeralds in Mom's anniversary ring. She was beautiful. Time to move on before she caught him staring. "So, Ethne, tell me about your name. I've never heard it before."

As the smile disappeared, the gray shades dropped back down over her eyes, and she fingered the edge of the sleeve of the sweater-thing she was wearing and pulled it downward. Then she grasped her left forearm just as she had the other day at the meeting with Jackson Williams. "I'm named after my grandmother. Ethne Claire."

"Oh." That was an underwhelming and uninformative response, but as her legs again wound around each other, her body language confirmed that was all he would get.

Sean materialized at the end of the bench and tousled her hair. "Ethne's Celtic for fire."

"Stop it, Sean." She jumped up and ran her fingers through the fiery mane, obviously trying to tame it.

"Can you see why?" Sean teased.

Still arranging her hair, she continued, "I can't believe you, Sean. We're not in grade school anymore."

No, she sure wasn't.

~*~

The guys were seated at a table facing each other in the far corner of the restaurant. So Daniel had been in the military. Now Ethne could see it—the short haircut, the rod-straight posture. She should have figured that out the first moment he'd stepped into Vaughn's office, but she'd been too surprised and confused for the clues to sink in.

She made her way from the restroom and slipped into the empty chair between them.

Sean spoke first. "So, looks like you were able to get your hair back under control. No harm, no foul?"

"No harm, no foul." She glanced toward Daniel.

He jerked his gaze away from hers and pasted it onto the orange paper placemat in front of him. His face was red. It wasn't hot in here. In fact, she was glad she had her sweater. She'd have been freezing without it.

"Server's come and gone. Food should be here soon." Sean scooped some salsa onto a tortilla chip and shoved it into his mouth. "S'great. Best salsa around." He went back for more. "Try some, Daniel."

Daniel shook his head. "Maybe in a minute."

The awkward silence from earlier when she and Daniel sat outside on the bench returned, but only two of the three seemed to notice. Sean was a one-man, chip-devouring machine.

Finally, as Sean paused for a drink and the crunching stopped, Daniel began. "Thanks so much for coming tonight. Especially on such short notice. I really wanted to talk with you both as soon as possible."

So, the invitation tonight was for more than a simple social time—a bonding time—for the beneficiaries of Vaughn O'Connor.

Sean pushed the chips and salsa to the side. "Shoot."

"I've done a lot of thinking and praying over the past couple days. Your father was generous and more than fair, but I don't care what his will says, I can't accept anything. I don't deserve it. Everything's yours."

Silence hovered over the table as a young woman with long, brown hair pulled back into a ponytail placed the food before them and refilled their water glasses. "My name's Leeza." Her nametag read Liza. "Let me know if you need anything else."

As she left, Sean muttered under his breath, "Maybe a phone number."

"Sean!" Ethne's whisper scolded.

"What? She's crazy cute. Um-hmmm."

Ethne shook her head and turned back toward Daniel. "I'm sorry. You were saying?"

"You two are the rightful heirs. Not me. I want to get this ironed out before our next meeting with Mr. Williams. I don't figure that's the time and place to rock the boat."

Sean winked at her. "Hey, dude, Eth and I have already talked about this. Our father wanted you to have part of his estate, and we do, too. It was important to him to fulfill the obligation he had to your family. And we want to do everything we can to honor him and his wishes."

Who are you to question me? Honor your father!

"It just feels wrong," Daniel replied.

How many people would have fought for their share out of greed? And yet, the fact that he fought to surrender his spoke volumes about his character. "It may feel wrong to you," Ethne replied, "but it's not. My father made a promise. A promise Sean and I intend to keep. The wrong would be in our not doing so."

Despite their words, the struggle still blanketed his face. He was obviously an honest person, a nice person. And a very handsome man. From the little she knew of him, he'd be a good catch—if someone was looking. But she wasn't. She'd already broken one of the promises she made to herself when she left Crescent Bluff, and nothing would make her break the other. Besides, maybe he'd already been caught.

"Case closed?" Sean smiled and then motioned toward Liza. He winked at Ethne. "Game on."

4

This time, when Ethne stepped into the foyer, she was not alone. At the meeting in his office this morning, Jackson Williams suggested an estate sale might be the best way to divide the physical assets—whatever they were—among the "beneficiaries." They could use the proceeds, along with any insurance money to pay off outstanding debts, and then the rest would be divided equally. When he said he knew a company that would organize and oversee the sale for a reasonable percentage, she and Sean quickly agreed. Daniel, though, sat silent.

Each of them was armed with a stack of sticky notes. Hers were shocking pink, Sean's canary yellow, and Daniel's were fluorescent green. Their mission was to lay claim to whatever they wanted to be held aside for themselves by placing their colored squares on the items. This wouldn't take very long—at least not for her. There wasn't much she wanted. Grandma's buffet in Vaughn's office, and maybe her old bedroom furniture. The four-poster bed, chest, dresser, and nightstands had been Mother's when she was a little girl, and they'd been passed down to Ethne. The set was solid wood and was a perfect candidate for Resurrections. Plus, Sean wouldn't want any of those items.

"Hey Daniel, I'm going out to the shed," Sean announced. "There's some great old tools out there. Wanna come?"

"No, thanks. I'll, uh, just go sit on the porch." Not waiting for a response, Daniel set his stack of sticky notes on the table in the foyer and strode out the front door.

"Did I say something wrong?" Sean shrugged. "He's a guy. I thought he might want some tools."

"You go on. I'll talk to him."

Daniel sat in one of the oak rockers and stared back toward the road. She eased into the chair next to his. "Sean didn't mean to upset or offend you. He just thought you'd be more into tools than furniture."

"It's not that."

She was pretty sure she got it. He'd tried to play along just because he thought he should, but he was an outsider, and it wasn't working. "I think I understand. I haven't been home in ten years, and even though I grew up in this house, I feel like an intruder myself. You don't have to claim anything if you don't want to. But you are starting a new chapter in your life, and maybe you could find some things you could use. Even if it's only temporary."

"A new chapter... Maybe I should go back a few pages," he continued, but his gaze never found hers. "When I joined the Air Force, I was so positive that's what I wanted—a life of service to my country. But after six years, that assurance is gone. I prayed about it and felt it was time for something different, so I decided not to reenlist. And here I am...free, but things aren't exactly working out like I thought they would. A few months ago, everything seemed so black and white. But now..."

She got that, too. "Things don't always turn out like we think they're going to. But there's always the possibility they'll work out better in time." Listen to her—suddenly the optimist. But it was true. Her life today was much better than it had been when she'd left home. Not perfect, certainly, but so much more than she imagined.

"Maybe."

"So what is it you left the Air Force to do?"

"I'm a physician."

A huge weight thudded against her chest. "A doctor. I didn't know. Mr. Williams never said you were Dr. Daniel Spenser."

For the first time since she came out onto the porch, his gaze met hers. "Doctor, Captain, whatever. It's just a title. It doesn't change who I am."

Well, he was certainly right about that. Nothing he could do, no title he bore, no amount of education he had acquired could change one fact. He was a man. Being a doctor was simply the warning label on the package. "So, Dr. Spenser, what did you imagine happening when you left the Air Force?"

"I wanted to move back home and practice family medicine. You know, really get to know my patients. Build relationships with them. It's not that easy in the military. People are transferred from one place to another all the time. You begin to get to know them, and then they're gone. But in the civilian world, everything's so convoluted now. Medicine's big business. Practices are huge and there's so much red tape to deal with. I just want something small. Personal."

In school, when she made suggestions, her teachers always said she had good problem-solving skills. Vaughn, though, considered her ideas nothing more than an interruption, a nuisance. *Children are meant to be seen and not heard.*

But this was a no-brainer. The solution was as obvious as the purple petunias dancing on the porch in the morning wind. Even Sean would have reached this same conclusion had he been here rather than in the tool shed. "Stay here. I'll be back in a few minutes."

~*~

Daniel stood on the porch as Sean struggled with the keys to the front door. The old brick building had been someone's home a lifetime or two ago. Bouquets of wilted flowers were piled to his left and right, just like images he'd seen on TV when some celebrity had died prematurely. Only to a much lesser degree. But Crescent Bluff was a small town, so while modest by the world's standards, this demonstration of love and respect was every bit as significant as anything he'd ever seen.

The black letters stenciled on the plate glass window to his right spelled out "Crescent Bluff Primary Care." The three-story building stood one block off the old town square—just around the corner from the restaurant where they ate the other night.

This week had been surreal. At any minute, he totally expected to wake up and find out he was stuck in some sort of a strange time warp—just like the characters in those old sci-fi reruns he and Dad used to watch on TV when he was a kid. Yeah, these last few days had definitely been otherworldly.

He probably should have left days ago. He didn't want anything from Dr. O'Connor's estate, so there'd really been no reason to stay. Except that Ethne and Sean had asked, and it had seemed important to them. But more significantly, a quiet, familiar Voice deep inside kept urging him to stay. He'd learned years ago to listen when his Father spoke—even when he didn't understand. Especially when he didn't understand.

Besides, what else did he have to do? His parents' house was empty, and he had no job, so he stayed. Still...the whole situation was weird. Just plain weird.

"Probably need to put some graphite in the lock to smooth it out." Sean turned toward him and smiled. "I must not be holding my mouth right, as Dad used to say."

One more jiggle, the key turned, and Sean pushed open the door. A pulsing beep sounded as he quickly pressed numbers on a keypad inside the door. When all was quiet, Ethne gestured toward the interior of the building. "Guests first."

Daniel stepped through the door and then paused while his eyes adjusted from the blazing brightness of the morning sun to the cool darkness produced by the drawn shades blanketing the windows. Each second revealed a new facet of the old building. Despite the obvious renovations, the bones of the original home stood firm. The waiting room to the right had once been the living room, and the receptionist's area to the left was the old dining room. His heart raced as *deja vu* swept over him.

He turned back toward them and was met with knowing grins.

"Is this small enough? Personal enough?" Ethne lifted her eyebrows to accentuate her questions.

This, yes, this was exactly what he envisioned for his office. But how could they have known? "I...I mean..."

Sean bolted around him and assumed the role of tour guide. "Come on. Check it out. On the left, down the hall is Dad's office and a small lab. On the right are the exam rooms."

While Sean was totally at home here, Daniel was a trespasser. He stayed in the center of the hall, peering into the rooms from afar. He stopped at the door to the office. Nothing was out of place—no partially completed paperwork spread over the desk waiting for the occupant's attention the following day. All loose ends were tied up, as if Dr. O'Connor had known he wouldn't be coming back.

Sean pointed to a staircase at the end of the hall. "When Mom and Dad first got married, they lived upstairs, so there's a full three-bedroom apartment on the two upper floors. Wanna go see it? It needs some renovating, but it'd be great for you."

Daniel's thoughts bounced around like ping-pong balls. Before he could return one, another flew his way, and then another. They were offering to sell him this practice. He could live upstairs to save on rent. How much did they want? He had some money saved. But surely not near enough. Maybe he could get a loan. Maybe Jackson Williams knew a banker who could help. He had to think about it. And pray about it. "I, um… Maybe we can go up later. We need to talk."

Ethne was still stationed in the front doorway with obviously no intention of coming farther in. So he walked back toward her as Sean followed.

"You don't like it." Sean concluded.

"Oh, no. It's not that. I just…" He stepped into the warmth of the sunshine streaming through the open door. "Thanks, anyway, y'all. It's a kind gesture."

Ethne knit her eyebrows together in obvious confusion.

"It's the money," he explained. "I have a pretty good idea of how much a practice like this is worth, and I can tell you, I don't have near enough saved. Plus, I have no collateral to put up for a loan."

She grinned as if she'd just gotten the punch line to some joke. "Dr. Spenser, I took you for a smarter man than that. We're not offering to sell you the practice. We want to give it to you."

"Yeah, dude." Sean laughed. "What will we do with this place? You'd save us the trouble of trying to find a buyer." A sudden gravity replaced his lighthearted tone. "Besides, Dad would have wanted this. I'm sure."

The ping-pong balls flew even faster, and Daniel couldn't connect with any of them. All he knew was this was too much. "Like I said, it's a very kind gesture, but I couldn't—"

Ethne placed both hands on her hips. "Forget about this gesture business. Is this what you had in mind? I don't know all the financial details, but Jackson Williams does. And if you want it, I'm pretty sure he can make it happen. Consider it part of your inheritance."

It was way too much. "Guys, I—"

This time her voice was softer. "Daniel, we're not saying there'd be no debt involved. I don't know the financial status. But isn't it worth looking into before you simply write it off? And you'd be doing a service to the town. They need a doctor."

A sudden peace flowed over him. The ping-pong balls dropped. He had been praying about this for over a year. Not this specifically, but about going into private practice in a small town. And this seemed perfect...if he could raise the money. He'd definitely pursue it. If it worked out, then great. If not, he'd just trust there was something better. God had led him this far, and he had no reason to think He'd stop now.

Trust, Daniel, trust.

Trust he would. "I think maybe I'd like to see that upstairs apartment after all."

~*~

As Ethne stood at the bottom of the stairway, footfalls echoed overhead. She had managed to make it into the building and down the hall. But going upstairs was out of the question. Besides, Sean would make a fine enough guide. He'd been too young to remember much. One of them upstairs would be enough.

"Eth, are you coming, or what?" Sean's voice tumbled down the stairs.

"I'm fine. I'll just wait down here. Y'all take your time. No hurry."

"C'mon," the voice from on high continued. "I told him you could give him some ideas for what kind of furniture he needs and where to put it."

"It's OK, Sean," Daniel replied. "I'm sure she's a busy lady. I can figure it out."

"No, man. She's really good at this. Always has been."

"Oh, Ethne, you've rearranged your furniture again. What a lovely job you've done! I would have never thought to put the bed in the middle of the room. You are such a creative person."

"It looks ridiculous, Mary. Tell her to put it back."

"But, Vaughn, it's her room, and she's just exploring her creativity."

"I don't care what she is or isn't doing. It looks stupid. It's my house, and I'll not have it turned into some sort of disorganized obstacle course. When she pays the bills, she can decorate it any way she wants. Put it back now. Do you understand?"

She'd been so excited to surprise Mother with her new room arrangement that evening. But later, before she went to bed, Mother explained the practicality of having the bed near the wall and the electrical outlets. So they moved it back...to where it had stayed and had still been when she left eight years later. She'd moved other pieces of her furniture many times over the years. But never the bed.

Rebellion overcame her. She would go upstairs. She'd been running away all these years, but now Vaughn O'Conner could no longer dictate what she could and couldn't do. "I'm coming." She scaled the stairs before she could change her mind.

Avoiding the door to the coat closet in the far, left corner, her gaze swept the apartment. The main room was much smaller than she remembered. Still plenty large, just not the cavernous space etched in her memory from when she was five. The dining area was in the far, right corner, and the kitchen was in the left.

"Well, what's the verdict, Eth?" Sean stood with his arms folded across his chest.

"You could put a couch here, a couple of chairs there grouped around the fireplace. Or maybe you'd want a sectional. You could have a small conversation or reading area over by the windows. At any rate, you've got plenty of space to do just about anything you'd want."

They followed her to the kitchen doorway. It was a quaint 1920's design. She loved the old painted cabinets, wooden counters, and black and white tile floor. She'd repaint the cabinets and refinish the counter and floors, but most people would want to gut it. "You'll probably want to update this, and when you do, maybe take out some walls and make the whole area open concept. That's really popular today."

"I don't know." Daniel spoke for the first time since she'd begun her appraisal of the space. "Maybe, maybe not. I kind of like this old stuff."

She turned toward him and smiled. At least they had one thing in common. "Me, too."

He returned her smile, and she tried to look away but couldn't. Some unseen force held her gaze to his. Then she saw something in his eyes she hadn't seen for years. Something she promised herself she would never accept from or feel toward a man. Attraction.

"Told you she was good," Sean said, his voice full of pride.

Without moving his gaze from hers, Daniel replied softly, "Yes. Yes, she sure is."

Swallowing the fear that had risen into her throat, she pried her gaze away and turned toward the stairs. "I think we're done for today."

The door to the coat closet she had worked so hard to ignore came into view. *Spare the rod and spoil the child.* She'd been running away all these years only to discover now the path she was on was nothing more than a huge circle. She was right back where she'd started.

5

Sitting in a booth at WingNuts Grill, Ethne sipped tea and munched on peanuts while she waited for Molly. The restaurant's stark wood and metal decor offered no hint of the jumbled, crowded store that had birthed it.

For as long as she could remember, this building had been a hardware store owned by the Smiths. She'd often begged Vaughn to let her go with him whenever he needed supplies for some home project. Young and blind to truth, she hoped every trip would be the beginning of a new reality. That Vaughn would hold her hand as they walked through the aisles. Smiling, gently leading her to a particular shelf and then patiently waiting while she found the parts he was looking for. Then when they checked out, Mrs. Smith would pull the big plastic bowl from under the counter, and Vaughn would let her choose a lollipop—for being "such a good girl," as Mrs. Smith always said.

But that never happened. Vaughn was always in a hurry with no time to let her find the parts. Instead, her job had been to watch Sean. And while she tried hard to be a good girl, Vaughn always refused the candy. It would decay her teeth. And Mrs. Smith stopped offering.

Instead, when Vaughn was distracted, choosing whatever items he needed for his current project, Mrs. Smith would slip a yellow lollipop into Ethne's pocket—yellow because it wouldn't leave as dark a telltale stain on her tongue as a red one—and whisper, "Sweets for the Sweet. Promise me you'll brush your teeth really well when you're finished."

After they got home, Ethne would steal away to the farthest corner of the backyard to enjoy her reward in secret. Then, she'd brush her teeth just in case Mrs. Smith ever asked. Even today, lemon flavored lollipops were her favorite.

"Ethne, how are you?"

She jumped as a now familiar male voice startled her back to reality. "Dr. Spenser. This is a surprise."

"I can tell. Sorry. I didn't mean to scare you."

He looked neither doctor-ish nor captain-ish today. His previously meticulously styled hair was tousled on top, and he was in a black t-shirt, khaki shorts, and boat shoes—much more casual than she'd seen him before. Even his smile was relaxed. "I was just lost in thought. That's all," she offered.

"How about some company? I'm alone, too."

She folded her hands and placed them on the table in front of her. "Actually, I'm only temporarily alone. Waiting on a friend."

A glimmer of what appeared to be disappointment crossed his face. It was probably pretty lonely being in a town where you knew no one. Or maybe just three or four people. "But my friend is running late, so you're welcome to join me until she arrives."

"Sure." He slid into the seat across from her and set his iced tea on the table. "You were right about Jackson Williams. He knew all the buttons to push. He should have a contract in place before long for me to buy your dad's office. He's working out all the details with the bank, and he's not even charging me for his services. He just keeps saying he's doing it for his friend."

He stretched his hand out toward hers, and the memory of the interest in his eyes from the other day bounded back. She quickly withdrew her hands from the table and placed them in her lap. Allowing him to rest his hand on hers would be overstepping a boundary. The only reason he was sitting here right now was because they'd been thrown together by some weird twist of fate. That was it. They weren't even friends, and things needed to remain that way.

He continued as if he hadn't even noticed her slight. "Everything has fallen into place perfectly, and it's all because of you. So, I just want to say thanks." He quickly flipped his hand up into a handshake position.

Smooth. Funny how a ninety-degree angle could make such a difference in intent. She lifted her right hand from her lap and placed it in his. "You're very welcome. I'm so glad it's all working out."

His hand was warm, and his smile formed attractive little crinkles at the corners of his eyes, his chocolate-kiss-brown eyes.

His voice was soft. "Me, too."

"Well, hello there. Sorry I'm late."

Despite what the clock said, Molly's timing was impeccable. Ethne pulled her hand from Daniel's. "No problem. This is Captain...Doctor..."

He scooted out of the booth and offered Molly his seat. "Daniel. Daniel Spenser."

"I'm Molly Bowen. Nice to meet you, Daniel."

"Same here."

"Molly was my best friend all through school. We haven't seen each other in years."

Daniel lifted a couple of fingers to his forehead in a casual salute. "Well, you ladies must have a lot to talk about. I'll leave you to it. Thanks again, Ethne." He walked away.

Molly leaned forward. "Who in the world was that fine specimen of manhood?"

Years ago, Ethne would have bared her soul to Molly. They'd had no secrets. But time had a way of changing things. And this whole situation was too complicated to discuss with her right now—maybe ever. The abridged version would be more than sufficient. "His father and mine went to medical school together. Daniel just got out of the Air Force and is considering buying my father's practice."

"He might be the one to make you do something none of the rest of us could. Move back." She winked, and then her smile disappeared. "Seriously, I've missed you so much, and with everything the way it is now, you should consider coming home."

And what would she come home to? The situation had changed, but the memories still haunted every corner.

On the many nights Ethne had slept over at Molly's when they were kids, they'd lain awake planning their lives. They'd be roommates in college, and then when they graduated, they'd get an apartment or small house together. They'd even work for the same advertising company. And if they ever got married, it would be long after they turned thirty.

But everything changed the summer before their senior year. Molly met Adam, a Baylor student who was a youth intern at church. Then after graduation the following year, she went away to Baylor while Ethne just went away. And absolutely nothing turned out as they'd planned. Men had a way of messing up things.

"Molly, if all this had happened a few years ago, I might have been able to move back." *Doubtful.* "But too much time has passed, and now I have my business to think of. I can't just pick up and leave it."

"But you wouldn't have to leave it. You could expand. Open up a Crescent Bluff location."

She and Alicia had been talking about the possibility of opening a store in Waco—close enough that whoever managed it could live here in Crescent Bluff if he or she wanted. But the timing wasn't right. They'd have to raise the capital—which shouldn't be a problem—and then train someone to run it. That part would take months. And right now, everything was running along seamlessly with both their Fort Worth and Weatherford locations. Why rock the boat? The timing wasn't right.

Besides, even if all those requirements were checked off the list and the timing was right, she had absolutely no intention of moving away from the main shop. "We are talking about expanding to this area—maybe Waco—but that's a ways off. And if and when we do, I won't be the one to run this location."

"But you could be."

"No, I couldn't…wouldn't."

"But…you could." Molly grinned. "You could, if you would."

This topic was a dead end. "Moving on. How are Adam and the girls?"

~*~

Daniel dropped peanut shells into the empty bucket on his table. He'd moved far enough away from Ethne and her friend to make sure they felt as if they had privacy, but he hadn't been able to move so they were no longer in his line of sight. The restaurant wasn't big enough for that. Fortunately, he was at an angle where he could watch her, but she couldn't see him without turning in his direction.

The past year had been interesting. He'd known for a while it was time for him to leave the service, so he hadn't re-upped. But he had no clue what he was supposed to do next. No matter how hard he prayed, he had no sense of direction. These last months had been like driving down a mountain road that was so curvy he could see only a few feet in front of him, and someone had taken down all the yellow road signs. He had to keep moving if he wanted to get off the mountain. Even when it meant taking his foot off the accelerator and tapping the brakes or letting the car coast slowly because he had no idea what lay around the next curve or even what direction the road would turn.

So that's what he'd done. Kept creeping forward until the last few weeks. And now he was flying down a flat, straight, West Texas highway. The scenery was whizzing by so fast that he was having trouble taking everything in. All he could do was hang on until he came to a stop sign.

In all his time praying about this next segment of his journey, he could never have imagined, never anticipated, or even thought to pray for what was happening in his life right now. The only thing he wanted was to be the best steward possible of this gift that was being presented to him.

Soft laughter rose from the ladies' table and pulled him back into the present. Molly was placing her hand on Ethne's and smiling. Man, he'd almost screwed up that one. He hadn't thought through the gesture before he made it. He came from a family of "huggers" and resting a hand on another person's was generally nothing more than a sign of friendship, of shared experience. But she'd certainly read it differently. And in this day and time, he didn't blame her.

Plus, she was right. Something clicked the other day up in the apartment. He'd thought she was beautiful from the time he first shook her hand in her father's office. Who wouldn't? With her copper hair and emerald eyes, she looked as though she should be hiking the hills of Ireland rather than tromping around Central Texas. But her heart…to want to give him something as valuable as her father's practice, to place another person's contentment above her own, reflected an inner beauty scarce in today's all-about-me society.

Well, it looked as though he might be headed back onto that curvy road again soon. What he'd found at the end of the first leg was more than he could have ever imagined. He couldn't wait to see what might be at the end of this second one. He was so ready for a change.

His phone vibrated, and Savannah's picture popped up. He sent it to voicemail. He'd call her back later.

The calendar on his phone read "May 22." A part of him wanted to laugh. How appropriate she should call him today for the first time in years. He remembered the date but doubted she did.

6

Ethne backed the truck up to the dock door. Round Top had been a goldmine. It was a good thing Resurrections didn't own a semi, or they would have had to rent a separate warehouse to store all the new treasures she would have purchased. As it was, the smaller truck, although filled to the brim, at least provided limits.

That was the funny thing about this business. Sometimes she struggled to discover one thing she could use. Another time she'd find enough stuff to open an additional store. She learned early on, when she found a treasure, to buy it—whether she needed it right then or not. Because chances were, she could never go back and get it later.

She jumped out of the truck and left it for the guys to unload. As she turned the key to the building and pulled open the back door, a beeping tone sounded. Her memory took her back to the porch at the clinic when she'd waited for Sean to enter the alarm code.

Daniel had been so confused, so surprised, by their offer. She was glad Sean had agreed to her idea. After all, by right, half of the practice already belonged to Daniel anyway. The rest of it could have been considered interest for his father's original investment...and Vaughn's failure to live up to his end of the contract. In actuality, Daniel had done them a favor by accepting their offer and keeping them from having either to find another buyer for the practice or to sell off the equipment and any other assets.

The beeping grew louder and faster. She quickly punched in her code before half the Fort Worth police force descended on her parking lot. She breathed in the warm, musky aroma of sawdust and paint. It was good to be back home.

She had done something she thought she would never do and had escaped relatively unmarred. Being in the house and apartment where she grew up had been challenging to say the least, but here she was—safely home in Fort Worth. She'd gone back for Mother and for Sean, and she never had to return to Crescent Bluff again.

~*~

Ethne looked up from the spreadsheet on her computer as Alicia bounded through the door and hugged her.

"Welcome home, Eth. Missed you!" she exclaimed. "How did everything go? I was praying for you." She slipped into the chair facing Ethne's desk.

"Thanks, Alicia. It was interesting…hard, but I made it. We should go out to dinner one night this week, and I'll fill you in on the details."

Alicia was one of the few people who knew the truth. When they'd been thrown together as roommates their freshman year of college, neither one of them would have ever guessed they would end up as best friends and business partners. Alicia had been a safe harbor in the storms of Ethne's life.

"I was going over the sales figures, and I see you guys were quite busy while I was gone."

"I know. Isn't is exciting? The Weatherford store's really starting to take off. Last weekend's promo was a huge success. Your Resurrection Decor-Gestion service was quite the hit." Alicia looked down at her tablet. "We have all our slots filled for the next month. I'll e-mail you the list of appointments and my notes."

Ethne had known offering a decorating-suggestion consultation service would be a good move. They did that with clients inside the stores. Why not go outside? People were always asking for suggestions about accessories and furniture for their spaces. "That's great news!"

"Glad you think so, because, um…" she paused for a second, "you have an appointment today at eleven with a potential client who has a new, empty house."

"Nothing like hitting the ground running."

"I know. He originally visited the Weatherford store, but this location is actually closer to where he lives. And I wouldn't have made the appointment for today, except he was already going to be in town for another meeting or something."

Ethne pulled out her leather padfolio to make notes. "That's OK. Any information I need to know?"

"I'll e-mail you the details. But most important, he's single and handsome—let me rephrase that—unbelievably handsome." Alicia raised her eyebrows and winked. "As much as I wanted to work with him, I figured I better not. I'm afraid I would have wanted to suggest a lot more than simply furniture and accessories."

"Alicia!"

"Nothing like that. Just a date or dinner. All work related...of course."

"Of course. How could I possibly think otherwise?" Alicia's interest in men certainly made up for Ethne's lack. "Are you sure you don't want to reconsider and take the appointment?"

"No. This program was your idea, and it's only fitting that you should have the first client."

Nick stuck his head in the door. "Welcome back, stranger. Is there anything left in Round Top?"

"Just trying to provide job security for you and the guys."

"Hey, we appreciate that." As he grinned, his eyes sparkled. "Seriously, I'm glad you're home. Let me know when you have the time to come back and share your visions for the new pieces."

Ethne nodded. "Will do."

As Nick headed back down the hall to the shop, Alicia placed her hands on her hips and stared in silence.

Ethne ignored Alicia's unspoken chiding. "Have you seen the stuff? It's amazing. Plus, I brought some pieces from home—an old buffet and a bedroom suite. All solid wood."

No response.

"What?" As if she didn't know. Alicia had been singing the same song for months now.

"I don't know how you can continue to ignore him. He's obviously interested in you."

"And I don't know how you can continue to badger me about

this."

"I just thought with your father dying and all, maybe you'd feel free to move on with your life."

Vaughn had died, but the memories would live forever. "Even if I wanted to date, I wouldn't date Nick. He's a nice man, but he's an employee, and dating someone who works for you is never a good move—personally or professionally."

"I only want to see you happy."

"Well, take a good look. I'm very happy. Believe me. I don't need a man to accomplish that."

~*~

The phone on Ethne's desk beeped. Alicia. She pushed the answer button. "Hey."

"Your eleven o'clock is here." The excitement in Alicia's voice bubbled out of the speaker.

"Already?" He was early. She glanced at the clock display on her computer screen. No. He was right on time. How could it possibly be eleven? She was so engrossed in going over the books and cataloging the new inventory that the morning had flown by—that's how. "I thought you were e-mailing me the info about him."

"I did."

"Oh."

"You didn't read it, did you?"

"Not yet. The time got away from me."

"I could suggest he browse around while you review the notes if you'd like."

She didn't want to get off on a bad foot with this special client. Being late would be unprofessional, and they could always use another good online rating. "No. That's OK." Besides, it would be good for her to start over from ground level—to ask her own questions. That wouldn't seem abnormal, since she hadn't been the one to make the appointment. "I'll be right out."

She stepped into the powder room off her office, brushed her teeth, ran her fingers through her hair, and applied some lip gloss.

Butterflies filled her stomach. This was a special day. The inaugural client for a new program that could potentially open all kinds of doors and increase business growth for their company was here. And she was ready—notes reviewed or not.

As she walked by her desk, she grabbed her jacket off the back of her chair and slipped it on. Then she picked up a pen and the leather bound padfolio on its corner. She'd transfer her handwritten notes to the computer later. Something about taking notes on a laptop, staring at the screen while a client was talking, made her feel detached and seemed less personal than writing the information by hand.

She stepped out of her office and headed down the hallway to the showroom floor. Behind the sales desk, Alicia sported a Christmas-morning grin and nodded her head toward the far corner. The back of the client's head arched above the top of an old high-back chair she'd picked up in Waxahachie. She took a deep breath and made her way toward him. Rounding the chair, she extended her hand, "Hello, I'm—"

"Ethne." He stood and grasped her hand.

"Daniel?"

His hand was warm. Just as it had been in WingNuts when he'd briefly shared her booth that day. When he'd almost held her hand. When his eyes had been such a delicious shade of chocolate brown.

Today he looked like a model from *Cowboy Weekly,* if such a publication had existed. Brown plaid pearl-snap shirt, blue jeans, and brown ostrich cowboy boots. Surprise aside, she couldn't help but answer his grin with one of her own. "This is unexpected. Alicia didn't say—"

"I didn't tell her that we sort of knew each other. It's kind of a weird situation, and I thought you should be the one to decide how much info to give your coworkers. And when and how to do it."

He was so thoughtful. Not many people—especially guys—would think that through. "Thanks, Daniel. I appreciate your thoughtfulness." Her hand…it was still in his. As she relaxed her grip, he released her hand. "So, what's the status of the practice?"

"The closing on the property is set up for Friday. Everything fell into place with the bank. They seemed pretty willing to take a chance on an ex-military man." He grinned.

Friday, less than a week. She'd just left Crescent Bluff and had no desire to return anytime soon…if ever. "That's much sooner than I anticipated. I'll have to check my calendar."

"I mentioned that to Jackson."

So they were first-name friends now.

"But since he's the executor of your father's will, you and Sean don't need to be there—unless, of course, you want to. You're certainly welcome. I mean, y'all are the reason I'm getting the practice."

A reprieve. "Thanks, but I'll probably pass. I've already spent too much time away from the office the last couple of weeks. I don't know how much more I can take off without negatively impacting my business."

"Sure." What appeared to be a brief glimmer of disappointment shadowed his face, but as quickly as it had come, it was erased by a smile.

On with business. Business. That's exactly what this was. And she prided herself in her ability to push aside anything personal where the success of her business was concerned. He was a new client, just like any other client. That was all. She straightened her shoulders. "So, have you had a chance to browse around the store?"

"Only the Weatherford store. I saw so much awesome stuff, I decided I would need help choosing what was best. That's why I signed up for your service."

"Well, let's get started then."

~*~

Daniel followed Ethne to the back corner of the showroom to an old dining table, chairs, and hutch.

"Have a seat, Daniel. We don't have an official conference room, but I think this is out of the way enough that we should be able to work without any distractions."

He slipped into one of the chairs. She was more of a distraction than anybody else that might come into the store possibly could be.

She looked great. More beautiful than he remembered—if that was even possible. She was the type of girl he'd be interested in, if he was free to date. Which he wasn't right now. And if the past years proved anything, he might never be.

"Daniel?" She was staring at him, brows knit, obviously waiting for an answer to her question.

"Sorry. I was thinking about… My mind was… You, uh, have such great stuff here… Could you please repeat the question?"

She grinned. Her eyes sparkled, and the emeralds returned. "I asked if you'd brought the dimensions of the rooms you want to decorate."

He hadn't even thought to do that. But it might not matter. "No. I didn't, but I can get them and e-mail them to you."

"That would be fine." She pushed her notebook toward him. "Could you do a quick sketch of the layout?"

"I can, but that may not be necessary. I decided to take Sean's advice. I'll be living in the apartment above the clinic, at least for a while. So you may actually be able to draw a more accurate diagram than I can."

"Oh…" Those gray shades from the other day dropped over her eyes.

She'd been so hesitant to even step through the clinic door into the waiting room the day they'd all gone to check out the practice. And then Sean had practically forced her to come upstairs to the apartment. He got it. There had to be a lot of pain there for her. A lot of memories. Her first home, and now, her father gone.

Sometimes, he still felt the same way when he returned home. Walking into the den, expecting Dad to jump out of his recliner and give him a big hug. "Hey, I'm sorry. I hadn't thought about how painful this might be for you. Maybe it would be better if Alicia helped me."

A loud clatter sounded from the room setting behind the hutch, pulling Ethne back to the present. "Everything OK over there?"

Face flushed, Alicia rounded the corner. She held up a feather duster. "Sorry to disturb you. I was, uh, just dusting and accidentally bumped into one of the planters on the floor."

"As long as everything's OK."

"It is." Her face was now scarlet. "I'll just move to another section of the showroom." She disappeared as quickly as she'd appeared.

"You're right, Daniel. I probably don't require exact dimensions right now." Her smile was stiff. "Why don't you tell me what you need."

"Everything. All I have are some clothes and a foot locker full of personal possessions."

"No furniture from your previous house or apartment?"

"No. I always lived in the BOQ—Bachelor Officers' Quarters. They're furnished apartments. They were affordable and had all the amenities I could possibly have needed. That was easier than trying to move around a bunch of furniture and other belongings whenever I was transferred. So, just a foot locker."

She picked up her padfolio and her pen. "Why don't we walk around the store? You can show me what you like, and I can make notes and offer suggestions of items that might work in the space."

~*~

Ethne glanced at her phone as the door chimed Daniel's exit. Two hours. He'd been here almost two hours. How was that even possible? He seemed to like everything she suggested. Either that, or he simply didn't care that much about how his space would be decorated. If he hadn't had another appointment this afternoon, who knows how much longer he would have stayed.

But she'd done it. And he'd been right. She hadn't needed measurements to plan furniture layouts for the apartment. Every inch of the floor plan was etched on her heart. Not being in the actual space, only looking at sketches on paper, she'd been able to make herself think two dimensionally. She'd managed to divorce herself from the realities, the memories. She did it today, and she could continue to do it.

As she walked to the back and placed her padfolio and the key he'd insisted she take on the counter, Alicia jumped up. "Well, well, well. You and Dr. Handsome certainly hit things off." Alicia's eyes sparkled with excitement. "And look at that…a key."

"That's just so I can get into the apartment if he's not around. Apparently, he's still going back and forth between Fort Worth and Crescent Bluff."

Alicia crossed her arms over her chest and smirked. "Right."

"Alicia, he's a good potential customer. That's all."

"Oh, I think he's got great potential in a lot more areas than just furniture and accessories. He's a doctor, you know."

"Yes. I know."

"A handsome, unmarried, available doctor who's just moved back home and is probably lonely and in need of some female companionship."

"You sure you wouldn't like to work with him?"

"Nah. It's kind of like going to the candy shop. I love to taste all the samples, but I always buy the same thing. Peanut butter fudge. He's not my flavor, but I can sure enjoy sampling."

She was right about that. Daniel wasn't a jock with a flashy red sports car.

"You know, Eth, maybe you should allow yourself to sample a little bit, too. You might be surprised. This might be the perfect flavor for you."

"Alicia."

"Just offering a suggestion."

"Really? Well, I have one for you. If you ever decide to make a career change, don't go into espionage."

"What do you…"

"Despite the feather duster, it was obvious you were spying, not cleaning."

Alicia grinned. "That bad, huh?"

"That bad."

7

Compared to Dallas or Houston, Fort Worth would be considered a small town, and that was one of the things Daniel had always liked about it. He could be anywhere in about fifteen minutes—twenty minutes at the most. The appointment with Ethne had run longer than he thought it would, and he was cutting it close. But Savannah wasn't known for being on time, so he should still be at the house first.

He drove down the old brick boulevard, past the quaint shops and galleries in Arlington Heights, turned north, and headed toward Westover Hills, to the only house he'd ever called home. Since leaving for college and the Air Force, he'd lived other places, but none of them had ever been home. "Home is where the heart is," Mom had always said, and no matter where he'd been in the world, his heart had always been here, although a Voice deep inside was telling him that was about to change.

He was falling in love—with a town, with a people, and with a dream. Everyone in Crescent Bluff had been so nice, so welcoming. He loved the old building that housed what was to be his new practice and the upstairs apartment. And now, with Ethne's help, he'd be able to turn that old space into a new home. His home.

Ethne. He hardly knew her, but what he knew he liked. She was self-sufficient and independent. One of the few women he'd met who hadn't thrown herself at him, and that was perfect. It should make working together on the apartment easier.

The guys on base had always ribbed him about being old-fashioned when it came to dating. He wanted to be the pursuer rather than the pursued. He was way out of step with today's dating scene. They joked that was the reason he was still single. He'd been happy to let them think that. After all, it was true. Just not the complete truth.

But, man, Ethne was good-looking. Even a tree stump could see that. If he'd been in the market, he would have pursued her. But he wasn't…yet.

The next few weeks and months would be challenging. Getting the practice up and running—hopefully most of Dr. O'Connor's patients would carry over—and fulfilling his promise to Savannah would require maximum use of his organizational skills. Time management had always been a strength of his, and it should serve him well until the divorce was final and she was back on her feet. So, the last thing he needed now was another romantic distraction.

He slowed as he neared the iron gate and pulled into the driveway until he could reach the keypad. He punched in the code, and the gate swung inward. The lawn service must have just come. The yard looked great. Mom had insisted on keeping them and the maid for him while she was gone. At first, when he thought he'd be living here, he'd wanted to argue with her, but now he was glad he hadn't. Maintaining the house was one less distraction he'd have while he settled into a new city and a new practice.

He parked his pickup to the side of the house in the turn-around space. He'd leave the empty spot in the garage for Savannah so she could keep her car out of sight from the street.

This whole plan Mom and Donna had cooked up was shaky at best. Dangerous, at worst. They should have gone to the authorities, but Savannah hadn't wanted to. So here he was—a plan he didn't agree with dropped into his lap. He'd support them until the first sign the idea was headed down the tubes, and then he'd call the police.

He let himself into the mud room through the side door and then headed on into the kitchen. The white cabinets and marble countertops installed in the recent renovation really brightened up the room. Mom's designer had done a great job.

Even though the furniture was new, the positioning was not. The breakfast table still sat next to the wall of glass windows overlooking the pool area. That was one of the things he'd always loved about the U-shaped design of this house—the view of the pool from every room. The floor-to-ceiling windows made him feel as if he was outside no matter the season.

His phone vibrated, and he pulled it out of his pocket. His cheeks tightened into a grin. He pressed the green answer button. "Mom. How are you?"

"Daniel, sweetie. I'm fine. Just fine."

"You ought to be sleeping. Isn't it the middle of the night there?"

"How could I sleep after I read your e-mail? Oh, Daniel, I am so excited for you. Your own practice. And your father would be so proud that his favorite son has taken over the practice he and Dr. O'Connor founded."

Dad had always introduced him as his favorite son. The first time Dad spoke the words, they'd puzzled Daniel.

Daniel laughed, and he and Mom repeated in unison the next words Dad had said so many times. "It's such a wonderful coincidence that my only son just happens to be my favorite son."

Priceless memories filled the silence between them.

Mom cleared her throat. "The institute is updating our contact records. I have your cell number, of course, but could you e-mail me the office number when you get it, and maybe an emergency contact there in Crescent Bluff?"

He'd been so busy he hadn't really had time to make many friends. Maybe he could send her Jackson Williams' number. Or the number of the church. Yeah, the church. "OK, I'll get those to you."

"Well, I guess I better get some sleep before I have to face my students tomorrow. Sweetheart, I've lived a long time, and God's given me many blessings. But the biggest, most wonderful one He ever gave me and your daddy was you. You, Daniel, were a gift, a true gift."

Tears burned his eyes. He was the one who'd received the gift.

"Love you, sweetie. I'll look forward to getting your e-mail."

"Love you, too, Mom."

He dropped his phone into his pocket and then wiped away the tears with his sleeve. He headed down the hall toward the bedroom wing to grab some more clothes and a couple of reference books to take back to Crescent Bluff with him. He needed to remember to get that inflatable mattress out of the garage before he left, too.

Voices floated down the hallway. "Uncle Danny! Uncle Danny!"

They were here. Mom must have given her the code.

As he stepped out into the hall, he was tackled around the legs with the energy only five and seven-year-old boys could muster. "J-Squared. Hey, guys."

"Mom said we're sleeping in your room," Jeremy spoke first.

"That's right. Why don't you and Jared go choose which bed you want."

As they raced past him, Savannah rounded the corner from the main wing of the house. Although over ten years had passed, she still looked as she did when they were in college. She'd been the popular blonde cheerleader, and he'd been the socially awkward science geek. "Hey, Vanna."

"Danny." She fell into his hug. "Please tell me you're staying here with us."

He loosened the embrace and backed away slightly. "Can't do that."

"Yes, you can. You just won't. This house is plenty big. We can stay in this wing, and you can stay in the master bedroom wing." Her eyes filled with tears. "Please, Danny."

"We're not kids anymore. It wouldn't be appropriate. Plus, you're a married woman."

"I wish I weren't."

He'd ignore that comment. The last thing he wanted was to rehash their past. "Besides, I'm opening a new practice in a small town close to Waco, and I need to stay there to get it up and running."

A tear tracked down her cheek.

"Hey, I'm only a phone call away, and I'll try to get up here and see you as often as possible until this whole thing is over. OK?"

She nodded and sniffed. "Looks like I don't have much of a choice."

Jared bounded into the hall. "Me and Jeremy picked out our beds. Mom, come see Uncle Danny's cool Legos." And he was gone again.

A soft smile crept across her face. "I keep telling him you're not his uncle, just a friend, but he doesn't seem to get it."

"Yeah, it's always been confusing to me, too. One thing I know for sure, uncle was never on my to-be list."

"When we were in high school, we were closer than I was to any of my cousins. And then college—"

Every decision has its consequence. "Let me carry your stuff in and help you get settled before I leave."

She grasped his hand. "Stay, Danny. Please stay."

~*~

Ethne glanced at the time display on her desk phone. Was it really eight o'clock? Alicia had gone home right after closing at five, but she wanted to stay and catch up. If she left all the loose ends until tomorrow or the next day, she wouldn't be able to sleep. As it was, she had caught up on everything that happened during her absence and was ready to start fresh tomorrow designing Daniel's space. Daniel's space…Vaughn and Mother's old space.

A wave of nausea washed over her just like the one that hit her the other day when she and Sean first took Daniel to Vaughn's office. The oppressive space…it wasn't hers. And never would be.

She turned off her desk lamp and headed down the hallway toward the back of the building. Someone had left a light on in the shop. She stepped through the doorway and walked over to the bank of light switches. As she reached out toward the one that was still flipped in the on position, a bass voice sounded.

"Don't touch that."

Even though the voice was familiar, she still jumped. "Nick! You almost scared me to death. What are you still doing here?"

"Working. Finishing up cataloging all the new stuff you bought. You got some great pieces." He stood up from his desk and stretched. "But I'm done, and since you're finally leaving, I think I'll go, too."

He grabbed his keys, turned off the light, and then followed her to the back door. As he set the alarm and closed the door, the reality of the situation knotted her stomach. Maybe Alicia was right. She couldn't remember a time ever working late that Nick was not here, too. This was the first time they'd ever left together, though. "Nick, did you really work the whole time?" she asked.

His face flushed and his ears turned bright red. "I, uh, had plenty of work to do."

"But nothing that couldn't have waited until tomorrow."

He jammed his hands into the front pockets of his jeans. "Look, I just wanted to make sure you were OK. This isn't the safest neighborhood after dark."

"But it's not dark."

"Not yet. But how was I supposed to know how long you were working tonight?"

She had no comeback.

He rocked up onto his toes. "Hey, I was going to stop at Ricky's and get a brisket sandwich on the way home. Wanna join me?"

She wished he hadn't done that. Now came the hard part. Nick was a great guy, and the last thing she wanted to do was hurt him. Plus, they had to continue to work together. So, how honest should she be? If Alicia had asked, she would have gone. But Nick was a guy...and an employee.

"Nick, I... Thank you for staying with me, but—"

"Never mind..."

"It's just that I'm really tired. It's been a long day on top of an even longer couple of weeks. I'm not even that hungry."

"Sure, I understand."

No, he really didn't, but this was not the time and place to go into it all. And chances were, it never would be. "It's nothing personal." Not personal with him, anyway. "Please understand, I've made a commitment not to date employees." That was good enough. It was true without going too deep. He didn't need to know anything else.

"Who said anything about a date?"

Heat covered her face. Despite his words, she'd known his intent. Or at least, she thought she had, but maybe she was wrong.

"It's just two co-workers having a sandwich together, Eth. That's all. No ulterior motive."

Men always seemed to have ulterior motives, but maybe Alicia was wrong about him. She took a deep breath. "Sorry. I'm exhausted and brain dead. It's been a hard couple of weeks. Actually, a barbecue sandwich sounds great."

~*~

Ethne scooted onto one of the benches at a small wooden picnic table on the patio overlooking the main street that ran through the Stockyards. Nick dropped onto the bench across from her. Today's temperature was moderate for a Fort Worth summer day. The high had been only in the upper eighties. The combination of the overhead fans and the Texas wind made sitting on the patio enjoyable. "This is the perfect end to a long day stuck in the office. Thanks for the suggestion."

"Sure." He stared into his glass of iced tea for a few seconds before he continued. "I like all the stuff you got at Round Top—especially that bedroom set. I'm not sure what you paid for it, but it's solid wood, and it's in great shape. We wouldn't even have to refinish it. Whoever owned it over the years took really good care of it."

"I'm glad you like it, but I think we should refinish it."

"There are a few small scratches on some of the surfaces, but we can cover those up using some wax and steel wool, and it'll be ready for sale in no time. There's really no reason to refinish the whole thing."

Yes, there was definitely a reason to refinish it. "I understand where you're coming from, but I still say we should refinish it."

"So, Ethne, one of the things you pay me for is my advice. Money-wise it doesn't make sense. The man hours required to completely refinish some pieces that really don't need it would eat up a huge chunk of the profit."

She struggled to keep her voice even. "Nick, I appreciate your input, but I want it refinished. I don't care how you do it—paint it, sand it and finish it with tung oil, whatever. And the credenza, too."

"Ethne—"

"Nick, please..." Her voice was louder than she'd intended.

"Hey, I didn't mean to—"

She took a deep breath. "Sorry. I'm just tired. It's been a long day piled on top of a whole stack of long, emotional days." He deserved an explanation, but she wasn't in any shape to give it right now. "Just trust me, please."

"Sure. Whatever you say, boss."

He'd never called her that before. Although his tone was light, the weight of the words made his comment feel like a slam. She'd explain it all to him later when everything wasn't so raw and her emotions were more under control.

"We've got to stop meeting like this."

A now familiar voice drew her back to the present. "Daniel." The smile on his face erased any possibility he might have overheard their conversation or sensed any tension. "Nick, this is Daniel Spenser. He was in the shop earlier today. He's our first Decor-Gestion client."

The two men shook hands. "Nice to meet you, Nick."

Before Nick could respond, the overwhelming need to explain their being together ambushed her. "Nick is one of my employees." That was unbelievably insensitive, but the damage was done. "What I meant to say was, we're co-workers. He's the manager of our shop. He and his guys are the ones responsible for the transformations—resurrections—as it were. Nick's like a miracle worker—the person who makes the vision a reality. We couldn't do without him." Now she'd marched right through insensitive and on into patronizing.

Daniel nodded. "Well, based on what I saw today, you do great work."

"Thanks." The tone of Nick's response was obligatory, not sincere.

The server appeared and placed their sandwiches on the table.

Daniel spoke. "It was good to see you. I guess I better get a table before my order's ready."

Suddenly, her mouth shifted into high and words tumbled out before she could stop them. "Why don't you join us? We've got plenty of room." She scooted over and made space for him.

He looked first at her and then at Nick. "I don't want to interrupt."

"Oh no, you wouldn't be interrupting anything. Would he, Nick?"

Nick's face glowed bright red. "No. In fact, you'd be helping us. I'm more tired than I realized, but I didn't want to leave Ethne here alone." He stood and picked up his plate. "I think I'll have them pack up my dinner to go and head home. Nice to meet you, Daniel. See you tomorrow, Eth." And he was gone.

"Well…" Daniel still stood in the aisle.

Her face burned. "Now there really is plenty of room." She gestured toward the spot Nick just vacated. "My invitation still stands."

Daniel slipped into the seat across from her and set down his glass of tea and metal number placard. "Hey, Ethne, I'm sorry if I did anything—"

"It wasn't you. It was me. I'll apologize to him in the morning." And that was exactly why she'd always made it her policy to never go out with a male coworker—no matter how casual the invitation.

The clomping of boot heels on the sidewalk beside the patio and the buzz of conversations of those wearing them filled the silence between them. The sun had dropped behind the buildings, painting an orange glow striped by long, dark shadows onto the cobblestone street outside—the time when day and night merged and, for a brief moment, light and darkness became one.

As the server set Daniel's plate in front of him, Ethne cleared her voice. "So, I'm surprised to see you're still here. I thought you were headed back to Crescent Bluff when you left the store."

"I had another appointment, and it ran longer than I thought it would."

That's right. She'd forgotten.

"Plus, I picked up some stuff from home to take back with me—more clothes, some books. But you're right. I figured I'd be gone long before now."

"You should just spend the night at your house up here and then head back to Crescent Bluff in the morning. That way you won't have to drive in the dark."

"I can't." His answer was quick.

"You can't? Why not?"

"I, uh…"

For some reason, she had caught him off guard. While she'd asked the logical question, he obviously hadn't expected it, and he certainly didn't want to answer her. In all honesty, it didn't matter to her where he spent the night. She'd just been making small talk. So, although his response had fueled her curiosity, she'd let him off the hook. "Oh, I get it. Another one of those incidences where if you tell me, you'll have to kill me."

"Something like that." He grinned. "Actually, I prefer to drive at night. Especially when I'm by myself. There's less traffic, and it gives me uninterrupted time to think and pray."

Vaughn always wanted to leave on their vacations at night, but not so he could think and pray. So she and Sean could sleep in the car. But they were always excited, and it never worked. They spent most of their time dodging his arm as it flailed over the backseat. *If you make me stop this car, you'll be sorry.* And the times he actually did pull the car over, she had been sorry. Very sorry.

"Thanks again for the consultation today. I can't wait to see your suggestions."

"Sure. Give me a couple of weeks, and I should have the initial plans done."

"Sounds great."

From a bar down the street, a steel guitar filled the evening with its mournful song. "So, Daniel, do you like country music?"

"Not especially, but I can't say that I particularly dislike it, either. Why?"

"Listen to that moaning melody. It's sad, depressing. I'm just wondering why anyone would like that."

He pushed his plate aside and leaned forward. "Ah, because it tells a story that all people can relate to. The human tragedy. The quest for love. That's one thing all of us have in common. We all want to find that one true love—the person who will love us as we are…in spite of who we are. And when we don't, it's sad. Mournful."

"I think you're generalizing way too much. Not everyone wants that out of life."

His chocolate kiss eyes sparkled in the twilight. "I beg to differ. The desire to be loved is universal. The issue is not whether someone wants to find love, but whether the finding it is worth the pain of searching. The problem is, just as the songs often say, we look in the wrong places, so we never find the right love."

She was in no mood to debate the merits of the single life. "Whatever. The music is still depressing."

He grinned as he slid his plate back in front of him. "Not nearly as depressing as letting this sandwich get cold."

8

Barely visible in the pink, predawn glow, the first estate sale signs had appeared a little north of Hillsboro, and they'd increased in number the closer Ethne got to Crescent Bluff.

Jackson Williams' prediction had been right. The will had sailed through probate, and now, less than a month since she'd first returned home, she was going back for a second time. Her first visit had been for personal reasons. This one was all about business.

She'd completed the plans for redecorating Daniel's apartment and had a few samples of accessories and potential paint colors and finishes in the back of the truck. Plus, how perfect was it that the estate sale and the semi-annual Hill Country flea market had fallen on the same weekend? Completely perfect. Jackson Williams never left anything to chance, and his planning skills had worked out for her benefit, too. She could kill two proverbial birds with one proverbial stone. Or in her case, three birds—the estate sale, the flea market, and Daniel's design consultation.

As the rising sun inched its way above the horizon, Ethne turned off the highway and headed down the back road toward the house.

Jackson suggested she come last night and make one final check to be absolutely certain there was nothing else she wanted before the sale was opened to the public. But that would have meant driving in the dark, after a full day—no, a full week—of work and then having to rent a room and sleep in an unfamiliar bed. She was a morning person, and it made much more sense to spend the night in her own bed, get up early in the morning—before sunrise, if necessary—and drive the couple of hours to Crescent Bluff fresh and well-rested.

Besides, she'd gotten everything she was interested in the first time. But since Jackson had been so kind to arrange the estate sale, the least she could do was honor his wishes and make one final check.

And she understood. Once the items were sold, she and Sean could never get them back. Jackson was just simplifying his life by doing everything he could to eliminate the possibility that either of them would change their minds or have second thoughts.

She turned the box truck onto the two lane, country road that led to the house. Far ahead, someplace around the next bend, a blue glow pulsed its way into the brightening orange morning. A police car. As the road made its final curve, she slammed on the brakes. Pickup trucks, cars, and all sizes of vans lined both sides of the road. The sale wouldn't officially open for another two hours, but the pickers were already here. Some of them had probably been here all night.

She threaded her way along what the vehicles had now transformed into a single lane road, crept up to the turn into Vaughn's driveway, and stopped. As the policeman approached, she grabbed her purse to retrieve her driver's license.

When she lowered her window, the officer smiled. "Good morning, Ethne."

He knew her. She knew him, too. Justin something. She glanced at his nametag. Lake. Justin Lake. They'd been in the same Sunday school class growing up—at least until the unanswerable questions invaded her heart, and she'd stopped going. Everything had become too hard, too painful, too confusing, so she escaped by volunteering in the nursery on Sunday mornings. Rocking a baby was uncomplicated and required absolutely no soul-searching. "Hello, Justin. It's good to see you. It's been a long time."

"Sure has. I was sorry to hear about your father."

"Thank you."

"Mr. Williams said you'd be coming by to make one final walkthrough."

"Yes, and here I am. You know when Jackson Williams makes a request, no one refuses." She smiled politely.

"Yep." He grinned back. "Drive on up to the house. I'll let them know you're on the way."

As he spoke into his shoulder com, she steered the truck past the patrol car and began what would be her final journey down this driveway. Once this weekend was over, the house and property would be put on the market and sold, and an era of her life would be gone forever. And she…she would finally be free.

Ethne parked the truck at the top of the circle where she parked it a few weeks ago. Today, the house was lit up like a Christmas tree, as Mother would have said. Every window Ethne could see was bright and welcoming.

Vaughn would have had a fit. *When you leave a room, turn off the light. What do you think I'm made of? Money?*

She walked up the stairs onto the front porch and grasped the doorknob. Out of habit, she turned back and glanced below the pot of purple petunias. Today, no turtle smiled up at her. He was gone, his services no longer needed. The door was unlocked.

As she stepped into the foyer, a young, professionally dressed woman stood. A nametag on her blazer read *Crane Estate Management.* "You must be Ethne. I'm Lindsey Crane."

The normally open foyer now held two long industrial tables covered with neat stacks of clipboards and legal pads. Each table displayed its own metal cash box and an electronic tablet for processing credit cards. On a chair in the far corner next to the door into Vaughn's office sat another policeman. This was a much bigger deal than she'd imagined. But that was Jackson Williams. Why would he do something on a normal scale when he could surrender to excess?

Lindsey held out one of the clipboards. "Everything for sale is listed on here, and every item in the house has a numbered sticker that corresponds with the descriptions on the list. The sale won't begin for another couple of hours, so take your time walking through the house. If you find something you want, mark it on the list and we'll set it aside for you. And of course, there will be no charge."

Of course not. Whether she wanted it or not, all this stuff belonged to Sean and to her. And to Daniel. At least for the next few hours, anyway. She reached out and took the clipboard. "Thanks, Lindsey. We appreciate your managing this for us."

"You're welcome. You have some real treasures here. We should be able to make you a sizable profit."

A sizable profit. The last thing she wanted was to profit from

Vaughn's death. She hadn't wanted anything from him in life, so why should his death benefit her?

No. Deep in her heart, a voice told her that was wrong. She had wanted desperately for them to have that special relationship only a father and daughter could have. But it was not meant to be. She'd never been good enough, smart enough, pretty enough to earn his love.

"Thank you, Lindsey. I won't be long." Ethne turned and headed up the stairs toward the only room she wanted to check.

The door to her bedroom was open. Whoever staged the house had moved in a couple of chairs and a side table from the storage shed out back. When added to the existing bookshelves and window seat, the pieces gave the room the feel of a cozy library. Someone had found an old picture of Mother and placed it beside a book laying opened on the table between the chairs. Even the picture and the frame had a reference number on them. Ethne picked up the brass frame and carried it to the window now whitewashed by the morning sun.

She dropped down onto the window seat. When she was a child, people often told her, but she'd never been able to see it—until now. She looked just like Mother.

She remembered this picture. It had been on her nightstand for months after Mother died. Until one day it was gone. Just gone. Vaughn scolded her for being careless and losing it, but she hadn't. Vaughn said maybe it was better anyway. She needed to move on with her life. Mother would have wanted that.

How does a child who's lost her mother simply move on with life?

The memory of the last time she held this picture burst into her mind. It had been that Thursday. Vaughn left for work early, and she was responsible for getting Sean and herself off to school. Her stomach had been upset when she first got up, but Vaughn told her she was probably just hungry and to eat something. She wanted to stay home, but he reminded her he was a doctor and insisted she'd feel better if she went on to school.

She and Sean walked to the end of the driveway to catch the bus, and that's when she threw up. She waited for the bus to come, and after Sean got on, she went back home, grabbed the picture, and crawled into bed. Hopefully, she'd feel better before Vaughn got home, and he'd never know she disobeyed him by missing school. After pulling the blanket over her head, she closed her eyes and begged sleep to come and erase the nausea.

In her dream, she'd been walking through a field of fragrant flowers looking for Mother. As she opened her eyes and her room came into focus, the floral sweetness only became stronger. One of the risers on the stairs creaked through the closed bedroom door, and she snuggled deeper under the covers. Someone was in the house. Her heart had pounded wildly in her chest as she willed her breathing to be silent so the intruder wouldn't know she was there.

The front door opened and closed, and a second set of steps ascended the stairs. She couldn't understand the words, but she knew the tone of the voice. Vaughn. If there was an intruder here, Vaughn would catch him. Soft female laughter answered his words as an upstairs door shut.

Ethne silently slipped out of bed, opened her door, and tiptoed into the hall. She peeked over the bannister into the foyer below. The key from the belly of the little turtle lay on the console table in the hall.

More laughter came from the direction of her parents' bedroom. She wasn't yet a teenager, but she understood what men and women did behind closed bedroom doors, and she hated him for it. She hated that he could dishonor Mother's memory in that way.

That was the last day she'd seen the picture. The next day when she returned home from school, the little frame had disappeared. She never confronted Vaughn, and he never scolded her. But she now knew…somehow, he had discovered she'd been there and had taken the picture as punishment.

That was not the first time she'd smelled that fragrance and the first time the key was used by someone other than her or Sean. And it wasn't the last. She had definitely smelled the fragrance of that perfume many times over the years. Most recently at Vaughn's funeral. And that had not been the only sweet scent lingering in the air when she came home to an empty house after school. There had been many others. As a young child, she'd assumed the various fragrances belonged to Mother. Some had, but now she knew, not all.

She looked at the number on the frame and marked it off the list on the clipboard. This was the only item she wanted from the house.

~*~

Ethne turned into the clinic parking lot, pulled her car into the slot next to a white pickup, and killed the engine. Daniel must already be here. They were supposed to meet at eight o'clock, and it was two minutes until that time. He was early, but that was just fine. She was relieved when he agreed to the morning appointment. The last thing she wanted was to waste time hanging around Crescent Bluff. She grabbed her laptop and sample bag and walked up to the front door.

The shades were drawn, and all the windows were dark, so she tapped on the door. No response. She knocked more loudly the second time, and then the next. Nothing. Maybe he was already upstairs in the apartment. She pushed the doorbell once. Then twice. Still, no Daniel.

She pulled her phone out of her pocket. Fortunately, she'd entered his number last night before she left work. She called. Straight to voicemail.

Now that she thought about it, maybe that wasn't Daniel's truck. He'd been driving a small sedan that day they first brought him to the practice. Vaughn constantly had to call towing companies to haul off random vehicles people left parked in the clinic lot. Especially on weekends. Apparently, that was still the case.

Now grateful for his insistence after the consultation, she pulled the key he'd given her out of her purse. She'd go inside and wait. He'd certainly be here soon. Today, the key turned smoothly. He either put graphite in the lock as Sean had suggested or changed it altogether.

Praying he hadn't changed the code, she quickly punched in the numbers on the keypad. The beeping stopped. She exhaled her relief and closed the door. The drawn shades blackened the room, so she paused a moment while her eyes adjusted. Furniture had been pushed to the center and covered with canvas tarps. In the dimness, their silhouettes resembled snow drifts, but the musky smell dispelled that impression. Someone had been painting.

She reached to turn on the lights and then stopped. Within the darkness created by the closed shades, she could hide. Almost as if she wasn't really here but was experiencing everything virtually.

She tiptoed farther into the waiting room. Today it was easier than it had been when she and Sean had brought Daniel here the first time. As difficult as it had been that day, she had conquered the past. She was able to walk all the way down the hall and up the stairs to the apartment. It had been hard—especially when she turned to leave and the closet door came into view. It was only a small victory, but people had to crawl before they could walk. And now she was about to chalk up another one.

She took a deep breath and inched her way through the waiting room and on down the hall to Vaughn's office. Entering, she balanced herself on the edge of one of the chairs facing the desk and stared at the spot where Vaughn should have been. At the high back leather desk chair where he'd sat the last time she'd been in this office on the afternoon of graduation day when she'd announced she'd be leaving forever in a few hours. He stared at her stoically and said, "And that's the gratitude I get for raising you all these years?" His words had not held the slightest tone of sorrow, only anger.

Tears of mourning filled her eyes. Not mourning for his death, but for the relationship that never was and now never could be.

"Well, I'm glad to know I won't be needing this."

She shot out of the chair and spun to face the hall. Grinning in the doorway stood a version of Daniel she'd never seen before. Brown, spiked, bedhead hair, eyes heavy from sleep—or lack of it, and a face covered with a day or two's black stubble. Bare-chested and barefooted, he wore a pair of low-slung pajama pants and held a baseball bat in front of him as if he'd been preparing to swing at an incoming pitch.

The second their eyes connected, his smile disappeared, and he propped the bat against the doorjamb. "Ethne, are you OK?"

She quickly wiped the tears away from under her eyes. "I'm fine."

"I'm sorry if I scared you."

"It's not that."

"Hey, I know it's painful now, but it'll hurt less as time passes. I promise."

He thought she'd been sitting here grieving over Vaughn's death.

Slowly, Daniel made his way to her and gently placed a hand on her shoulder.

A foreign longing overcame her. She ached for him to draw her close, to smooth her hair, to softly wipe away the remnants of her tears with his fingertips. She longed to feel his skin against hers. Out of self-preservation, she quickly stepped away. "According to my records, we have…had…an eight o'clock appointment today."

"And your records would be correct. I overslept. Sorry. I was up late last night painting the waiting room, and my phone was accidentally set on silent, so I didn't hear the alarm when it went off."

"We could reschedule for later today."

"No. You're talking to an ex-military man, a master of the two-minute shower. If you can give me five minutes, I'll be ready to get to work."

9

Daniel bounded down the stairs and practically jogged to the door of his—well, it wasn't really his yet—Dr. O'Connor's office. He owned the space, but nothing in the room had been changed to make it his. Of course, none of the places he lived in the last several years had been his, either. They all belonged to Uncle Sam.

He rounded the doorway and stepped into the office. The empty office. He didn't blame her for leaving. The loss of her dad was still fresh and had to be really tough on her. He could relate. Some parts of grief were universal. She'd feel better in time, but this early in the process, it would be hard for her to imagine that.

He looked down the hall into the dark waiting room. The front door was ajar, and her bags sat on the floor next to it. He'd probably have gone outside for some fresh air, too.

Ethne sat on the top front step of the porch facing the street. He cleared his throat to avoid startling her as he had a few minutes ago.

She whipped her head around toward him. Although the earlier tears were gone, her smile was forced. As she stood, she glanced at her phone. "Amazing."

He nodded his head. "Thank you. Thank you very much." He did his best Elvis impression, and it worked.

She smiled for real. Then she cocked her head and glanced at him out of the corners of her eyes. "The process is amazing. Not the end product. Four minutes and fifty-seven seconds."

Everything about her response was a good sign. He was more than happy to play along. "You were timing me? Really?"

"Just wanted to make sure you were a man of your word."

"And...?"

"So far, so good."

"And just exactly what's wrong with the end product?"

The smile was gone again. "Nothing. I was just kidding."

"You know what they say. Always some truth in kidding."

"I've always wondered. Who exactly is the 'they' that says all that stuff all the time?" She paused briefly but not long enough for him to reply. "I guess we better get to work. I have some samples to show you and some possible design plans for the apartment."

Playtime had been fun, but now it was over. He turned and held the door open for her. "After you."

~*~

He did look amazing. Unbelievably amazing. Damp hair tousled from the shower. Chocolate-kiss eyes. Shorts, flip-flops, and a T-shirt—thank goodness he had put on the shirt. But Ethne wouldn't confess such to him. That might lead him on and give him a false sense of interest. Even though she'd vowed never to marry or even date, she couldn't help the reaction to what her eyes saw and what she felt when he placed his hand on her shoulder earlier. He was a handsome man, movie star handsome.

There had to be a reason he was still unattached. If, in fact, he was. She'd never asked, and he'd never said one way or the other. Their relationship was strictly business, and she didn't go about prying into clients' personal lives unless they offered. Which he hadn't. So she wouldn't.

Daniel was opening the blinds in the waiting room. "Do you want to meet down here or go upstairs to the apartment? All I have upstairs is an inflatable mattress and my foot locker. I can uncover some of the chairs and an end table in here if you'd like."

Relief washed over her. "I think we can do most of what we need to do today right here."

The sun shone through the windows and brought the walls to life. He'd chosen a warm beige color, very close to the shade she'd used for the offices and behind the front desk at work. She would have recommended gray for this space—it was cooler, more calming—but she wouldn't say anything now since he'd already started. Besides, he hadn't contracted her to consult on the office—

only the apartment. He could make this work, though.

"What do you think of the paint color?"

"It's nice. Gives the room a warm feel. A lot like what I have on some of the walls at work."

"It's exactly what you have on the walls at work. Sahara Sand, right? At least that's what Alicia said when I asked about it." He grasped a drop cloth and pulled it off some of the furniture. "And look at this. What do you think?"

As the cloth receded, a gray upholstered chair with wooden arms and another one with a coordinating gray, black, and white vertically striped woven fabric appeared. He picked the gray one up and moved it next to the wall and then placed the striped one beside it. "And..." Then he pulled out a square end table with a wooden top and straight-lined black metal legs and set it beside the chairs.

She could hardly breathe. He had fantastic taste and a special eye for decorating. How unexpected to combine these colors and styles. "I would have never chosen these items to use together, but the whole effect is quite stunning. A perfect balance of warm and cool tones. Amazing, Daniel. Absolutely amazing." Now she had an even better feeling for his style.

"Uh-oh. Did I hear the 'A' word again? Did you say 'Amazing Daniel'?" He winked at her.

Her breathing caught. He was a client, just like the hundreds of clients she'd helped in the store over the years. Nothing more.

No, that wasn't exactly true. They'd been thrown together by some weird twist of fate. The odds of her knowing him otherwise were miniscule. They already had some history, even though they hadn't known it until a few weeks ago. Trying to pretend he was nothing more than a regular client was ridiculous.

She should attempt to be friends with him. This whole decorating process would be simplified if they were. When she tried with other men in the past, it had been a disaster. Case in point, eating barbecue with Nick the other night.

But Daniel seemed to have no ulterior motives. Except for that weird handshake-thing the other day at WingNuts Grill. And now, she was pretty sure she overreacted and read something into his actions that hadn't been there.

Once all the legalities were finalized and decorating his apartment was completed, she'd have no reason to return to Crescent Bluff, and she'd likely never see him again, unless he came back into the store to buy something else.

So, even though he was a client, he was a safe candidate for a temporary friendship. A nice, safe, albeit handsome, candidate. "No. I said 'Amazing, Daniel.' A pause and a comma make a big difference in the meaning."

"OK. I just wanted to make sure you weren't retracting your statement from earlier." He grinned. "Let's see what you brought."

As he moved toward the door to retrieve her bags, his stomach growled long and low. "Sorry."

He was hungry, and the banana and coffee she had at home before dawn had been gone for an hour or so. Today would be long and busy. She could stand a little refueling. "Why don't we discuss all this over breakfast? How about The Perks?"

~*~

She chose a large table in the back corner. It was away from the hustle and bustle of the packed dining room, and she'd have enough space to spread out her samples for him to review. She scooted into the booth and dropped her bags beside her while he set the tray down and took the seat across from her.

"So, you really haven't eaten here yet? How long have you been in Crescent Bluff now?"

"Long enough that I should have been here before today." He smiled as he doled out the breakfast sandwiches and coffee.

As she grasped her English muffin, he asked, "Mind if I bless the food?"

She couldn't remember the last time she'd prayed over a meal. Or over anything, for that matter. He'd quickly bowed his head before he ate at the barbecue restaurant the other night, but she'd already been eating, so he hadn't prayed aloud. "Of course. I mean, no, I don't mind. Of course, please bless the food." Although her cheeks were on fire, he didn't seem to notice.

His blessing was short, conversational, as if he was speaking to someone sitting in the seat right next to him. Completely opposite from Vaughn's formal discourses, heavily laden with "Thee's" and "Thou's."

He held out his coffee mug and grinned. "Cheers to a great day."

She picked up hers and pushed it forward until the musical clink of porcelain rang out. "Cheers."

She sipped her coffee.

He took a bite of his bagel sandwich. "Wow! Amazing. Absolutely amazing, Ethne." He grinned. "Did you catch the little pause there? I was referring to the bagel. The bagel is amazing."

Oh, brother. "Yes, I caught it."

"Good. Just wanted to make sure there was no misinterpretation." His chocolate-kiss eyes teased.

They ate in silence for the next few seconds. No exciting conversational topic pushed its way into her mind, and he seemed lost in thought. Probably about the amazing bagel sandwich.

"What's so funny?" His brows knit, forming attractive crinkles around his eyes.

"What?"

"You're smiling—no, grinning. Have I got something on my face?"

"No. Just enjoying my breakfast, but I guess we should get started. I need to get on the road before all the good deals are gone."

"Deals?"

"At the flea market toward Austin. It doesn't officially open until noon, but most of the time they let people in the trade in early, and that's when you can get the best deals. And they do have great stuff. It's my favorite one."

"Well, contrary to popular opinion, I can multi-task, even though I'm a guy. So go for it."

She pulled her computer and the large blue plastic envelope marked with his name out of her bag. "Let's start with the overall design first, and then I'll show you some ideas I have for finishes and pieces. Please stop me at any time if you have any questions. And remember, these are only suggestions. If you have any ideas or don't like some of mine, please speak up."

"Right. Resurrection Decor-Gestion. I remember."

She couldn't help but cringe. The name sounded dumb when she heard it out loud now. Yet she and Alicia had thought it was so cute a few weeks ago. Oh, well. It wasn't the first bad decision she'd made, and it certainly wouldn't be the last. As long as the majority of decisions she made were good, she'd be just fine.

She opened the laptop and began. She was only doing the living room and dining room, so the presentation was short. He sat quietly, watching the screen and munching his bagel as she presented her ideas for furniture pieces and arrangements for the rooms. "Any questions or comments?"

He shook his head.

The silence weighed heavy on her shoulders. He didn't like it. Perspiration prickled her forehead and upper lip as she opened the plastic envelope. "OK, let me show you the finishes I had in mind." She arranged the paint and fabric samples along with pictures of accessories by room on the table top. "I think the hardwood floors are in good enough shape that you can use area rugs and save a chunk of money, so I didn't suggest any flooring. But I can if you want."

Studying the computer screen and the samples she had clustered by room, he cupped his coffee mug in his hands and took a drink. A long, silent drink. He definitely didn't like it.

"So, as I said, those are just my initial ideas. We can always tweak them or throw them all out and start over if you don't like them. They're only suggestions." She was babbling. She took a deep breath to reset. "I mean, is this at all what you had in mind?"

Still staring at the samples, he slowly shook his head. "No, not at all."

She had always prided herself in having a knack to understand what their customers wanted, and she'd thought she had a pretty good idea of what he liked after their meeting at the store, but somehow, she'd fallen flat on her face today.

His gaze raised to meet hers. "Ethne, I could have never imagined this, but it's perfect. Absolutely perfect." A huge smile lit up his face. "No, let me rephrase that. It's amazing! All designed by the amazing Ethne. And did you notice? No pause, no comma."

She answered his smile with one of her own. "You really like it?"

"Of course I do. Who wouldn't?" He reached out and covered her right hand with his. "It's great. Thank you."

His touch was warm, and completely appropriate. She wouldn't pull away her hand as she had at WingNuts. "Sure, I really enjoy making an old space new. In some ways, it's like bringing to life a design that was hidden by time."

"Resurrecting it, right?"

She smiled. "Right."

"So, you know how when you really like something, a little is not enough?"

Her heart pounded as she now drew her hand away. The conversation had headed down the wrong path. "Daniel—"

"I wonder if you could help me pick out some art for the walls in the waiting room at the office. I want something unusual. Not those mass-produced, meaningless paintings you see in various forms in every medical office. I'd be glad to pay for your services."

Relief flooded over her. "Payment's not necessary. I'll be happy to help you. Any ideas of what you might want? I can keep an eye out at the flea market today."

"That's the problem. I don't know what I want, only what I don't want."

"Why don't you come with me, then? That is, if you're not busy. They always have some unusual pieces."

"I think painting the waiting room can wait. Sounds great."

What had she just done?

10

Today had not been her day. Sometimes she bought more than they could possibly use and other days, like today, nothing. She'd have to settle for the thrill of the hunt. They hadn't even found anything for the walls in Daniel's waiting room.

They turned down the final aisle, and Daniel stopped. "What about that on the back wall?"

He pointed to a huge, round, wooden clock with black iron hands and mismatched numerals of varying sizes and fonts. The red oak matched the color of the wood on the arms of the waiting room chairs and the table tops. It must have been at least five feet in diameter. But she could see it in the space. "That would look gorgeous. Let's check it out."

As she approached the booth owner, she held out a business card. "Hello."

The white-haired man stepped forward. "Howdy. How can I help ya?"

"I own some second-hand stores in the Fort Worth area, and we may be interested in the clock. What can you tell me about it?"

"Ain't much to tell. Came from an old mill outside Hillsboro. It's big, and it don't work."

She fingered the price tag. "Five hundred dollars? Don't you think that's a bit much for a clock that doesn't even work?"

"Well now, value's a funny thing. I'm a-thinkin' you wanna talk me down so you can buy it cheap and sell it high." His blue eyes sparkled as he grinned. "Wouldn't that be right, missy?"

Normally, she loved this part of the game. He'd act as though he was losing money, and she'd act as if she didn't have any. And in the end, they'd reach a compromise that satisfied both of them. But this was a little different. "I'm not buying this to resell. It's for him." She nodded her head back toward Daniel.

"Oh, so you're buyin' it for your fellah, huh?"

"He's a client. A friend."

"Oh, well in that case, I could knock off fifty."

"Fifty? I was thinking more like two fifty."

"I'll just bet you were. Four fifty's the best I can do."

Daniel stepped up and held out his hand. "Hello, sir. Daniel Spenser. That's a fine clock."

"Jimmy John King. Thank you, son."

"You say four fifty's the best you can do?"

"Yessir. Rock bottom. I had it marked at eight hundred earlier today."

Daniel turned toward her. "Ethne, I think that's a fair price." He turned back toward Jimmy John and continued, "It's fair, but it's above my budget. I just got out of the military, and I'm setting up a medical office in the area. My max would be two fifty, but that's about it. So thanks, anyway, for your time."

He ignored Daniel's offer. "What branch, son?"

"Air Force."

"You gotta be kiddin' me." Jimmy John grinned and pulled up the sleeve of his shirt to expose a tattoo. "Me, too. Where were you stationed?"

"Germany, mostly. How about you?"

"'Nam. Got me a purple heart. If it hadn't been for a GI doc, I wouldn't be talkin' to you right now. Never did get to thank him." He extended his hand to Daniel. "Thanks for your service, son."

Daniel stood rod straight and shook Jimmy John's hand. "Thank you for yours, sir."

"So you want that big ol' clock?" Jimmy John stroked his chin. "I've tried all morning to sell that thing. Ain't nobody gonna buy a clock that don't even work. You'd be doin' me a favor to take it off my hands so I ain't gotta load it back into my trailer again."

"That's very generous, but I couldn't do that, sir."

"Sure you could, and you're gonna. It'd kinda be payin' it forward." Jimmy John grabbed a pen and wrote "SOLD" on the ticket. "Come back by when you finish your lookin', and I'll help you get it to your truck."

Daniel extended his hand again. "Thank you very much, sir."

When they were out of earshot, Ethne stopped and looked up at Daniel. "So, what exactly happened back there?"

"Two ex-military men helped each other out. He helped me financially, and I helped him emotionally. Pretty amazing how things work out sometimes, Ethne."

"Yes. Very amazing Daniel."

He laughed. "I don't believe I heard a pause there."

"I don't believe you did, either."

~*~

The last row of the flea market had been a goldmine. In addition to the clock, an old iron gate, a metal and glass medical cabinet, a pair of pews for seating on the front porch, and an antique oak examination table—which Daniel insisted could be used as a console table in the waiting area—rattled in the rear of the truck as they headed back to Crescent Bluff. And all for less than three hundred dollars. Ethne glanced over at Daniel. If he ever decided to leave medicine, he'd be a great negotiator.

Shadows had lengthened as the sun began its descent toward night. Daniel's voice broke the silence. "Wow, this day's flown by. Thanks for your help."

"I don't think you needed me at all. You did great on your own."

"Not true. I wouldn't even have known about this place or been able to get in early without you."

"A minuscule contribution. I still can't get over your idea to use that old gate as wall art. It'll look great in the reception area. Let me know if you ever want to change careers."

He chuckled. "Too bad one of us isn't in the food service business right now."

"A few miles after we get on the interstate, there's a German restaurant at one of the exits. I thought you might enjoy eating there since you used to live in Germany." She hadn't even known where he was stationed. Hadn't even thought to ask. From the first moment she met him in Vaughn's office, she began constructing a fence between them. She'd left little peepholes in it so she could see bits and pieces, but nothing large enough to get a complete view.

Well, maybe it was time to install a gate. If they were to be friends, even temporary ones, she needed to learn more about him. Besides, it could only make her job as his decorator easier. She loved everything he picked out today, but she would never have chosen any of it for him.

"Some schnitzel sounds great!"

As they crested the top of the hill, piercing blue light swept across the landscape. A patrol car blocked the entrance onto the highway, and the policeman was directing traffic to stay on the access road. Oh, great. There must be a wreck. Ethne slowed the truck and rolled down her window. "Good evening, officer."

"Sorry, ma'am. Highway's closed. You'll need to stay on the frontage road."

In front of her, a trail of red taillights reached all the way to the horizon. It would take them days to get home this way. "What happened? Any idea when the highway will be opened?"

"No, ma'am. Wreck between a couple of passenger vehicles and a chemical tanker. Surrounding area's being evacuated, too."

Why did this have to happen now? Today had been a long day, and she was tired and hungry. By the time she got home to Fort Worth, she'd be exhausted. Just her luck.

Daniel leaned over into the sightline of the policeman. "I'm a physician. Any injuries? I'd be glad to help."

"Thank you, sir. Everyone involved has been transported to the hospital. Now move on up, please."

As she drove the truck forward, guilt squeezed her chest. What kind of a person was she? She hadn't even thought about the people who'd been in the vehicles. They hadn't been real people to her. They may have been out on a family ride this beautiful summer evening, and now… In the midst of the tragedy, all she'd thought about was how she was being inconvenienced. How cold and self-centered of her.

She crept up behind the last car and stopped and then turned toward Daniel. His eyes were closed, his mouth barely moving. He had to be praying. She waited to speak until he opened his eyes and turned toward her. "That was kind of you to offer to help."

A puzzled look covered his face. "Kind? Not particularly. Why wouldn't I offer?"

Vaughn had never offered to help in similar situations. "I don't know. It wasn't the first thing that crossed my mind."

A smile warmed his face. "Of course it wasn't. It was a medical emergency, not a decorating emergency."

She didn't know him well but enough to realize he didn't mean it the way she heard it. Suddenly her life's work felt trivial, unimportant. She'd never saved anyone's life. But he had.

"My dad always carried his medical bag and a box of first aid supplies in the trunk," he continued. "When I was about twelve, we were headed out to the Grand Canyon for vacation, and we came across a car that had run off the road in the middle of nowhere. He stopped and helped them. I remember thinking they could have died if Dad hadn't come along. That was the first time I thought I might want to be a doctor, too."

"Yeah, I guess no one's ever died from an uncoordinated wall color crisis."

"C'mon, Ethne. No good work is worthless."

He'd read her mind.

"What you do brings joy and peace to people's lives. We're complicated creations with many facets. Not every moment's a crisis. Your work improves quality of life, and that's as important to emotional health as medicine is to physical health."

He sure knew how to make lemonade out of lemons, as Mom used to encourage her to do. Still, the truth was she'd thought only of herself. Why was she so self-centered, so void of empathy? And why was he so caring? Of course, helping others was his job. He'd taken an oath to do so. But Vaughn had, too. And yet, Vaughn had never stopped. He'd always had some excuse. He was headed to some important function and stopping would make him late. The picture of the Good Samaritan from one of the children's Bibles in Sunday school flashed in her mind. She'd never sat beside an honest-to-goodness Bible character before.

"Looks like we may be stuck here awhile." He unfastened his seatbelt.

She had to get home, to escape to her miniature fortress. Traffic wasn't moving at all, and people in front of them had turned off their cars and were out milling around.

"You might want to consider turning off the truck to conserve gas."

Some of the cars behind them were turning around and heading back the way they'd come. "I have a better idea. Are you up for an adventure?"

He grinned and then nodded. "Always."

She got out her phone and tapped in the address for his office. Then slowly and carefully she turned the truck around and headed back the way they'd come.

"I'm guessing German food's off the table for tonight."

"Sorry."

"That's OK. I'll just have to take a rain check."

He'd doubtfully ever get to cash in on that one, but no need to call notice to that fact now.

A soothing female voice urged from her phone, "When possible, make a U-turn."

"Hey, Lucille. Get with the program," he admonished. "She can be such a nag sometimes."

"She sure can. Always wanting everything done her way."

"Exactly, but she'll come around eventually. She always does." He smiled.

After a half mile or so, "Lucille" zeroed in on their location and began giving them directions for a new route home.

Before long, her stomach spoke up. The Frito-chili pie they had for lunch at the flea market was long gone. Assuming Lucille was leading them back into civilization, they should be able to find something to eat soon. But as Daniel noted, she often had a mind of her own.

As the roads narrowed and the sky darkened into night, Lucille led them farther into the countryside. Daniel had drifted off to sleep a while back, so Ethne was alone—except for the crickets singing through the window she'd left rolled down since the traffic jam.

She long ago lost any sense of direction or location. When they turned around, they headed south and then west. Eventually they should hit a highway, and Lucille should command them to turn north. She grabbed her phone to check the map. The blue dot showed their location and the road, but the letters in the upper left corner spelled out "No Service."

She pulled over to the side of the road and placed the truck in park. "Daniel, wake up." She kept her voice gentle. No response. She placed a hand on his shoulder. "Daniel."

He jerked awake. "Sorry. I was painting until three this morning. What's up?"

"Do you have any service on your phone?"

He leaned forward and pulled his phone out of his back pocket. "No. Do you?"

"No. We're lost. What do you think we should do?"

"The lack of cell service shouldn't affect the GPS. It should still work. But if you're concerned, we could turn around and go back the way we came, or stay put until morning."

Spending the night in the truck was not an option. "No. We'll go on. Surely, the highway can't be too much farther. We've got to be close."

He shrugged his shoulders, leaned his head back against the seat, and closed his eyes. "You have the conn."

She continued on for about another hour, until the road slowly transformed from paved to gravel, to dirt, to nonexistent. She slammed on the brakes as a boulder marking the end of the trail jumped up into the wash of the headlights. The map on her phone showed a continuation of the road, but it was nonexistent.

Maybe they should have turned around earlier and gone back. Putting the truck in reverse, she tried to revive her memory of the three-point turn. She hadn't had to do one since Driver's Ed. At least this truck had a backup camera.

She glanced first into her mirror and then into the one on the passenger side before beginning the turn. The glow from the dashboard was just bright enough to reveal her sleeping passenger's face sporting a slight smirk. The last thing she wanted from him right now was an "I told you so." She'd take her time, and she'd turn this truck around. Then they'd see who was gloating.

She turned the steering wheel sharply to the right and slowly backed up. Step one down. She put the truck in drive, turned the wheel to the left, and pulled slowly forward. This was a piece of cake. Putting the truck in reverse again, she turned the wheel to the right. The truck died. She pushed the gearshift into park and tried to restart it. Nothing. Again…nothing. And again…still nothing.

"Check your gas gauge," the sleeping passenger with the smirk suggested.

"It can't be the gas. The light hasn't come on, and the bell hasn't dinged." But the headlights were on and the dash was illuminated, so it wasn't the battery. Maybe he was right. The gas gauge had read half a tank when she left home this morning. She promised herself she'd stop and get some gas once she got to Crescent Bluff, but she hadn't. The truck was getting great gas mileage. It was still around half a tank when they left for the flea market. And even now, it still read half… "Oh, no. I think you're right. The gas gauge must be broken." As she turned off the truck, night engulfed them. "Any ideas?"

"We've only got one choice as far as I can see. Stay put until morning."

He was right…and had been right earlier. If she'd done what he'd suggested, they might not be in this mess. He had to be angry because she hadn't listened to him, but he was hiding it well. She should apologize, but she wasn't ready to endure the torrent of I-told-you-so's her apology would unleash. She may as well get it over with. "I'm sorry, Daniel. If I'd listened to you earlier, we wouldn't be stuck out here." She braced herself for the well-deserved tirade.

"Hey, it's not your fault the highway was closed, or the GPS is wrong, or the gas gauge is broken. I'm just glad you're not stuck out here alone." He grinned.

That was it? Vaughn always acted as though her mistakes were the end of the world, because apparently, he'd never made one. She rubbed her left forearm. Under the sweater, a mesh of almost imperceptible scars striped her arm. Never-fading souvenirs of a time when two-year-old Sean had spilled his milk. "Thanks for not being angry. I really am sorry."

"No need to apologize for a situation beyond your control. And why in the world would I be angry? It's actually kind of funny."

The desire to lean over and hug him caught her by surprise. She'd definitely ignore that urge.

"Or it would be funny if I wasn't so hungry. I might have to revive my survival skills from basic training and forage for some grubs, nuts, and berries. I'm starving."

"Me, too. Maybe foraging through the truck would be more productive. Who knows what Nick and the guys might have left? There's always water in the console." She turned on the dome light, slid open the cooling compartment, and pulled out a couple of bottles. "That's a start."

He rummaged through the glove box, while she searched the rest of the console. Between them they found two energy bars, a packet of peanut butter crackers, two after-dinner mints from a Fort Worth hamburger chain, and some chocolate covered peanuts.

She spread a paper napkin over the arm rest between them and placed the fruits of their labor on it. For the first time in years, she wanted to say a prayer thanking God for the meager, though greatly appreciated food, and for the company. She would have been out here all alone in the middle of nowhere if she hadn't followed a whim and invited him to come. "OK, I guess dinner is served."

He reached up and turned off the dome light. "Probably should conserve the truck battery, but—" He turned on the flashlight app from his phone, decreased the intensity until it was a soft glow, and placed it on the napkin next to their dinner. "No reason we can't dine by candlelight." He winked.

There he was, making lemonade again.

~*~

An insistent drumming on the passenger door of the truck yanked Ethne into the world of the awake. "Y'all OK in there?"

someone asked with a muffled voice.

A man with a scraggly gray beard and what looked to be the same color hair under a straw cowboy hat stood outside Daniel's window. He was barely within an arm's reach of the truck—shotgun in hand, an ATV parked several yards behind him.

Daniel sat up and waved. Then he slowly opened the door. "Yessir, we're fine. Just out of gas and out of road." His voice was gravelly from sleeping.

"And a mite lost, I'll bet."

"Yessir, we sure are."

"You ain't the first, nor will you be the last, I reckon, what with them GPS things that don't work so good out here," he chuckled. "Well, gather up your missus, and we'll go up the road and get you enough gas to get you back to the station so you can fill up."

"Oh, but we're not—" Ethne began as she leaned closer to the open door.

Daniel held up a hand to silence her.

He turned toward her. "Ethne, most people in this rural part of Texas are ultra-conservative." His voice was barely above a whisper. "Do you want him to think we're not married and have just spent the night together?"

"He wouldn't... I mean, we wouldn't... It wasn't by choice. It was an emergency."

Daniel turned and replied to the stranger. "Thank you, sir. We'd really appreciate it."

They got out of the truck, and Ethne locked the door.

The man laughed. "Ain't nobody around here to steal nothing. Even if there was, they couldn't get very far with an empty tank."

He was probably right.

Daniel held out his hand. "Daniel Spenser."

The men shook hands. "Hank Stroud." Then Hank faced her. "And you must be Mrs. Spenser." He tipped his hat.

"No. We're not married. I'm Ethne O'Connor."

Hank held up his right hand—the one that wasn't holding the shotgun—in a casual "stop" position. "Hey, you don't owe me no explanation. Things is different nowadays with you young folk."

He didn't believe her. "No, really. I'm his consultant."

"Consultant. Uh-huh. Like I say. Ain't none of my business, no matter what you call it."

She glanced over at Daniel. His face was bright red, and he was biting his bottom lip in an obvious effort to keep a straight face. This was not funny, despite what he thought.

11

Nick sprawled over the armchair facing her desk. "Broken gas gauge? Really?"

"That's all I can figure." Ethne smiled.

Nick grinned back. "Glad you weren't alone." His expression was tender, like a big brother's.

Thank goodness the tension between them was gone, and everything felt normal again. But still, she owed him an apology. "Nick, about the other night at Ricky's. I'm sorry."

He stood and winked. "Water under the bridge. Now, let me see if I can figure out what's up with the truck. And then I'll get the guys to start on the dining room furniture for the Spenser project."

She took a deep breath of relief as he walked out of the office. The phone buzzed, and she pushed the answer button. "Yes?"

Alicia's best operator voice sounded over the speaker. "Dr. Handsome on line one. Dr. Handsome on line one."

Ethne didn't need any further explanation. Alicia had been teasing her ever since she'd related the night-in-the-truck story. "Thanks."

"Oh, definitely my pleasure. And I'm sure it will be yours, too."

Shameless. Ethne pushed the flashing red light. "Hello." Road noise sounded in the background.

"Good morning, Consultant."

An unanticipated smile crept across her face. "Good morning, Negotiator."

"Thanks for texting me when you got home yesterday. I would have wondered."

"Sure."

"Hey, I've had something come up, and I'm actually in Fort Worth. Since you owe me a German dinner, I wondered if you'd let me take you to lunch today. Kind of as a payment for all the trouble over the weekend."

The smile faded. This was not the direction they needed to be heading.

"There's this great little place my family used to go to on the circle."

Road noise filled the silence. She needed to stop this before it went any further.

"Ethne? Are you still there?"

"Yes. Sorry. I can't today, Daniel." Her words tumbled out. "I've, uh, just got too much to catch up on. You know, after being gone most of the weekend. I have another client coming in at two, and I still have some last-minute details to attend to." She closed her eyes and waited.

"Oh, sure. No problem. See you in a couple of weeks."

And the line went dead.

~*~

Well, Daniel should have seen that coming. He said exactly what he'd rehearsed, and it had sounded fine to him. Logical. Casual. But no, it was bad. She'd seen right through him.

When was the last time he'd asked a woman out? Eight years ago? Ten? He couldn't even remember for sure. However long, he was way out of practice. And he should be. Why in the world would he have practiced a skill he had no intention of ever using again?

At least he'd spent the last several years of his life—since Savannah left—telling himself that. He always believed the breakup was her fault. She hadn't been willing to go with him overseas. But now that time had passed and the wound was no longer fresh, he saw things differently. He had let his career take first place in his life. Above family, above personal relationships. Above God. And she must have seen it, too, because that's when he'd lost her.

How had Dad done it? If only he were still here to answer that question. And lots of others.

He went into medicine for Dad. Although he'd never pressured him, Daniel knew Dad's dreams and wanted to honor him. To make both Mom and Dad proud. But he wasn't a natural doctor like Dad. Medicine had been so demanding. And in wanting to please the parents who had rescued him, he'd lost sight of everything else for a while.

He wouldn't let that happen again.

He turned down the street he grew up on. Nothing there ever changed. The houses were still the same colors they'd been when he was a kid. Just fresher paint jobs. The manicured grounds displayed the same foliage. Some of it definitely more mature, but not different.

He pulled into the driveway and texted Vanna so she wouldn't be surprised. Then he pressed in the code. As the gate slid back, he drove through and waited until it closed again. He followed the driveway up to the side of the house and parked his truck next to the garage. All the curtains on the front of the house were drawn closed, but he could see through the windows in the garage doors. Savannah's car was there. The house sure looked dead, though.

He grabbed a few bags of groceries out of the backseat and headed toward the side door. As he placed his hand on the knob, the door opened to reveal Jared and Jeremy. "Hey, guys. How's it going?"

"Mommy said we can't go outside or open the door for anybody. Except you," Jeremy said.

"I'm glad you're obeying your mom. Here, take these, and I'll get the rest from the truck." He handed the boys the bags and returned to get the remainder.

As he stepped back into the mud room, Jared closed the door behind him and turned the deadbolt. Tears filled his dark eyes, and Daniel knelt down beside him. "Hey, buddy. Everything will be OK. Where's your mom?"

"In the shower," Jeremy answered.

"Why don't you guys let her know I'm here and then go get on your swimming trunks? I'll bet I can put all the groceries away and get changed before y'all are ready."

Their faces lit up as he headed into the kitchen. "What are you guys waiting for?"

They bolted toward the master suite, and Daniel began shoving items into the refrigerator. Then he dropped the non-refrigerated items in the pantry and headed toward his ex-bedroom. There should be an old pair of soccer shorts or something in the chest of drawers. Hopefully, they wouldn't be so small he couldn't squeeze into them.

The sound of laughter mixed with footsteps trickled down the hall. He grabbed some old board shorts and ran to the guest bathroom. He changed and then waited until he could hear twittering and shushing outside in the hall. Then he jerked open the door.

"We beat you!" Now the boys were more like themselves.

"Man, you sure did. You guys are fast!" Daniel pulled some towels from the linen closet. "Ready?" They headed back down the hall.

The pool looked great. That was one bad thing about living away from home: no convenient place to swim laps, although it didn't really matter. He'd been so busy getting the practice up and running, working out had been the farthest thing from his mind. Besides, there weren't enough hours in his days for one more thing right now. He'd look for a gym when he got back to Crescent Bluff and things calmed down.

"OK, guys. You can get on in. Just don't go past the ladder."

As he spread a towel out on one of the lounge chairs, Savannah walked onto the patio. Her hair was still wet from the shower.

"Hey, Vanna."

Her lips began to quiver and her eyes filled with tears. Her voice shook. "Danny."

She walked up and rested her head on his shoulder. He had no choice but to draw her close. "Shhhh. It's OK." He stroked her damp hair to give her enough time to collect herself and then relaxed his embrace.

"Danny, it's so hard. Will keeps texting and calling my cell phone and leaving messages. I'm scared he'll find us."

This was exactly why this whole thing was a bad idea. Trying to hide until after the decree. "Why haven't you blocked his number? You know I think you should call the police."

"No. What if he finds out where I am and kidnaps the boys? I couldn't live without them."

"That won't happen. He won't do that."

"You don't know that."

Her body trembled against him.

"Please come stay with us, Danny. Please," she begged. "I get so scared at night. I can't sleep. I hear every little sound. And I don't even want to let the boys go outside and play. This is the first time we've even used the pool."

He pulled her close again. "Savannah, this place is like a fortress. Plus, there's a twenty-four-hour security patrol. The number's on the side of the refrigerator. They can be here in minutes, if not seconds, if you think you need them. And there's no reason for you not to use the pool. The privacy fence is so tall even a giraffe couldn't see over it."

Her breathing became more even, so he drew away. "I'm sorry it's been so long since I've come by. Things have been really hectic these last few weeks. I'll try to get up here more often. But you can always call me if you need anything."

Eyes glistening, she nodded and grasped both his hands. "Do you ever think," she whispered, "how things might have turned out between us if I hadn't been such a self-centered snot in college?"

Years ago, when she'd left him, he'd often thought about that, wondering how life might have been if they'd made different choices. And he'd come to one conclusion. "We both wanted different things. We're better friends than lovers, Vanna."

"C'mon, Uncle Danny. When are you coming in?" Jared called behind him.

"You have very demanding kids. You know that?" He grinned as he squeezed her hands. "Why don't you go take a nap? The boys and I will be fine."

~*~

Ethne dropped down into the chair in her office. Her second "Decor-Gestion" customer had just left.

"So, how'd it go?" Alicia stood in the doorway.

"Good. They're remodeling their breakfast room. Once the construction's done, we'll do the redecorating. And then—assuming they like the design—we'll work on their den afterward."

"Great! I saw my third client the other day, so we're ahead on our monthly goal. I'd say your idea is a booming success."

"Our idea."

Alicia slipped into one of the chairs facing the desk. More than business was on her mind. "Well?"

"Well, what? Is everything OK?"

"Can we expect a visit from Dr. Handsome today? I mean, I figured he was more than simply a client since you spent the night together." Her eyes sparkled.

"We did not spend the night together."

"Uh-huh. Right. Weren't you in the same truck? On the same night? In the same place all night long? By definition, I'd say that's definitely spending the night together."

She was so infuriating sometimes, and she was loving every second of this. "Just because we were in the same place at the same time, doesn't mean we were 'together.'"

"Oh, aren't you just the epitome of self-control!" A smirk covered her face. "Hey, have you seen your grandmother's old buffet since the guys got it done? It's all finished except for the new hardware."

She followed Alicia to the shop. The buffet had been painted soft white and then distressed to make it look even older than it was. "It's gorgeous."

"Isn't it?"

"What do you think?" She hadn't heard Nick walk up behind them.

Ethne turned and smiled at him. "Beautiful job."

"Wait until you see the bedroom set. I was wrong. You made the right call to refinish it."

"You dared think otherwise?" Alicia laughed. "You should have known better than to doubt the Furniture Whisperer."

"Yes, I should have." Nick's voice dripped with pretended contrition. "As soon as the guys get the hardware installed, we'll make some space and move the buffet onto the showroom floor."

"No."

"No?" Both Alicia and Nick spoke in unison.

"It'll be really hard to sell from back here in the shop," Alicia continued.

"It's already sold."

12

Ethne eased the door closed behind her. The empty waiting room looked like something out of a decorating magazine. The clock was the perfect accessory for the back wall. An attractive blonde smiled at her from behind the counter. "Welcome to Crescent Bluff Primary Care. Do you have an appointment?"

"Yes. No. Well, not a medical appointment. I'm Ethne O'Connor. I have a two o'clock appointment with Daniel...Dr. Spenser."

"Of course." The receptionist glanced at her computer screen. Her face reddened and her smile disappeared. "You're Vaughn's daughter, aren't you? I saw you at the funeral."

"Yes."

"I loved that man." Her eyes glistened. "He was like a father to me."

She had no doubt Vaughn loved this young woman in return, but not in the way a father would or should.

"Please have a seat. I'll let Dr. Spenser know you're here."

Ethne sat down in one of the striped arm chairs and then set her computer case and portfolio on the floor beside her. She took a few seconds to soak in the feel of the room. The new decor—homey and inviting rather than sterile and clinical—had pretty much erased any of Vaughn's influence. The waiting room looked nothing as it had when she was a child. She had almost forgotten the history of the room until the receptionist reminded her.

She stood and walked over to the old oak exam table they'd gotten at the flea market. Daniel had been right. She ran her fingers across the top's carved front edge. It made a perfect console table. A fiddle leaf fig tree stood beside it on the floor, its rounded leaves softening the straight edges of the table. Fanned out magazines lay on the top. She couldn't help but smile. He'd done a great job.

"So? What do you think?" Daniel roused her from her thoughts.

"Well done." She turned toward him. "It's…"

He stood behind her smiling. He wore khaki dress pants, a blue shirt, striped tie, and cordovan oxfords. A white lab coat with "Dr. Daniel Spenser, Crescent Bluff Primary Care" embroidered on it in royal blue completed the look. He was clean shaven, unlike the last time she'd seen him, and his brown hair was meticulously combed into place. He looked even more professional than he had the first time they'd met at the house. And handsome. As she moved her gaze to his eyes, she could almost taste chocolate kisses.

"Ethne?"

"Amazing. You look, um, I mean the room looks amazing. You may have missed your calling in life."

"Thanks. I'm really happy with the way it turned out. But I never could have done it without your help. Your amazing help."

The blonde receptionist cleared her throat as she approached them. "Will that be all, Dr. Spenser?"

"Yes, Sarah. Thanks. I'll see you tomorrow morning."

"Sure thing. Nice to meet you, Ms. O'Connor."

"You, too, Sarah."

Daniel followed her to the door, closed it behind her, and then locked the dead bolt. He slipped off his lab coat and hung it on one of the hooks by the door. "Another day down."

"How's business?"

"It's been great. Amazing." He winked. "Really, I had to work hard to keep this afternoon's calendar clear for you."

"Thanks, but I doubt the consultation will take the rest of the day."

"That's actually good, because I couldn't quite reschedule everything. I have one more appointment later this afternoon." He reached down and picked up her computer case and portfolio. "May I? Computer images are OK, but I have an easier time visualizing stuff if I'm in the actual space. I thought we could meet upstairs." His face reddened. "As long as you're OK with that."

She spent the entire drive down here preparing herself for this moment. Convincing herself she could handle going upstairs if that's what Daniel wanted. After all, the first day they brought Daniel here, she made herself go upstairs with no issues.

Not being alone during those times had helped stave off any panic. And she wouldn't be alone today. She'd told herself she could do it, and she would. "Sure. I'm fine. Lead on."

Daniel climbed the old wooden stairway at the end of the hall.

Ethne took a deep breath and followed. The top step still groaned as it had over twenty years ago. "At some point, I need to get that fixed, although it does make a good burglar alarm." He opened the door to the apartment and stepped aside. "Well, home sweet home. Ladies first."

She would do this. For years, she'd been running away from the memories, and now it was time to face them. No, not just face them, but conquer them.

As she stepped through the doorway, relief flooded over her. The living room in no way resembled the living room from her early childhood. In fact, she wouldn't even call it a living room. It was more of a minimally-subsisting room.

A large inflatable mattress occupied the center of the area where she'd planned to place the sofa and chairs. On it laid a rumpled sleeping bag. In the dining area, two folding camp chairs flanked a footlocker that was obviously being used as a makeshift table. Under the window, some stacked cinderblocks and boards made primitive shelves that held books, a TV, and some of his personal items. A bunch of shoe boxes were stacked along the back wall next to the stairway to the third floor. Obviously, some sort of primitive filing or storage system.

"Told you I didn't have much. Just bought the TV last week. I figured it would be better to wait until after I got your suggestions before I chose anything else."

"It's easier to start with a blank canvas when you're painting a new picture."

"Only if you're an artist. Which you are." He grinned. "But some of us need paint-by-number."

"There's something to be said for not always coloring within the lines. Case in point, the accessories you chose for your reception room were so out-of-the-box, but they look…amazing."

His face reddened, and he looked away. She'd never seen him embarrassed before. He was generally so poised. Even when he'd stood up and protested that first day in the meeting with Jackson Williams, his voice, though raised and direct, was still very much under control. Maybe there was a lecture on controlling your emotions in med school. If so, Vaughn must have been absent that day.

"Thanks." He gestured toward the chairs and footlocker. "I, uh, guess we better get to work. I can't wait to see your suggestions."

She moved toward the chair facing the kitchen—the one with its back toward the door to the front closet.

"Oh, wait. Speaking of artists, before you sit down, I want to show you something cool I found."

He was walking toward the door to the closet. Her heart began to pound.

He grinned as he opened the door. "I have a feeling you or Sean might be responsible for these."

He motioned her over, but some unseen force glued her feet to the spot. She couldn't move. She couldn't look. Tears filled her eyes. Her heart raced.

If you don't stop crying, I'll give you something to really cry about.

The memories of what seemed like hours spent locked in there in the dark with a flashlight gripped her chest. She told her body to run down the stairs, but her legs were concrete blocks. She couldn't move, she couldn't breathe. Everything became fuzzy, and the room began to swim. She was going to pass out. She needed to sit down. Help, she needed help.

~*~

Daniel caught Ethne as her knees buckled. He held her close. Her fingers dug into his biceps. She was having what looked like a panic attack. He got in her face. "Ethne, look at me. You're hyperventilating. I need you to do what I say. Breathe in while I count, hold it, and then breathe out while I count again."

She breathed in slowly while he counted.

"Now hold it." He counted again. "Now exhale. Again." They'd do this as long as necessary until she calmed down.

After a minute or so, she was still pale and clammy, but her breathing was more normal and her heart rate had slowed. He helped her ease down into one of the chairs. "Don't get up. I'll be right back."

He stepped into the kitchen and returned with a bottle of water. "Here. Drink some." He handed it to her and then rested his hand on her forehead. No fever. He placed his fingertips on her wrist. Her pulse was a little rapid but nothing to be concerned about.

He sat down in the chair next to hers. "You OK?"

She nodded, although her face said otherwise.

"So, has anything like this ever happened to you before?"

She shook her head, and her hand trembled as she took another sip of water.

"I'm pretty sure you had a panic attack, and it may just be a one-time thing that'll never happen again. But I recommend you go see your PCP and get it checked out just in case. I'm about ninety percent sure that's what it is. But you need to figure out what triggered it."

Her eyes glistened as they filled with tears.

He reached over and covered her free hand with his. "Hey, it's gonna be OK. I promise."

"That's what I've been telling myself for almost twenty years. And it's a lie." Her voice was coarse, her words broken, as she spoke through her tears.

"Ethne, I—"

"It's the closet." The tears trailed down her cheeks.

"The closet?" He didn't get it. "I just saw some kids' drawings on the walls in there and thought—"

"I drew them—most of them. Sean scribbled some—to pass the time when Vaughn was having one of his spells. My mom would lock us in there out of his way until he calmed down."

He clenched his jaw. How could anyone do that to a child? "Ethne, that's abuse."

"She was trying to protect us." Her lips quivered. "I figured out really quickly what actions triggered his anger and was careful to avoid them. I learned to be quiet and obedient. To not do anything that brought attention to me."

He ran his fingers through his hair and tried to swallow back the anger that had risen in his throat. He'd noticed the slash marks on the outside of her forearm the day he'd had his first consultation at the store. That wasn't something a person brought up when just meeting someone. But now…

He reached his hand over and slipped up her sleeve to reveal the scars. "And these?"

"I didn't know you'd seen those," she whispered. "Most of them are from a time when Sean accidentally spilled his milk, and I was trying to get him into the closet to protect him. The belt buckle got me instead of him. Then there were other times…"

He had to move. He jumped up, held his head in his hands, and paced between the mattress and the chairs. He was furious but didn't want to do anything that might add fuel to the fire. He took a deep breath as he turned back to face her. "Did you tell anyone?"

She shook her head. "Only Molly and Alicia know. Oh, and my counselor. And now you. Sean was probably too young to even remember. He's never mentioned it."

"You should have told someone." His tone was sharper than he intended and probably sounded accusatory, although he didn't mean for it to.

"No. No. I couldn't do that to my mother. Our family's reputation meant everything to her. Besides, when we moved to the house, there was more space, and it was easier to stay out of his way." Her uneven breathing was the only sound filling the room.

"I'm sorry. I didn't mean it the way it sounded." He walked toward her and offered his hand. "Do you think you can stand?"

She placed her hand in his and took her time to stand.

"You OK?"

She nodded.

"Let's get you back downstairs." Placing his arm around her waist, he drew her close to his side. They made their way across the wooden floor to the stairs. He tightened his hold as they carefully descended.

A few minutes ago, he'd held her up, touched her face, her forehead, her wrist. That contact had been professional. This...this was personal. They reached the bottom.

He wanted to gather her against himself to take some of the burden she'd been carrying all these years. "I'm sorry, Ethne. So sorry."

He wrapped his arms around her, and she didn't pull away. She leaned her head on his shoulder, and he brushed his lips against her hair. It smelled like lavender. Then he rested his cheek on the top of her head.
It wasn't exactly the same, but he knew the feelings. He understood. He'd like to share his childhood with her, but now wasn't the time. Someday, he'd tell her that they had more in common than she could imagine.

~*~

The glass cooled her cheek as Ethne leaned her head against the window of Daniel's truck. Burned by the Texas heat, the early summer grass was already brown. The Bible talked about being purified by fire. But that only worked for some things. Grass died.

Now four people knew. Molly, Alicia, her counselor, Lynn, and Daniel. She'd never intended for more than the original three to find out. She'd thought she was over it. For years, she'd managed everything quite well, or so she'd convinced herself. But no. She'd only been avoiding the issue. She'd never be over it. Maybe it was time to go back and see Lynn again. That is, if she was still in practice.

"Take the next left turn." Gently admonishing them, the soothing voice from the GPS broke the silence in the car.

Ethne glanced over at Daniel. He'd been unusually quiet since they'd left the office. His face offered no clue as to his thoughts. About her, Vaughn, Mother.

He'd refused to leave her alone and had, instead, gently insisted she accompany him on this house call. A house call. She hadn't realized doctors even did that anymore.

Her usual response would have been to decline, but today was different. She hadn't wanted to be left alone at his office, and she'd been in no shape to drive home. She still wasn't. She might have to find a room in Crescent Bluff for the night and drive back tomorrow.

Daniel turned left onto a dirt road and followed it as it wound away from the highway toward the old farmhouse nestled far back in an oasis of live oaks. "Do you know Mr. Adams?" His words startled her.

She shook her head before she realized he was watching the road and not her. "No."

"Josh, uh, Pastor Lewis, called me and asked if I'd look in on him. He fell and broke his arm a few weeks ago, so he can't drive. He usually sees a physician in Waco, but his daughter couldn't take him today. So, I'm going to make sure he's still doing OK. Shouldn't take too long."

"I didn't think doctors today made house calls."

"It's probably not very common, but I'm sure there are some others who do."

Vaughn had made certain types of house calls. Only during the day, and only when the husbands weren't home. He would have never done this.

Daniel stopped the truck in front of the house and shifted it into park. He reached into the backseat and grabbed a scuffed up old black medical bag. "My dad's. My mom saved it for me."

The last time she'd seen Vaughn's bag, it had been pristine. As though it had never been used.

"Now, so that I look official." He pulled the stethoscope out of the bag and draped it around his neck. "Would you be more comfortable waiting in the truck, or would you prefer to sit on the porch?"

A breeze rustled the periwinkles in the pots on the front porch. "The porch is fine."

He turned off the engine. They got out of the truck, and she followed him up onto the porch. Weakness had replaced the dizziness from earlier. She felt as if she had run a marathon. Or at least how she imagined she'd feel. All she wanted to do was lie down and sleep. She dropped into one of the rockers.

Daniel knocked on the door. "Mr. Adams? It's Dr. Spenser."

After a few seconds, the door opened to reveal a short, elderly man who was about as wide as he was tall. His hair was snow white, and his eyes cornflower blue. If he'd had a beard, he'd have looked like Santa. Except for the sling.

"My goodness. Ain't you a young one."

Daniel chuckled. "The older I get, the more I like to hear that."

Mr. Adams stepped away from the door and gestured back toward the house with his good arm. "You and Mrs. Spenser come on in."

"Oh, we're not married." Daniel shot a quick look in her direction and grinned. "She's…a friend making house calls with me today. She's happy to wait on the porch."

"Friend, you say?" He shook his head. "I just don't get you young folk nowadays. When I was your age, I'd 'a snapped her up quicker'n you can blink." He stepped aside. "Well, don't just stand there. Both of y'all come on in. She's more than welcome, too."

Even in the bright summer sun, the old shiplap walls made the house dark and cool. She would have painted the walls a soft white or a pale gray to lighten things up.

"Where to, Doc?" Mr. Adams asked.

"Right here in your recliner's just fine. Ethne, would you mind waiting for us in the kitchen?"

"I'll be glad to. Take your time." She walked into the kitchen and sat on one of the ladder-back chairs around the old oak table. Daniel was taking Mr. Adams's blood pressure. She pulled her phone out of her pocket to check e-mail and to act as a distraction so she'd be less tempted to watch. It worked until the tearing sound of Velcro drew her attention away from her phone and back to them.

Daniel dropped the blood pressure cuff back into his bag and then slowly began to ease the sling off Mr. Adams's other arm. Although she couldn't understand their words, the tone of their conversation was warm, relaxed.

Daniel's movements were unhurried. His hands gentle. Just as they'd been this afternoon. Before then, the only men she could remember touching her, outside of a professional handshake or brief accidental brush, were either relatives or pastors. As she closed her eyes, her body recalled the tenderness of his earlier touch. And the strength of those same hands as he held her up to keep her from falling.

His movements had been, and still were, artistic. Strength clothed in gentleness. Like those of a potter shaping his clay or a violinist coaxing forth a beautiful melody. His hands were instruments of beauty and healing, not punishment. Vessels of love.

Something she'd never known a man's hands could be.

~*~

Daniel's truck tires roared over the old brick boulevard as he followed her through Arlington Heights. He would have never guessed Ethne's house was only about five minutes from Mom and Dad's.

She insisted she was well enough to drive home, and he insisted he follow her. All afternoon, since her panic attack, two emotions had been at war within him. Concern for her. And anger toward her father. When he was younger, he would have wanted to seek some sort of revenge, but he couldn't do that toward a dead person. Plus, maturity had taught him vengeance wasn't his job. His job was to heal. But it was still OK for him to be angry. He was pretty sure his Father was, too.

He followed Ethne as she turned off Camp Bowie, and then pulled into the driveway of a little 1920's bungalow. This house was so her. Remodeled and given new life. Resurrected. He pulled in behind her, and then as she got out, he did, too.

"I told you I could make it."

"You did." He followed her to the front steps.

"See. I'm just fine."

"I'm glad." Something about this felt like an under-the-porch-light-doorstep-after-date good night. Or at least how he thought it should feel. College had been the last time he'd experienced one, and that was a long time ago.

"I'll have Alicia call you tomorrow and set up a time to come install everything in a couple of weeks."

"Sounds great."

She unlocked the door and pushed it open. "Good night."

"Good night, Ethne." He turned to walk back to the driveway.

"Daniel?"

He turned back. "Yes?"

"Thank you. For everything."

"You're welcome."

He made his way to his truck. Today had been long, and he was tired. Mom and Dad's house was only a few minutes away. He could stay in the guest room and get up really early in the morning to go back to Crescent Bluff.

As good as that sounded, he'd be setting a precedent that would only cause trouble in the future. Besides, wasn't he the one who preferred to drive at night? He'd drive through at some fast-food restaurant and get a large coffee.

13

Ethne jumped as the doorbell sounded. Ten o'clock on a Monday morning. She wasn't expecting anyone. She'd hide out in the kitchen and wait for the caller to leave. The doorbell rang again followed by a series of loud raps a few seconds later. The visitor was persistent if nothing else.

She tiptoed into the living room and peeked out onto the porch. She couldn't see him, but she could see the truck.

"Ethne, it's Daniel," a muffled voice sounded through the door.

What was he doing here? He should have been at his apartment. The painting had been completed last Wednesday, and they were loading everything today.

Ignoring him would do no good. He obviously knew she was here. "Just a minute."

She ran to the bedroom and grabbed her robe from the foot of the bed. Pulling it on, she headed back to open the door.

He stood there holding a large bouquet of mixed flowers. "I wasn't sure what your favorite is, so I got a little bit of everything they had."

"Thank you. But I—What are you doing here? Don't you want to be at your apartment while they set up everything?"

"I trust you guys. This way I'll get to see it all at once when it's done. Kind of like a reveal on those TV shows. Besides, Alicia told me you weren't feeling well."

"She did?" Alicia didn't know Daniel knew the truth about her past. "After the episode in your apartment, she volunteered to go in my place today and was just trying to cover for me."

He held out the bouquet. "Well, now that you're not sick, what am I supposed to do with these?" His brow wrinkled as he waited for a reply.

"I certainly wouldn't want them to go to waste. But I wouldn't want to accept them under false pretenses either."

"You wouldn't be. I was pretty sure you weren't sick despite what Alicia said. But if it'll make you feel better, I have my medical bag in the truck. I can double check."

"So, that's what this is? A long-distance house call?"

"Kind of. I was hoping you'd let me take you to lunch at my favorite place." As a blush crept across his face, he glanced down at his feet.

When he looked back up and his gaze found hers, all she saw was chocolate kisses, and her breathing caught.

"Kind of as payment for all the grief you've suffered because of me."

"That's not necessary, Daniel. None of it was your fault."

"It would make me feel better if you'd come."

The easiest thing to say would be "no." But he had driven all this way. He had brought her get-well flowers, even though he'd rightly suspected she wasn't sick. And he believed his actions had brought about the panic attack she'd suffered. Didn't she at least owe him the opportunity to clear his conscience?

She stepped back and motioned for him to enter. "Why don't you put these in water while I get dressed. There's a vase in the cabinet above the refrigerator."

He grinned. "Thanks."

"What should I wear? Any special instructions?"

"Very casual. And wear comfortable shoes. There's a short walk involved."

He had on shorts, a t-shirt, and hiking sandals. That was a good hint. "I'm not a master of the two-minute shower like someone else in this room, but if you'll give me fifteen minutes, I think I can be ready."

"You got it."

"So what is your favorite?" His question followed her down the hall.

"Favorite what?"

"Flower."

"Daisies and zinnias. My mother always grew them in her garden because she said they were hardy and resilient. They would survive even in the worst conditions."

~*~

"Are we in Louisiana yet?"

Daniel glanced over at Ethne. Her smile betrayed the impatient tone of her voice. "No. I can stop at the next convenience store and get you something if you're feeling faint."

"I would've packed a snack if I'd known the restaurant was in another state."

He hadn't remembered the drive taking so long. "Sorry. It's been awhile since I've been there, and it's farther than I thought. But just to put your mind at rest, we'll still be in Texas. In fact, we're heading more toward Mexico than Louisiana."

She sighed and pushed her head back against the seat. She'd chosen jean shorts and an orange Texas Longhorn t-shirt. Fortunately, she'd worn tennis shoes because flip-flops would be totally inappropriate. This was the first time he'd seen her so casual, and she looked amazing. Her face was scrubbed clean and her hair pulled back in a ponytail-bun thing. Absolutely amazing. There was that word again. He pressed his lips together to hide his grin.

"What? What's so funny?"

"Nothing. Oh, here's the turn." They left the highway and headed toward one of his favorite places on earth. Dad brought him here that summer before high school, and it had changed his life. As he drove up to Fort Worth, he'd prayed it would have the same effect on her.

The road narrowed, forcing him to drive slower. "So, you didn't tell me you went to UT."

"That's because I didn't. Why would you think...? Oh, the shirt. Sean sent this to me when he got accepted. I think he expected me to wear it to some of his football games."

"And?"

"Football's not my thing. Besides, I had my hands full working evenings and weekends to support myself as I finished up college. I went to a local college. Put myself through school with no debt and started my own business."

"You should be proud of yourself and what you've accomplished."

"My father said I'd never be a success. That I wasn't smart enough. That I should just get married and have babies."

The pavement ended, and now they were on a gravel road.

"Proving him wrong has been my greatest motivation." Her eyes glistened as she turned away to stare out the passenger side window.

Oh, he understood. He'd known the pain she felt, the desire to prove someone wrong. He'd heard similar words, spoken out of hurt and anger, telling him he was stupid and would never amount to anything. And then Dad had brought him here.

Since her panic attack, he'd prayed daily for Ethne. And each time he'd prayed, a quiet Voice had urged him to bring her here. To the place where he'd found his peace, so she might have the same chance to find hers.

He hadn't been back here since before he left for the Air Force, but this looked like the right place, so he pulled off what had now transitioned into a dirt road. "We're here."

Dry-eyed, but red-faced, she turned back to him. "Where's the restaurant?"

"Who said anything about a restaurant?"

"You did."

"Nope. Don't think so."

"Yes, you did. You said you wanted to take me to your favorite restaurant."

"No, I said I wanted to take you to lunch at my favorite place."

"Whatever. It's the same thing. You're mincing words."

"You, Miss Consultant, are about to be proven wrong."

~*~

Ethne was starving. He'd been joking about the convenience store, but if the trip had taken much longer, his joke would have needed to become reality. And here they were in the middle of nowhere. No restaurants, no gas stations. Nothing. She pulled her phone out of her pocket. No cell service, either. Maybe she should have stayed home. This was beginning to look like a rerun of the trip home from the flea market. Except he seemed to know where he was and where he was going.

He slid on a camo backpack. "Ready?"

"Please tell me there's food in that thing."

"There's food in this thing."

"Then yes, I'm ready."

She followed him toward a small canyon, and they began a slow descent on a path along the wall. Cedar trees and other foliage she couldn't name seemed to grow straight out of the rock wall. But somewhere hidden in the crevices there had to be some soil for them to take root. Amazing that such a small amount of nourishment could grow such strong trees. Amazing. She grinned.

He turned back toward her. "What's so funny?"

She placed her hands on her hips. "Nothing. Just like nothing was funny before."

He smiled and then slipped off the backpack. "Would you mind holding this while I climb down this one part, and then you can hand it down to me?"

She grasped the straps, and he lowered himself down to a ledge on the side of the small canyon.

"OK. Hand me the backpack. And then I'll help you down."

Once he slipped the backpack on, he offered her his hand.

"I can do it." She turned around and backed down, holding onto the small saplings accessorizing the canyon walls rather than his hand.

The minute her feet hit the path, a distant roaring that hadn't been audible from above rushed through the small canyon. "Is that what I think it is?"

"And exactly what do you think it is?"

"A waterfall?"

"It is." He smiled. "A very special waterfall."

She followed him along the path until the roaring became so loud she could hear nothing else and water droplets transformed the Texas summer heat into a cooling mist. They rounded a bend, and there it was. Unfurling over the canyon ledge in front of them, silver ribbons of water mixed with the sunlight to paint rainbows in the mist. She reached forward and grabbed his arm to get his attention.

Turning, he raised his eyebrows and leaned toward her in response.

She placed her lips close to his ear. The fragrance of his cologne was earthy, enticing. "Amazing. It's absolutely amazing, Daniel." As she made a comma motion with her finger, he grinned and winked.

He pointed to a small opening in the rock ahead of them and then turned his lips toward her ear, "Just wait. The amazingness has only begun."

The slippery pathway demanded she take careful steps as she followed him into what appeared to be a small cave. Away from the summer sun, the dark air cooled her skin, and the thick rock walls lessened the roaring of the falls outside. Initials carved into the wall ahead proved others had visited this place, too.

He led her deeper into the cave until the walkway turned sharply to the left, and there they were. Behind the cascading water. The magnificence took her breath away. Surely, they had left Texas. She had to be in another state, or country, or universe.

High above the rocks, the waterfall whispered as it began its descent and prepared to thunder into the pool below. Once again, they could hear each other speak.

"Oh, Daniel. This is unbelievable."

"And the perfect spot to have lunch." He set the backpack down, pulled out one of those Mylar emergency blankets, and spread it on the rock floor underfoot.

"This is beginning to look so military. What else have you got in there? K rations?"

"No MREs in this bag. May I help you down?"

This time she took his hand. Its warmth revived memories of the gentleness of his touch that day at the apartment. "Thank you."

Looking through the wall of water before her was like looking through rippled antique glass that had settled in waves over time.

Except these waves were vertical instead of horizontal, and they were in motion. The effect was like an impressionist painting. A shimmering, softened suggestion of the reality beyond the water.

"Lunch is served."

He had transformed the space between them into a buffet of fruit and cheeses, crackers, hummus with carrots and celery, olives, and a small bag of chocolate kisses.

He handed her a bottle of water. "Mind if I bless the food?"

She shook her head.

Bowing his head, he leaned closer, almost as if he were sharing a secret with her. His words were hushed and warm. She felt them as much as heard them.

"Amen." He handed her a paper plate. "So, what do you think of my favorite lunch place?"

"I don't think words can adequately describe my thoughts. How in the world did you find this spot?"

"My dad brought me here one summer when I was having a hard time."

~*~

Daniel had prayed about this very moment for weeks now. "I'm adopted. My biological parents were high school students—unmarried. And I was nothing but the result of a lack of birth control. I never knew my father. He was killed in a car wreck before I was born, and my mother was into drugs. My entire childhood was spent in and out of foster homes."

"Oh, Daniel, I had no idea. I'm sorry."

"It's OK. I had some great foster parents, but that was the problem. I knew they were only temporary and when my mother got clean again, I'd get sent back to her. Things would always start out the same way. She'd be loving until her addiction took over. Then she'd lose her job, and we'd have no money for food. She'd scream I was a mistake, that she wished I'd never been born, that I would end up just like her. Many days the only food I ate was what I found in restaurant dumpsters. I used the cardboard from the boxes to patch the holes in my shoes. And I hated her for it. I swore I'd never forgive her, and that I'd prove her wrong. That I'd never go hungry, never have holey clothes."

As he set his plate down, she reached over and rested her hand on his. "I'm so sorry." Her eyes resonated with the same hurt he'd known.

"The last foster home I ended up in was with Mom and Dad. They were kind and loving. And when my mother died from an overdose, they adopted me. I couldn't believe they actually wanted me."

As she nodded, her words were coarse and broken. "I...understand."

He lay back and folded his arms behind his head like a pillow. The sun reflected off the curtain of water and cast images of sparkling diamonds across the cave ceiling. "Look, Ethne."

She lay back beside him. "Amazing."

He closed his eyes and let the rushing of the falls sweep the memories away.

"That's so unfair, so wrong." Her voice broke through. "Shouldn't parents be the first image of God a child sees? Why would anybody ever want to know the God who would let children be treated like that? Like you were treated? Like I was treated."

He raised up. "I've thought about that over the years." He offered her his hand to help her up. "Look at your reflection in the blanket. Can you see your image?"

She nodded.

"Does it look like you?"

"I certainly hope not."

"Exactly. That's because the blanket's imperfect. It's wrinkled and scratched. Plus, it's a two-dimensional object trying to reflect a three-dimensional being. And that just doesn't work. How can something that's flawed provide a perfect reflection?"

She pulled her knees to her chest and encircled them with her arms. Then she slowly rocked back and forth in silence, her eyes staring ahead toward the curtain of water.

He picked up his plate and bit into a carrot.

"So you were saying your dad brought you here?"

"Yeah. His dad had brought him here, too, when he was a kid. Grandpa told him that God's love is just like this waterfall. Pure, abundant, cleansing, ever-flowing. Loud enough to drown out the noise and clamor of the lying voices around us and inside us."

Her gaze still focused ahead. Her far-off stare gave the appearance she wasn't listening. But the glimmer of tears in her eyes confirmed she was.

"The trick is whether we choose to simply watch its beauty or immerse ourselves in it. Let it wash over us. Free us from being enslaved to the past."

As a tear trickled down her cheek, he scooted over and placed his arm around her. He wouldn't have been surprised if she'd pulled away. Instead, she leaned her head against his shoulder. "I'm not saying it's easy, Ethne. It's a constant battle. Some days the old voice of failure and worthlessness creeps back in and speaks its lies. Then I remind myself Whose I am, and how much He loves me. How He has forever adopted me."

He'd been obedient, and his job here was just about finished. What happened next was up to her. And God. "So, how about a kiss for dessert?"

She jerked away. "Excuse me?"

"No. No." His face burned as he reached behind his back and grabbed the bag of candy. Nothing like ruining the mood. "Chocolate, I meant."

Her shocked look morphed into a soft smile as she grasped the bag. "Maybe later."

One last thing to do before they left. He stood and kicked off his sandals.

"What are you doing?"

"The same thing I do every time I come here." He pulled his shirt over his head and dropped it beside his shoes. Then he held out his hand. "Come with me?"

She stood and moved toward the back wall of the cave. "Are you crazy? That's really dangerous."

"Yeah. It is, isn't it?" He still offered his hand.

She shook her head.

"Have it your way." He handed her his phone and his keys. "Hang on to these for me, will you?" Then he turned toward the wall of water. The first time he'd done this, Dad had been waiting in the pool at the bottom. Every time after that, it had been just him and his heavenly Father.

"See you later." He took a deep breath and ran through the curtain of water.

14

Ethne glanced over at Daniel. His hair was still damp and spiked in all directions from his run through the waterfall. He tuned the radio to some Christian station when they left the canyon and was now humming along with one of the songs. No conversation had passed between them thus far.

He jumped. Really jumped. She thought he was kidding around. But no. A knot formed in her stomach. It was a stupid thing to do. She was glad he was still alive. And, she was glad he came to her house today. That he'd taken her to his favorite place and shared his story with her.

But most of all, she was glad she shared her past with him. Alicia and Molly were the only other people who knew the whole truth, and neither one of them could really get it. They could listen sympathetically, but they both grew up in loving homes, and try as they might, they couldn't truly understand. But Daniel could.

He turned toward her and smiled. "You OK?"

"Just thinking."

"A long car ride's a good time to do that." He trained his gaze back onto the road and resumed humming as a new song came on the radio.

The lyrics said something about not being enslaved to fear because we're God's children. That was pretty much what Daniel had said earlier. And he obviously believed his words, but they only confused her. She'd spent so many years believing something different that she didn't know if she could change. Or if she even wanted to. Her life was going smoothly. It was working, and the last thing she wanted was to ruffle the waters.

The image of the waterfall burst into her mind. Daniel had

compared it to God's love, and as it fell into the pool at the bottom of the small canyon, it definitely ruffled the water below. No, it churned it up and mixed it together until the waterfall and the pool became one.

When he'd pulled off his shirt before he'd jumped, she'd thought she might pass out from not being able to breathe. At first, she'd figured it was only from fear, but it was more than that. Even now, the image still filled her stomach with butterflies.

She'd never had a boyfriend. And she'd spent most of her life telling herself she didn't want one because men couldn't be trusted. Mother had died from a broken heart because of Vaughn's unfaithfulness. Ethne had felt the pain caused by his anger. She never wanted to take a chance she'd become entangled with a man who could do that to her...or their children. She promised herself the abuse would end with her, and celibacy was the only way to ensure that.

But maybe she'd been wrong all these years. Maybe all men were not like Vaughn. Take Josh, her pastor, for instance. He was a fine man. But there was only one of him.

And how did one person really know what another was like? Seeing a man's heart was impossible. All that was visible were his actions. Actions that could be deceiving. And once people got married, it was too late.

But something happened today. Everything she'd convinced herself she believed all these years had been washed over the side of the cave. She didn't understand how, or even why. But when she watched Daniel run through the waterfall, everything changed.

Fear squeezed her heart. Certainly, fear for his safety, but greater than that, fear she would lose him. An overwhelming sense of emptiness filled her and caused her to do something she hadn't done in years. She prayed. It was quick. She couldn't remember the words she thought. Only the desperation that birthed them. And although the rough words may not have made it through the cave's rock ceiling, she'd had to do something and had known nothing else to do.

Daniel was different from any man she'd ever known. He was kind. His touch was gentle. And he had the ability to understand her on a level no one else she knew could. He'd lived through a childhood similar to hers. And he'd survived. No, he'd flourished. He was still flourishing.

He was handsome, intelligent, kind. So, why didn't he have a girlfriend? Or maybe he did. She'd never asked, and he'd never said. But what about today? She wouldn't have liked it if she had a boyfriend and he'd taken another woman on a picnic to the falls. Hopefully, he wouldn't do that to a woman. Vaughn would, but surely not Daniel.

She had to figure out a way to gently steer the conversation that direction. "So, why aren't you dating anyone?" Well, that was about as subtle as a bomb blast.

"Excuse me?" His face and neck reddened. "What would make you think I'm not dating anyone?"

"I'm sorry. I assumed…"

"You assumed no woman would be interested in me. Is that it?"

"No. I just—I mean—you've never mentioned a woman in your life." Her hands were clammy, and embarrassment burned her face; she could feel it. "I figured if you had a girlfriend, she would have helped you choose the furniture and accessories for your apartment. Most women would want to have some input…" She'd better stop before she dug the hole any deeper. "Sorry."

She looked out her window at the flatness that was this part of Texas. The music from the radio faded away as he turned it down and then off.

"Your assumption would be correct."

She turned back toward him.

He grinned. "Or at least partially correct. I'm not dating anyone, and I haven't dated anyone seriously for a very long time. Since college. We broke up when she decided she wasn't the type to marry an Air Force doctor."

"I imagine that was hard."

His grin disappeared. "It was. Sometimes still is. We dated all through college, and I had a ring in my pocket the night she broke up with me." He stared straight ahead in silence for a few seconds. "But I get it. Military life can be tough sometimes. All the moving and being away from family. And then add in TDYs and a physician's long hours. I would've hated for her to have married me and ended up miserable."

"What was her name?"

"Savannah." His gaze found hers for a moment, and then he looked back toward the road. "She made me understand how hard the life I'd chosen could be for a wife. That's why I stopped looking. It's just easier when the only person I have to consider is myself."

His words alone might have sounded selfish, but his reason for speaking them was filled with selflessness.

The revving of the truck engine lessened. "You know the hardest part, though?" He paused for only a second, obviously not expecting a reply from her. But she shook her head anyway. "My birth mother's voice in my head telling me Savannah left because I was stupid. Unlovable. A failure." He faced her. "The day after our breakup was the first time I came to the falls by myself. I needed a concrete reminder of Whose child I really am."

She had no response. She'd spent so many years running away from Vaughn, denying she could possibly be his child. But she had no destination. No One to run toward as Daniel had.

"What about you? Are you dating anyone?" His question pierced her thoughts.

"No."

"What about that Nick guy from work?"

"We're just co-workers."

"You may need to tell him that." He chuckled.

"No, seriously. We had a misunderstanding that night at Ricky's, but we got it all straightened out."

"So, tell me about your last relationship, then."

"Nothing to tell."

"Sure." The smirk on his face said he didn't believe her.

"Really. I've never had a boyfriend."

His face softened as he stared through the windshield. "Well, I know it can't be because no one's been interested."

She spent most of her high school and college years building a protective shield around herself. A barrier no man could break through. When college ended, it got easier. She was too busy getting her business off the ground, and men quit asking. She shrugged her shoulders. "The one who wasn't interested was me."

As he turned toward her, a look of understanding spread across his face. He got it. He covered her hand with his. "Remember the waterfall."

His touch was warm, gentle, just as it had been when he examined her after the panic attack. She forced herself to draw her hand away and turned her face toward the window. How could he make it sound so simple?

The feelings she'd smothered for so many years had suddenly begun to spark to life. If she would ever trust a man, it would be someone like him. The problem was, he was the only man she'd ever met like him. And he'd just confessed he had no interest in a romantic relationship.

As the music on the radio filled the car again and he resumed his humming, she pushed her head back against the seat and closed her eyes.

~*~

Daniel parked the pickup in her driveway and killed the engine. He waited a couple of seconds for her to react, but nothing happened. Before she fell asleep, she withdrew into a cocoon. Something had been on her mind. Maybe she'd been thinking about their conversation at lunch, and if so, that was great. Mission accomplished.

Now she looked so peaceful, he hated to disturb her. Resting his hand on her shoulder, he spoke softly, "Ethne, we're at your house." Her emerald eyes fluttered open, and she jerked up.

"I...must have...fallen...asleep." Her words were deliberate.

"For most of the trip."

She loosened her ponytail and ran her fingers through her fiery waves. As an old longing filled him, he moved his hand. He'd been a stranger to this feeling these last several years. After Savannah, he never intended to feel it again.

Maybe he'd made a mistake by inviting Ethne to go with him today. No, he'd been obedient and done what he believed he'd been asked to do. The issue was his self-control, or lack of it.

No matter what he wanted or felt, following that longing would result in a dead end. Just like the night they ran out of road when they got lost after the flea market. She'd made her stance on dating clear. Crystal clear, just like the flow of the waterfall.

"How about a cup of coffee before you head back home? I know I could stand some." She yawned.

He thought he might drop by to see Vanna and the boys before he headed back to Crescent Bluff. He glanced at his watch.

"Or maybe you've got something else going on."

"No, I just wanted to get back home before it got too late."

"I thought you were the man who liked to drive at night," she teased. "It won't be dark for a while. It's not even dinner time yet."

"Don't forget, I've got that newly decorated apartment waiting for me."

Her smile faded. "I hope you like it, Daniel." The teasing tone was gone.

"I'm sure I will." He smiled to assure her. "How can I not? You have nice stuff in the store and even nicer taste."

She stared in silence out the windshield. Something was on her mind, but she obviously wasn't ready to share it, and he wouldn't pry. Maybe the picnic was doing its job and he should stay in case she had any questions. "I think I might like that cup of coffee, after all."

"That's great." She grinned and scooted out of the truck.

He jumped out of his side. "You know, I would have gotten the door for you if you'd waited."

She looked up at him. "Thanks, but that's not necessary. It's not like we're dating."

That was true, but he wished it wasn't. Despite what he'd told himself all these years, he'd love nothing more than to have a wife and family. And now that he was out of the service and putting down roots, maybe the time was right. It was ironic, though, that the one person he was attracted to would never return his interest.

He followed her into the foyer.

She gestured toward the living room, and then she headed toward the kitchen. "Make yourself comfortable while I get the coffee."

As clattering sounds emerged through the doorway, he perched on the edge of the white slip-covered couch and studied the room. The items at Resurrections sure reflected her taste. Clean, simple, bright, and airy. He'd be more than satisfied if his rooms turned out half this good. A large clock, smaller but otherwise not too different from the one he'd gotten at the flea market, hung above a shelf between the far windows.

"Like my clock?" She set the flowers he'd brought earlier on the coffee table.

"Looks vaguely familiar." He smiled. "You didn't mention you had one, too."

"I didn't mention it, because I just got it. One of my pickers found it when an old mill closed, and I liked yours so much I bought it for myself. It never made it to the showroom floor." She grinned back. "Accessories by Daniel. If you ever decide to give up medicine, let me know."

Her mood was much lighter than it had been in the truck. "I'll keep that in mind."

She returned to the kitchen.

He eased back into the sofa and studied the bouquet. There were some daisies mixed in, but he wasn't sure about zinnias. He had no idea what they looked like. If he ever bought her flowers again, he'd ask the florist.

She returned and placed a tray on the coffee table. The dishes on it were the same design but all different pastel colors.

"Cool dishes."

"They were my Grandmother O'Connor's." She picked up one of the saucers and turned it over. "See the number forty-three? That's the year this piece was made. Came from a factory in West Virginia. I only have about a dozen pieces, but one of these years, I'll take the time to see if the factory is still in business and find out if I can get some more."

She poured the coffee from the pink pot into the blue cup and offered it to him.

"Cream or sugar? Honey?"

"Thank you. Black's fine…honey."

She pressed her lips together to suppress a grin as she poured coffee into her butter yellow cup.

"Just kidding."

Shaking her head, she squeezed honey into the steamy liquid and then curled up in the far corner of the couch. The memory of the first time they'd shared that park bench outside Nacho Mama's flashed into his mind. She sat as far away as possible from him then, too. She'd been cool, aloof. He thought it was because of her father's death. But now he knew differently.

That evening, he couldn't have foreseen the turns their relationship would take. That they shared similar hurts. That he would have been led to tell her his story. He could never have imagined he'd hold her in his arms to comfort her. That in those few seconds, a commitment he'd made to himself would be shattered, and everything would change.

And that's where the problem had started. He shouldn't have done it. He was walking a tightrope, and he didn't know how much longer he could keep his footing, because the winds were billowing. His only choice was to trust the One Who could calm those storms.

"Hello, Daniel. Anyone home?" She leaned her head to one side, her brow knit.

"Sorry. Did you say something?"

"Yes. How's your coffee?" She grinned. "Maybe you're the one who needs a nap."

"Maybe. The coffee's great, though."

"Good." She set her cup on the table. "Thanks again for the flowers. They're beautiful."

"No biggie. You're welcome."

"You're wrong. It's a very big biggie." Her eyes began to shimmer as they had at the waterfall. "That's the first time a man's ever given me flowers."

How could that even be possible? He mourned the experiences her father's behavior had stolen from her. "Well, I'll make sure it's not the last."

The tears formed little silver half-moons as they filled her lower lids, and then one escaped and trickled down her cheek. A delicate waterfall. "And thanks…for sharing your story." Her voice was barely above a whisper.

He set his cup on the table and scooted closer to her. She closed the gap between them and laid her head against his chest. He hugged her gently and slowly rocked back and forth.

"I think I've been wrong all these years."

He felt her words as much as heard them.

"I've judged millions of people by the actions of one. I shouldn't have done that, but it was the only way I knew to protect myself."

He stroked her hair. It was soft, like copper satin. He rested his cheek on the top of her head and whispered, "It's OK."

They sat in silence for the next few minutes. Over the years, he'd forgotten what this felt like—the closeness of another person. And he missed it. As her breathing became regular, he reached forward, picked up a napkin from the coffee table, and offered it to her.

"Thank you." She leaned her head against his chest again and whispered something about a kiss.

"What?"

"A kiss."

Weird timing. All those studies about women and chocolate must be true. "There's still some left in the truck, if they're not melted."

He drew away to stand, but she grasped his hand. "No. Not a chocolate one."

"Well, that's all I…"

Her face reddened, and she bit her lower lip.

His heart began to race. He stood and drew her into his arms.

She turned her face upward.

He rested his forehead against hers. "It's been a while since I've done this, but hopefully, it's like riding a bike, and you don't forget."

"Don't worry. It'll be OK. Because…" Her gaze left his and then crept back. "I've never been kissed before."

Slowly, he relaxed his embrace. He brushed his fingertips against the velvet that was her face. As she leaned into his caress, he whispered her name, "Ethne." Cupping her cheeks with his hands, he gently raised her face upward to his. Gazing into her eyes, he leaned forward until her eyelids fluttered closed. And his lips met the satin of hers. The kiss was soft, sweet, measured. As a first kiss should be. He hadn't forgotten.

As he drew away, her arms tightened around him, and she pulled him against her body. Her eyes were deep emerald pools, inviting him, drawing him in. His heart pounded like a jackhammer. Hunger mixed with passion surged through him. Fire burned every inch where their bodies touched.

She drew his face down to meet hers. This time when their lips met, her hunger fueled his passion. Her body pressed against his. Desire exploded like the force of the waterfall striking the pool below it. Enough. He drew away before he broke her trust. Before he did something they both might regret.

She wrapped her arms around him and rested her head against his chest. The silent seconds felt like hours. Maybe he was wrong. Maybe he really had forgotten.

Then her words vibrated within him. "You must be some kind of amazing bike rider, Daniel Spenser. Absolutely amazing."

15

"Have you heard anything from Dr. Handsome?" Alicia dropped into the chair facing Ethne's desk. "I'm just wondering how he liked his rooms."

"Not yet, but I'm sure he liked them." She wasn't as confident as her tone suggested. Daniel hadn't called last night when he'd gotten home as she'd expected him to do. The nausea she'd awakened with this morning had only worsened as the day progressed and the minutes crawled by. Maybe he'd used her, and if he had, the only person she could blame was herself. She was the one who had practically begged him to kiss her. At least the first time, but not the second. And certainly not the third. Or fourth. As her heart raced at the memory, fire raged through her body.

"Are you OK?"

"I'm fine. Why wouldn't I be?"

"Your face is all red."

A large vase of flowers cradled in Nick's hands rounded the door followed by the rest of him. "Special delivery."

Alicia jumped up and grinned. "Oooo. What a surprise!"

"For Ethne," Nick continued.

"For Ethne?" Alicia's voice registered the shock Ethne felt.

Nick set the vase on her desk, stepped away, and crossed his arms over his chest.

"Well, aren't you going to open the card and see who they're from?" Alicia was practically gyrating with anticipation.

The soft aqua glass vase held a rainbow mass of zinnias mixed among snow white daisies. She fought to keep her voice even. "They're from Daniel. Dr. Spenser."

"To know for sure you have to open the card." Alicia grinned.

"I know for sure."

Nick grinned. "He must be one satisfied customer. Well, I'll leave you ladies to it," he said as he left.

"Ethne?" Eyes wide, Alicia dropped back into the chair. "Well?"

Ethne's heart fluttered so much she could hardly breathe. "As Nick said, I'm sure it's just a thank you for helping him decorate his rooms."

"There's only one way to find out." Alicia stared at her, waiting.

Ethne removed the small white envelope nestled among the perky blossoms and slid out the card. Time crept in slow motion as she soaked in each second of this moment. A milestone. She never planned to receive flowers from a man. Or kiss a man. Or be overcome by such deep feelings of trust toward a man. In less than twenty-four hours, her life had changed.

The card must have been written by the florist. It wasn't Daniel's handwriting. She wasn't sure how she knew, but she did.

"Well?" Alicia was liable to launch herself from the chair and snatch the card away if Ethne didn't read it within the next two seconds.

"It says, 'Thanks for the wonderful decorating job. And thanks, too, for the amazing bike ride yesterday. Daniel.'" The signature actually read, "Love, Daniel," but she left out that one little word.

"You guys went bike riding yesterday after I told him you were sick? He must have thought you made some sort of miraculous recovery."

A miraculous recovery. Maybe she had. Maybe she was still. "We didn't go bike riding yesterday." Her face warmed even more.

"Then why..."

As Ethne held her finger to her lips, she stood and walked toward the door. She pushed it closed and then turned back toward Alicia.

"Is everything OK, Ethne?" The sudden disappearance of her smile matched the seriousness of her voice.

Alicia would love this. "It's a code."

"Code?"

"Yes." As Ethne's stomach turned somersaults, she took a deep breath and then spoke the words she'd thought she would never say.

"He kissed me."

Shrieking, Alicia rocketed out of the chair. She jumped up and down, clapped her fingers together, and then pulled Ethne into a bear hug. "Are you serious?"

Emotions that had been dammed back all these years exploded, and tears silenced Ethne's voice. Taking a deep breath, she nodded. "Yes," she whispered.

"Dr. Handsome and Miss Absolutely-never." Alicia laughed. "Well, spill. How was it?"

She'd been up half the night mulling over that very question. Scary, tender, sweet, surprising, gratifying, fulfilling, life-changing, earth-shattering, world-rocking. "Amazing. Absolutely amazing." Amazing Daniel. No comma there.

Alicia whispered, "I've been praying about this—that God would bring you the man you could trust—since college." She let Ethne go and then took both of her hands. "I'm so happy for you. You've suffered enough. You deserve to be happy."

Ethne's phone vibrated against the top of her antique oak desk. She reached over and flipped it face up to read the display. Her heart began to race. "It's Daniel." She giggled uncontrollably like a middle-schooler.

"Well, let me leave you and Dr. Handsome alone." Alicia walked out the door and pulled it shut behind her.

Ethne took a deep breath and swiped the answer button. "Hi."

"Hi, yourself."

Electricity tingled every inch of her body.

"I only have a couple of minutes between patients, but I wanted to let you know what an amazing job you did."

"And you did an amazing job yourself."

He chuckled, and she could imagine those cute little crinkles forming around his chocolate-kiss eyes. "And I love the design work you guys did, too."

Silent, comfortable seconds passed as she absorbed his electronic nearness. Memories of his cologne's earthy fragrance and the pressure of his body against hers wrapped her in contentment.

"I sent you a little Thank You surprise."

"I got them, Daniel. Daisies and zinnias. They're gorgeous."

"I'm glad you like them."

Silence. She closed her eyes, her tongue tracing her lips and remembering the warmth of his against hers.

"Well, gotta go. Maybe we can get together this weekend."

"I'd love that."

"You could check out my bedroom. Uh—"

His face was probably that same shade of red it had been when he'd offered her the chocolate kisses at the falls and embarrassed himself. She grinned.

"For decorating purposes only."

"For decorating purposes only," she echoed.

~*~

Daniel set his tray on the table and then slipped into the booth. He glanced at his phone. Josh was late. Well, maybe not for a pastor, but the time really didn't matter. He had no more appointments today. Lunch with Josh was the only thing left on his schedule. And even though the preacher hadn't said so on the phone, Daniel had a feeling today's meeting was more than just a casual lunch.

The phone burned in his hand. Part of him wanted to call Ethne...again. But a newly revived part of him suggested he shouldn't call, but he should drive up to Fort Worth after lunch and surprise her. Waiting until the weekend to see her would be an eternity.

The excitement in her voice this morning made all the hassle of trying to find a florist that had some zinnias worth it. Who knew they weren't a normal florist flower? But Becca of Becca's Bouquets offered to cut some from her own garden. Now that was service. She'd won his business today and from now on.

"How's it going?" Josh's words pulled him back into the present.

As the pastor set his tray onto the table, Daniel stood and gripped his hand. "Hey, Josh. Good to see you."

"Same here." Josh slipped into the booth across from him and unloaded the tray. "Mind if I bless the food before we begin?"

As Daniel bowed his head, Josh prayed, but despite the spoken words, the only thoughts Daniel had were reruns of the same ones he'd had all last night and this morning. His time with Ethne yesterday.

The trip to the falls had been meant as life-changing for her. But he hadn't imagined it would, once again, be life-changing for him. He was back driving on that curvy road with no street signs or guardrails, but this time he wasn't alone. She was in the seat beside him. And he hoped, no prayed, she'd reach the same destination he had. *Peace, Father. Please give her peace.*

Silence. Daniel jerked open his eyes to reveal Josh grinning at him.

"Something I can pray about with you, son?"

His relationship with Ethne, if you could even call it that, definitely needed prayer, but it was too new. Too undefined to talk about with anyone. "The practice. I've managed to keep most of Dr. O'Connor's patients, which has been much easier than building a patient-base from the ground up. But I want it to be more than a basic medical office. Like a community service."

Josh's smile widened. "Glad to hear you say that. I've heard good things about your work. Your patients like your manner. Problem is a lot of people who need medical care either can't get to the office or can't afford it."

This conversation was headed the exact direction Daniel wanted it to. This practice was an answer to prayer, and he had promised he'd be a good steward of the gift he'd been given. "I'm trying to keep my schedule open one afternoon during the week so I can make house calls if needed."

"Don't get me wrong. House calls are great. Just not enough."

"I'm listening."

"A church member has donated the use of a small storefront in a depressed area of Waco, and we want to offer a medical clinic there one Saturday a month to start. We have some nurses who've already volunteered, but we're looking for a doctor. I'd hoped Dr. O'Connor would help, but…"

Awesome. "I'm in."

"You're in? You mean I don't even get to use my persuasive preacher skills on you? All the time I spent planning my argument is going to waste?"

Daniel folded his arms over his chest and leaned back. "Well, I can play harder to get if that would make you feel better."

Josh laughed. "No need. I'll e-mail you the clinic address and the details. We hope to start the second Saturday of next month. If you want to go check it out beforehand, just let me know, and I'll get you a key."

"Thanks." Daniel took a bite of his corned beef sandwich. In a matter of just a few days, his life had taken a dramatic turn. The practice, Ethne, now the clinic.

"You sure there's nothing on your mind?" Josh leaned back in the booth.

Daniel shook his head. "Just trying to soak it all in. God's provision and answered prayers."

Josh stabbed his salad. "I hear Ethne's been helping you redecorate the old apartment above the clinic."

How had he heard that? Daniel hadn't advertised the fact. He nodded. "She's done an amazing job." Amazing. He bit his lip to curtail the grin.

"She's a strong young woman. Driven," Josh continued, oblivious to the private joke Daniel and Ethne shared. "I always knew she'd be a success at whatever road she chose to follow. She had a lot to overcome after her mother's death, and she's sacrificed experiences and relationships so many women her age have to get where she is today." He placed his fork on the table and looked straight into Daniel's eyes. "Know what I mean?"

They weren't just two men shooting the breeze. Josh was a pastor and Daniel was a physician. Their career choices held both of them to a higher standard of confidentiality than two regular guys talking about a girl. Still. He could hint without saying anything. "I think I do."

Seeming satisfied, Josh forked some more lettuce. "Good. You're not here by accident, Daniel Spenser. Not at all."

16

The shades were drawn and the door locked. Not what Ethne had expected. But then, wasn't that the definition of a surprise? Something unexpected, unannounced, unplanned. The only problem? She wasn't supposed to be the one surprised but the one doing the surprising. Maybe she should have called before she left Fort Worth. The old Ethne would have made sure she had an appointment time. But a new woman was standing on the porch. One completely unfamiliar, yet one she hoped she'd get to know better in the near future.

She reached to press the bell, but her finger stopped midway. What exactly was she doing? A few kisses, a handsome face, a kind heart, and some flowers had obliterated any shred of common sense she once possessed. She'd go back to the car and call him.

She turned to leave, but the door to Crescent Bluff Primary Care swooshed inward. She squealed, and he jumped. In the silent seconds that followed, she drank in the sight of him. Chocolate-kiss eyes, warm and enticing. T-shirt, shorts, flip-flops. The camo backpack from yesterday tossed over one shoulder.

A smile lighting his face, he raised one arm and leaned against the doorjamb. His body language radiated nonchalance, but his laser gaze penetrated to her core. "Ethne. This is a surprise. What are you doing here?"

Exactly. What in the world had she been thinking? She needed to keep it casual. "Not much for surprises, huh? I can always go back to Fort Worth if you can't handle it." She continued her turn toward the street.

He reached out and grasped her wrist. "Oh, I love surprises. Some more than others." Stepping backward, he drew her across the threshold into the clinic and closed the door behind her. "And I can definitely handle it. The question is, can you?"

He wrapped his arms around her, drew her close, and rested his chin against the top of her head. His cologne's earthy scent brought back memories of last night.

She leaned her cheek against his chest. Every place her body touched his tingled with electricity. An unfamiliar, almost uncontrollable yearning overcame her, and all she wanted to do was absorb his nearness. "I missed you."

"It's been less than twenty-four hours." His whisper electrified her.

Maybe she shouldn't have come. She'd never done this before— had a boyfriend, been a girlfriend. If that's what they even were. And if there were rules for such things, she hadn't read the book or seen the list online. "It felt longer than that."

His chuckle rumbled his chest. "Yes. Yes, it did." He slowly lifted her face to his and looked deep into her eyes, asking for permission. "A lot longer."

She leaned closer, and he briefly placed his lips on hers.

She craved more, but her gaze fell on the backpack behind him. "I should have called. Looks as if I might have come at an inopportune time."

"Yeah. I was headed out. To Fort Worth. To surprise my new...girlfriend."

Butterflies filled her stomach. "No one's ever called me that before."

"Maybe you'd prefer consultant?" He winked.

"Speaking of which, as far as work is concerned, this is officially a business trip. I'm following up on the installation for our first Decor-Gestion customer."

His arms tightened around her. "Well, if it's business, I like the perks. You don't need to do that, though." The playful tone had disappeared. "I took pictures of everything and was leaving to bring them up to the shop to show you. So, I guess you could say, I had a business trip planned, too."

"Alicia bought back pictures. They're good for some things, but not this. There's nothing like being in a space. I want to see if we've missed anything."

~*~

Daniel was trying to protect her, to save her potential anguish. The last time she'd been upstairs, she'd had that panic attack, and he didn't want a recurrence. But often, the best way to get over fears was to face them and find out they weren't so big. Plus, he wouldn't let anything happen to her. "If you're sure, but it's really not necessary. Alicia and the guys did a great job."

She drew away and placed a hand in his. "I'm sure. Ready?"

She wasn't wasting any time. "Ready."

The only sounds were the droning of the air conditioner as they climbed the stairs. The top riser squeaked, and he rested his hand on the doorknob. He turned and looked directly into her eyes. "You're sure you're sure?"

"Yes."

He pushed open the door and led her in.

She stepped through and inched toward the center of the large room. With the lights off, the afternoon sun flooded through the old casement windows, bathing the room in peaceful warmth.

He placed his arm around her and drew her against his body, protecting her. "So, what do you think?"

"It's really different. It doesn't even feel like the same place, and it looks even better in person than in the computer designs."

"As I said, you guys did a great job."

"Then, you really like it?"

"It's perfect, Ethne. Amazing."

She leaned her head against his shoulder. "In that case, Dr. Spenser, I hope you'll go online and leave us a favorable review."

"Favorable? As in five stars?"

"At least."

"You know, physicians are held to a strict code of ethics…in some areas of their lives, that is. But I'm not above bribery in others."

"Let me get my purse, then."

"That's not exactly the kind of bribery I had in mind." His eyes locked onto hers, and he leaned down.

The bell downstairs rang, followed by pounding on the clinic door.

He rested his forehead against hers. "Press pause." He squeezed her hand and then led her out of the apartment and down the stairs.

The pounding intensified. "Coming." He jogged down the hall toward the waiting area.

He unlocked the door and swung it open. "I'm sorry, the clinic's…"

Sean stood, arm around that server who'd waited on them at Nacho Mama's. A white towel streaked with red was wrapped around her hand. "Liza's cut herself bad."

Daniel stepped aside. "Take her to the first room on the right."

~*~

Ethne handed Sean a bottle of water and then sat in the chair next to his. Her great big, grown-up, football-playing, high-school-coaching, macho brother had been rocking back and forth since Daniel took Liza back to the exam room, and now he was as white as Daniel's lab coat. "You OK, Sean? Don't pass out on me. Drink."

"I think she just about cut off her finger."

She placed her hand on his bouncing knee. "She'll be OK. Daniel's with her."

"She was making lunch. The blood was…everywhere."

"Good thing you were at the restaurant—"

"We were at her apartment. Today's her day off."

"So…you just happened to be at her apartment?"

He shook his head. "You know all that stuff I said at the restaurant a few weeks ago? Well, I don't know what happened, but what started out as just a game got serious real quick." His knee began bouncing again.

Ethne completely understood. She had no experience with romantic relationships—other than what she'd observed growing up. And those observations had been enough to make her promise herself she'd never get involved with any man. Until Daniel. Now, that promise had no meaning. She'd known Daniel for a few weeks, but the amount of time seemed irrelevant. She was in a relationship with a man.

Only hours had passed since he'd kissed her and she'd kissed him back. And yet, as confusing as it all seemed, she was sure of one thing. Meeting him had changed her life. Had changed everything she believed about men. Everything Vaughn had been, Daniel wasn't. And everything Daniel was, Vaughn could never have been.

The man Ethne loved stepped back into the waiting room with Liza on his arm. "All better. All sutured up."

Sean jumped up. "Is everything OK?"

"Yep. It was pretty deep, but luckily it was on the fleshy part of her finger. Not as bad as it may have looked. Fingers just bleed a lot." Daniel handed Sean several sheets of paper. "Here's some after-care instructions. Call if you have any questions or concerns. And, Liza, call the office tomorrow and make a follow-up for the end of next week."

She nodded. "Thank you, Dr. Spenser."

~*~

Daniel closed and locked the door and then turned back toward Ethne. The timing couldn't have been more perfect. Over the years, he'd discovered interruptions could be more than just a pause in the action. Often, they were really redirections. God stepping in, as it were.

Ethne closed the space between them. As her arms encircled his waist, she turned her face upward and snuggled against him, reviving the earlier yearning.

"Now, where were we, Dr. Spenser? Oh, yes, time to press play again."

He guided her head down onto his chest and brushed her hair with his lips. "I think it's good Sean and Liza showed up when they did. Not good she sustained the injury, but good that it interrupted us."

Ethne turned her gaze back toward his, confusion marking her face. "What?"

She didn't get it. She had no understanding of the emotion and feelings her nearness exploded within him or the amount of self-control required to maintain and grow the embryonic trust she'd placed in him.

He could explain sexual chemistry scientifically—the body's response to visual and physical stimuli. How dopamine and norepinephrine combined to increase attraction. Yeah, a clinical explanation would be a surefire mood-kill.

She rested her head against his chest. She was an enigma. Like sunshine and rain, two opposites that when combined made a beautiful rainbow.

Life's circumstances had matured her and pulled her into adulthood long before many of her peers. She was capable, intelligent, accomplished. Yet, in some areas she was young. Naïve. Lacking a worldliness present in most women her age. And she had no idea—absolutely no idea—how challenging it was just being close to her.

When Savannah broke up with him, he'd thought he might never recover. But he had, and if she hadn't left, and God hadn't stepped in, he might have never met Ethne. And not to have known her, not to have loved her or be loved by her...now, that might just be an unrecoverable tragedy. He wouldn't let anything ruin his chance with her. "You up for a road trip?"

17

In silence, Ethne stared out the car window and gazed toward the dilapidated strip-centers and abandoned gas stations lining the highway leading into Waco.

She knew redirection when she saw it. She was the queen of deflection when it came to men and dating. And until a little while ago, she'd always been the giver—not the receiver. But that didn't mean she couldn't recognize it when it happened. For some reason, Daniel hadn't wanted to kiss her, as proven by his admission of gratitude that Sean and Liza had shown up.

She'd be the first to admit she had no idea what she was doing. She pretty much told him that before he kissed her after their trip to the waterfall. But she'd always been a fast learner. And for the first time in her life, she wanted to learn about men. No…about one man. Him. All he had to do was tell her. Show her. Teach her. But he had to want to, and maybe he didn't.

As the truck slowed, Daniel turned right into one of the shopping center parking lots. The remnant of a dry cleaner was on one end and an old barber's pole marked the other. A sign leaning against the inside of one of the windows in the center section read "Community Health Center."

"We're here."

"Where?"

He shifted the truck into park, unfastened his seatbelt, and turned toward her. "My newest project. Or should I say, Josh's newest project for me."

Daniel turned off the engine, and she reached for the door handle.

"Don't, Ethne." He jumped out of the truck and jogged around toward her side.

No need for frivolities. She was perfectly capable of opening her own door. She grasped the lever and popped the door opened as he rounded the front of the car.

"Ethne, I asked you to wait."

"No, you didn't. You told me to wait. I'm not some helpless damsel in distress."

He crossed his arms over his chest. "Is that what you think's going on here?" His chocolate brown eyes captured her gaze and held it tight. "Believe me. I know you're not helpless. Opening your door's a symbol of my respect, not your weakness. No ulterior motives. No subliminal message. But if it makes you uncomfortable, I'll stop offering."

Respect. Vaughn had never opened Mother's car door. Never opened the door to the house or to a restaurant for her.

Tears threatened, but she forced them back. She'd cried more in the few weeks since she'd met Daniel than in the last twenty years of her life. Slowly, she reached out and drew the door closed.

His face softened, and he dropped his arms to his side. Then he moved closer and opened the truck door. He held his hand out to her and smiled. "Thank you, Ethne."

His hand was warm, his grip strong. She stepped out onto the pot-holed pavement, and he closed the door behind her. "Daniel, I don't know the rules of the game. I'm a rookie, and I'm still learning how to play."

He grasped her hand and led her to the door of the clinic. As they stepped onto the sidewalk, he turned toward her. He rested his hands on her shoulders. "The rules of the game are the same as the rules of life. They're really pretty simple. Love God first, and other people second. That, Ethne, is all you need to do." He drew her close and then placed a kiss on her forehead.

He made it all sound so simple. If only it was.

Daniel inserted a key in the lock, turned it, and then pulled the glass door open. A wall of heat forced them back. The temperature must have been at least ninety inside the building. Stale mustiness advertised that the air conditioner hadn't run in weeks, if at all this season. They stepped into the sauna.

The waiting area was in disarray, with paint cans and cloths scattered over the floor. The walls were a patchwork of old and new paint colors. Three chrome-framed chairs with cracked red vinyl seats and backs had been clustered together in the center of the space. Parallel doorways into exam rooms, like soldiers on review, lined the back wall.

Daniel slowly surveyed the room. "Renovations aren't as far along as Josh indicated at lunch today. He wants to open in two weeks, but I don't see how we'll be able to."

"Well, you haven't gotten to know him very well. Once he sets his mind to something, there's no stopping him."

Daniel walked to the thermostat on the back wall, pushed the lever down, and the machine rumbled to life. Cool air crept into the room. "Well, at least the AC works."

He walked back to the front and locked the door. "I'm actually glad the painting isn't done yet."

He pulled a black permanent marker from his pocket and walked over to the left-hand wall. He began to write something on the wall.

"What in the world are you doing?"

"Same thing I did in Crescent Bluff. Writing Bible verses on the walls."

"But no one will see them if you paint over them."

"Doesn't matter. That's not the purpose. I'm dedicating this space and all that goes on here to God. And saying, 'Thank You.'"

She moved to stand behind him and read over his shoulder as he wrote:

Heal me, Lord, and I shall be healed; save me, and I shall be saved; for You are the one I praise. Jeremiah 17:14

Then she followed him as he walked to the wall on the right side of the room and wrote another verse.

See, I am doing a new thing! Now it springs up; do you not perceive it? I am making a way in the wilderness and streams in the wasteland. Isaiah 43:19

He turned and held the marker out toward her. "You're welcome to write one if you'd like."

She shook her head. No Bible verse came to mind. She couldn't even remember the last time she'd read the Bible. "No, thanks."

Something in his eyes told her he understood why she'd turned him down. He dropped the marker back into his pocket and then pulled his phone out, held it to his mouth, and began dictating.

As she moved and stood in the center of the waiting room, he walked around speaking a list into his phone of what they needed and what else had to be done before the opening. He made a pass by her, stopped, leaned close, and pecked her on the cheek. He winked as he continued. "Twenty chairs for the waiting room, two coffee tables, four end tables." Then he walked back toward the exam rooms.

She pulled her phone out of her pocket and pressed "4." And Nick had been upset with her when she'd accepted that donation from the clinic in Burleson.

"Hey, Eth."

"Hey, Nick. How would you like to free up some space in the warehouse?"

"You're speaking my love language."

"Remember all those chairs and occasional tables donated by that clinic south of town?"

"You mean all the junk that's eating up my valuable warehouse space? Don't tell me you've got a buyer for that crud."

"I found a free clinic that needs some stuff. I thought we could donate it."

"You are absolutely amazing, Eth."

Amazing. A smile tightened her cheeks. This whole scenario with Daniel was amazing.

"Give me an address and thirty minutes to load a truck, and we'll get rid of it today. Where are you, anyway?"

"Waco."

"Waco? Why in the—"

Daniel stepped out of the last exam room.

"Following up on the Spenser delivery. Just wanted to see how everything looked for myself and make sure he was happy."

"And?"

Daniel slipped his phone into his pocket and made his way to her.

"He seems happy."

He placed his arm around her and leaned close. "Amazingly happy." His whisper tickled her ear.

As a delicious shiver electrified her entire body, she suppressed a giggle. "Yes, he's amazingly happy. I'll give you the details tomorrow. Bye." She ended the call.

"I hope you won't be sharing too many details tomorrow with whoever that was." Daniel winked.

She made a show of rolling her eyes. "Nick. I remembered we have some old waiting room furniture that was given to us several months ago, so we're donating it to the clinic."

Those cute little crinkles radiated from the corners of his eyes. His grin made her heart flutter. "Ethne, that's wonderful. Amazing."

"And don't worry. I won't share too much info with him…mainly because there's not much to share."

He withdrew his arm from her shoulder, removed the marker from his pocket, and then began writing on the wall beside the front door.

He has made everything beautiful in its time. Ecclesiastes 3:11

He grasped her hand and brought it to his lips. "You'll have plenty of stuff to share. I promise. We just have to wait on God's perfect timing, Ethne."

18

As the sun crept closer to the horizon, Ethne turned the truck into the parking lot of the old strip center. She steered around the two church vans and half a dozen SUVs and pickups parked by the entrance of what would soon be the clinic. Two weeks had passed since she'd last seen this place and since she'd last seen Daniel. Between his work and hers, life had been busy. And all the phone calls and texts they'd shared intensified rather than lessened the emptiness his absence created.

That's why she'd insisted upon making today's delivery. Nick had scheduled one of the guys, but she gave some flimsy excuse about needing to see if the clinic could use anything else in their warehouse...strictly for the tax write-off. He'd seen right through her and grinned. "I'm happy for you, Eth. Dr. Spenser seems like a nice guy."

She backed the truck up in front of the abandoned barber shop. The sidewalk was higher on that end, so in the absence of a loading dock, it would be the best place to unload the waiting room furniture. Sixties rock and roll—undeniable evidence Josh was someplace inside—blasted out into the parking lot through the open double doors. The church's current youth group probably cringed even more than hers had years ago when he played that same stuff.

She made her way to the door and scanned the open room. Knots of people with paintbrushes and rollers lined the walls. Gray paint now covered the Bible verses Daniel had written on the walls. Everything in the reception area seemed done except for some final touchups. Smaller groups worked in the exam rooms.

She saw him before he saw her. His hair was longer, more relaxed than when they'd met in Vaughn's office weeks ago. He wore navy blue soccer shorts and a gray T-shirt with "USAF" in navy stenciled across the chest. Navy and lime green jogging shoes completed his outfit.

A smile warmed his face as his gaze found her. Too bad the room was filled with people. She reined in her steps to keep from running to him. As they met in the center of the room, he grasped her hand. "Hi, babe."

He'd never called her that before. No one had ever called her that before. "Hi, Daniel."

"Well, look what the cat dragged in."

She turned back toward Josh. "Still torturing people with that old-fashioned rock and roll, I see."

Josh mimed being stabbed in the chest and then shrugged his shoulders. "You know what they say. 'You can take the man out of the band, but you can't take the band out of the man.'"

"I think it's more, 'You can't teach on old dog—emphasis on old—new tricks.'"

"Ouch." He winked. "Glad you're here, Ethne. And I know Daniel is, too. Now, let me get some kids together to help you unload."

Ethne led her small squad of teenagers out to the truck, while Daniel stayed inside to supervise furniture placement. She barked instructions like a drill sergeant, and the group unloaded the truck in no time. She made one final pass through the back to make certain nothing hid under the furniture blankets. It was empty.

After pulling down the back door and locking it, she turned to walk into the clinic. The sun had slipped below the horizon. Deep tones of gold, red, orange, turquoise, and purple blazed across the sky as the arms of night held on to the last remnants of sunlight before day completely disappeared.

Why? Why the beauty? Science told her the blackness of space lay beyond the earth's atmosphere. So, why not black sky? Why all the colors?

Daniel's hand grasped her shoulder and drew her close. "I was wondering where you were." He pecked her on the cheek. "Nothing as beautiful as a Texas sunset."

"Why?"

"Why? Well, I think it has something to do with particles in the—"

"No, not the science. Why all the colors if there's no function? No purpose? If there's nothing but blackness beyond?"

"Oh, my creative Ethne, you of all people should know that being beautiful is a function."

She snuggled her head against his shoulder.

"My dad would have said God was just showing off, but I think it's a little more than that. It's a glimpse into the heart of God."

"The heart of God?"

His whisper brushed her hair. "Yeah. Beautiful. The heart of God is beautiful."

She'd never thought of God as beautiful. Righteous, judging, punishing, just, powerful, omniscient…yes. But beautiful? Never.

"Josh wants to offer a prayer of dedication for the clinic. I'd love it if you'd join us. You don't have to, but at least come inside. This isn't the safest neighborhood after dark."

She slipped her hand in his and then followed him into the building. His arrangement of the furniture was perfect. Small clusters of chairs dotted the large, open area. In college, she'd learned that every public place should include small areas where even an introvert could feel comfortable and secure. Maybe they had a similar class in medical school.

"OK," Josh boomed. "Everyone circle up. We'll pray, and then you can go home."

She grasped Daniel's hand and offered her free hand to a woman, probably one of the nurses, on her left.

Laughter tumbled out of the center exam room.

"Jasmine Porter and Olivia Simpson," Josh called, "would you care to join us?"

Two teenage girls, red-faced from giggling, emerged and inserted themselves into the circle.

A smile warmed Ethne's face. Josh would have been calling out Molly and her ten years ago. He always had to keep his thumb on them.

One girl pulled the baseball cap off the head of the other, and a river of bright red hair the exact same color as Ethne's cascaded down the back of the now hatless teen. The only difference was the texture. The girl's was straight. Ethne's was curly, unless she used a flatiron.

Everyone bowed their heads and closed their eyes as Josh began to pray. Everyone but Ethne. All she could do was stare. Porter. Hadn't Josh called one of the girls Porter? Something Porter? Clamminess shrouded her. As anger gripped her chest, bile rose up into her throat, and she fought to breathe. She had to escape. She jerked her hands free and ran on tiptoe into one of the exam rooms.

~*~

Daniel glanced at the empty space Ethne had filled seconds ago. Something was up. Fran, who'd been on Ethne's left, caught his eye and nodded toward the front door. He shifted into stealth mode and followed while Fran repaired the broken prayer circle.

The sun had dipped below the horizon. At the far end of the parking lot, Ethne's silhouette shown black against the narrow orange band—all that was left of the earlier riot of color—where the sky met the earth. He tiptoed over until he was at her side and then slipped his hand in hers. "Ethne?"

She stared ahead at the bleak Texas landscape. He leaned forward until he could see her face. In the waning light, the tracks of her tears glistened golden against her cheeks. "What is it, baby?"

She shook her head.

He let go of her hand, put his arm around her, and drew her close. He leaned his head on top of hers. "I've been told I'm a pretty good listener."

"The hair," she whispered.

"What hair?"

"That girl's red hair."

"Oh, yeah. It's the same color as yours." He kissed the top of her head. "But your curls are a lot prettier."

She exhaled a long, shaky breath. "Her mother…Vaughn…they…over the years, they…"

"Ethne, stop. I know where you're going, and you can't draw that conclusion. You can't assume everyone with red hair is a relative."

"But you didn't know my father. He…"

If only he could share the burden of her pain. "I'm sorry. I know even wondering about the possibility has to hurt, but you need to let that thought go." He brushed her cheek with the back of his hand.

"I can't."

"So, say it's true. What could you do about it, anyway?"

She stiffened and drew away. "What do you mean, what could I do? I can't do anything about it."

"Exactly. The past is the past. You can't go back and change it. You can only move forward. True or not, Ethne, let it go."

"You don't know what you're asking." She wiped her sleeve across her face. "I hate him. How could he do that to Mother? To me…to Sean?"

He grasped one of her hands. "Look at me."

For the first time since he'd joined her, she made eye contact.

"Don't, Ethne. Even if it were true, it's certainly not her fault."

"It's not mine, either. It's not my fault Vaughn couldn't keep his promises. That he failed to honor his vows. It's not my fault he had affairs."

"That's not what I meant. Look. You have one choice here. You can choose to forgive."

She pulled away from him.

"Ethne, unforgiveness is a prison. Believe me. I know."

She snorted. "That's not even a real word, Dr. Spenser." She spat out his name and title like a bitter pill. "If I'm in prison, it's Vaughn's fault, not mine. I tried to forgive him over and over again. But he never repented. Never changed. He just kept on doing the same things."

"That's the problem. Your forgiveness changes you, not anyone else. Only God's forgiveness can do that." He paused a moment and then continued. "So…what will you do about it?"

"Why is it always me who has to do something?" She turned away.

The gravel behind them crunched, and Josh stepped to the other side of Ethne. "Everything OK?" he asked.

Ethne collapsed against him. He wrapped her in his arms.

Daniel would have held her like that.

Josh rocked her back and forth like a father comforting a child.

Daniel would have rocked her. He would have comforted her. He'd wanted to. He'd tried, but she refused him. His presence here was an unnecessary redundancy. He was nothing more than the backup in case the main system failed.

He turned and walked back into the clinic.

~*~

The streetlights washed the overnight bag in the passenger seat with a dull orange glow. Ethne had taken it with her in case someone asked her to stay the night, and someone had. She'd been so upset Josh had invited her to come spend the night with him and Hope rather than drive home tonight.

But she'd refused. Josh wasn't the person she hoped would extend the invitation.

She loved Daniel, and she was pretty sure he felt the same way about her. Yet she'd been so mean to him earlier tonight. He was simply trying to be kind and helpful. She understood that now, and in truth, she knew it then. But in the pain and shock of the moment, she lashed out at him. She pushed him away and cut him off.

So what would she do about it?

She owed him an apology if he'd even listen to her.

As she turned the truck into her driveway, the headlights fell on a box on her front porch. The candles she'd ordered from Austin must have arrived a day early.

She cut the engine, grabbed her bag, and trudged up the front steps. After unlocking the door, she tossed her bag on the floor in the foyer and turned back to pick up the box. Tears blurred the return address. She recognized the words and numbers, and just as she'd known the handwriting on the card that accompanied the flowers he'd sent wasn't his, she knew this was. Daniel had sent her a gift.

She set the box on the hall tree and sliced through the packing tape with the truck key. She raised the flaps and then pulled back the brown craft paper to reveal a navy gift box. She lifted it out. The bottom of the box was covered with gold foil. As she inched up the lid, the musty, warm scent of leather filled the foyer. She opened the book and turned the pages until she came to one inscribed with block printing. "To: Ethne, From: Daniel." Daniel had sent her a Bible.

An envelope remained in the box. She picked it up and removed its contents—a sheet of paper on which he'd written a list of Bible verses. Daniel had sent her a Bible and a whole list of verses.

And what would she do about it?

19

Ethne raced in through the warehouse door. Without missing a word of his phone conversation, Nick lifted his hands in the air and pointed to his watch. She didn't need his silent reprimand to confirm her lateness. But this was the first, and only, time in all the years since she and Alicia had started the business. Surely, after last night, she was due a pass.

She'd been awake until four this morning reading the Bible Daniel sent, and she missed the alarm because her phone was set on silent. Today's makeup consisted of the lip gloss she managed to slather on at a red light a block from the store. Curly hair, still wet from her two-minute shower—Daniel would have been impressed— was pulled into a high ponytail and piled on her head in a knot of orange curls the size of a small cantaloupe. No time for a flatiron this morning.

Daniel…when she got home last night, it was too late to call, so she'd texted him. But when she'd finally fallen asleep, he still hadn't replied. And could she blame him? She pushed him away when all he wanted to do was comfort her.

She dropped her purse behind the front counter and then stepped onto the showroom floor.

Alicia was talking to a young couple in the front window, but she inclined her head toward another couple looking at the old store counter Nick had converted into a kitchen island.

Ethne walked over to them. "Hi. Welcome to Resurrections." She held out a business card. "I'm Ethne. Make yourselves at home, and let me know if you have any questions." As they nodded, she moved to straighten the throw pillows on the couch in a nearby room setting. That gave them some space so they wouldn't feel stalked, but she was still close enough if they had questions.

She caught a glimpse of her reflection in a wall mirror. The heat in the car had dried her hair some and the mass of curls protruding from the top of her head had morphed into a representation of a chrysanthemum on steroids. The bell to the front door rang as two more groups came in. Well, this was as good as she would get today.

~*~

Alicia dropped into the chair facing Ethne's desk and kicked off her shoes. "What a day. My feet are killing me."

"I know. We were too busy to even stop for lunch. I'm starving." Ethne pulled a couple of fruit bars from her desk drawer and tossed one to her friend. "But I guess that's a good problem to have."

Only the crackle of Alicia's wrapper answered her comment.

"Right, Alicia? Being busy is a good problem to have."

She shrugged her shoulders. "Only if we have enough employees to provide good customer service."

So that was it. "Sorry I was late this morning. I had a rough night, and I overslept." That was the only explanation she could offer right now. She'd managed to corral her emotions enough to get through today, but opening the gate, even a sliver, would only start the stampede of feelings she'd wrestled with overnight.

"It's not just this morning. It's all the other times you've been out lately. Eth, I can't remember the last time I even made it over to check on the Weatherford store. And that's my responsibility. But I've had to stay here and cover for you."

"Hey, just because I'm out of the office doesn't mean I'm not working. It's not like I've been lying on a beach somewhere. How are we supposed to have stuff to sell if I don't go out and look for it?" By now the volume of her voice had increased enough that she sounded defensive even to her own ears.

"I know that. It's just…" Alicia's words trailed off as she dropped her gaze to her lap.

"It's just what?"

"Like yesterday. Going to Waco."

"I was delivering the furniture to the clinic."

"Any of the guys in the back could have done that."

And now, she wished one of them had.

"But you're the only person who can help out on the floor. You're the only person who does our inventory adjustments. And they're so far behind, I'm not even sure what's in stock and available to sell."

The truth echoed deep within. Alicia was right. Despite the assurances Ethne had made to herself, her feelings for Daniel had compromised her work ethic.

"Don't get me wrong. I'm thrilled for you and Daniel. I want you to have him in your life. And you need to be free to spend time with him. But we can't sacrifice the business we've poured so much time and money into." Alicia walked over to Ethne and rested a hand on her shoulder. "We need to hire another full-time person."

A knock sounded on the door. "Come in," Ethne offered.

Nick stuck his head around the door. "Oh, sorry. I can come back later."

"No, Nick," Ethne replied. "Have a seat. I want to ask you something."

As Alicia returned to her chair, Nick sat in the one next to her. He cleared his throat. "What's up?"

"Alicia and I were just discussing possibly hiring another person to work on the floor. What do you think?"

Nick cast Alicia a sideways glance…which she returned. They'd already talked about this.

"I can see where we could use some more help," he replied. "Especially since you've been out more than usual recently. If you can't justify hiring a full-time showroom employee, maybe you could split the time with the warehouse. I could use someone to help with paperwork, and I think I have enough in my budget to cover a few hours a week."

"Why don't you and Alicia put your heads together and come up with a proposal?"

"Will do." Nick stood. "Oh, and I was wondering…do we have a policy about employees dating?"

"Nothing official," Ethne replied. "I'm OK with it as long as it doesn't interfere with their work."

"Good." He pointed at Alicia. "Pick you up at eight. We can, uh, put our heads together." He stepped into the hall and closed the door behind him.

"Alicia?"

Her face glowed bright red, and she shrugged. "Now that he's over his previous crush, I decided to try another flavor from the fudge store besides peanut butter."

"And?"

"It's yummy."

The memory of Daniel's chocolate-kiss eyes gripped Ethne's heart. Her rejection of him last night had filled them with such pain. And then he'd left. She wanted to share everything with Alicia, but she couldn't. Not yet. She didn't even know where to start, where to end, or how she felt about her possible discovery.

She stood and walked over to her friend. "Thank you for loving me enough to say the hard things. I'm sorry I've neglected my job lately. You're right. We need another person." She drew her into a hug. "Now go on home and get ready for your date with that nice man."

As Alicia closed the office door, Ethne picked up her phone and tapped in Daniel's number. Straight to voice mail. She hung up and texted him. No reply. She loved him, and in anger and pain she'd hurt him when, just like Alicia, he'd said the hard things. She wanted to apologize, to make it right. But how could she if he wouldn't communicate with her?

Her life was falling apart. She'd thought Vaughn's death would end his grip on her, but it hadn't. Even from the grave his reach impacted her. Because of him, she had pretty much destroyed the one positive outcome in this whole mess that was her life. Her relationship with Daniel. She had pushed away the man she loved, and she might never get him back. All because of Vaughn.

So, what would she do about it?

~*~

The doorbell roused Ethne into the land of the living. She'd fallen asleep working on the Resurrections inventory. Maybe whoever it was would go away. As the irritating ringing repeated, she set her laptop on the coffee table. The clock on the wall read nine, much too late for a door-to-door salesman. She tiptoed into the foyer and peeked through the peephole. Daniel's face stared back.

Turning away from the door, she took a deep breath and then glanced in the hall tree mirror. The chrysanthemum on her head had shifted and loosened, making her curls look like Fourth of July fireworks exploding from the side of her head. Black bags, evidence of last night's lack of sleep, underscored her eyes. Dried drool tracked white across her right cheek, and her mouth was probably a biohazard. Not exactly the best ammunition to win him back.

Pounding replaced the dinging. "I know you're in there. Don't make me use this."

She looked back through the peephole. He held up his phone in front of the lens. He'd pushed in the numbers "911," and his finger was poised below the dial button.

"One minute." She rummaged through her purse until she found a packet of makeup wipes and a piece of gum. She peeled off the wrapper and crammed the peppermint rectangle into her mouth, hoping it would do its job. A quick scrub of her face with the wipe, and she was ready. She flipped the deadbolt and pulled open the door. "Daniel."

"Hi." A tentative smile warmed his face.

He wore—very well—gray dress pants, a form-fitting blue and white striped dress shirt, and old-fashioned brown penny loafers. He must have come straight from the office.

"How are you, Ethne?"

"Better than I look."

He jammed his hands into his slacks pockets. "I got your texts. I didn't answer because what I need to say should be said face-to-face. Not in a text."

Her heart pounded. Her selfishness had driven away the only man she'd ever loved. "I'm sorry about last night, Daniel. I was so mean to you."

"Thank you." He shifted his weight from one foot to the other.

"Think we could have the rest of this conversation inside?"

She really was brain dead. "I'm sorry. Of course." She opened the door wider, and he stepped into the foyer.

He looked down at his feet and then raised his gaze to meet hers. "I probably should have called. But I was afraid you'd tell me not to come."

"You're welcome here any time, but I would've at least cleaned up if I'd known you were coming." She closed the door. "I got the Bible. It was thoughtful of you to send it to me." Her words tumbled out. As long as she kept talking, he couldn't voice what he'd come to say. "I have an old Bible someplace, but I couldn't tell you where. And the list of verses you sent... I was up most of the night reading. When I saw the box on the porch, I thought it was some candles I ordered. I was so surprised—"

"Ethne." He held a hand up to silence her. "I'm glad you got it. But that's not what I came to talk about."

She would not let Vaughn's actions steal the one thing she wanted above all else. "Please forgive me," she whispered.

He shook his head. "I came to apologize."

"Apologize? For what? Being kind to me? Trying to help me see the truth?"

"Last night, when you pushed me away, it really hurt. I wanted to be the one holding you, comforting you, suffering with you. I wanted to help carry your pain. Instead I watched Josh take the place that should have been mine. So I left."

"I'm sorry—" Fear shook her voice.

"No, I'm sorry. You see, I realized you needed Josh because you know he loves you unconditionally. And it's my fault you don't know that about me because...I've never told you. He held out his hands. "Come here."

Tears swam in her eyes as she fell into the strength of his embrace and his arms enfolded her. She drew him close, and the earthy scent of his cologne wrapped her with warmth. He lifted his hands and freed her hair. As she leaned her head into his fingers, he stroked her curls.

"I love your curls." He kissed the top of her head. "I love your nose." He kissed her nose. "Your cheeks." His lips brushed each cheek. "Your lobulus auriculae."

"My what?"

He leaned his cheek against the side of her head. "Your earlobes."

His whisper electrified every cell in her body, and from someplace deep inside an uncontrollable giggle erupted. She pressed her body into the strength and warmth of his.

"Ethne, I love you with all that I am. I want to be your one and only. Forever. Forgive me for not telling you that before now."

She drew just far enough away to see his chocolate-kiss eyes and whispered the words she'd vowed she'd never say to a man. "Oh, Daniel, I love you, too."

He leaned down to kiss her, but she turned away. "I, uh, haven't brushed my teeth since this morning."

A chuckle rumbled through his body as he tightened his embrace. "You smell delicious. But even if you didn't, I'd be up to the challenge. Trust me."

~*~

The little stone church sat back from the road in a grove of live oak trees. Ethne pulled her car off the brick boulevard and parked in one of the visitor spots. She'd passed this building twice a day every day for almost ten years. Yet she never had the desire to go inside. Until today.

She waited until five minutes after eleven and then walked inside. The service had, as she'd hoped, already begun. She slipped unnoticed into the back pew. Shining through a stained-glass window above the entrance behind her, the sun bathed the pulpit area up front in a patchwork of warm, jeweled light.

A lone musician sat on a stool on the dais. Guitar in hand, he sang some song about being enslaved to fear. She'd heard these words and this melody before…that day in Daniel's truck, after he'd run through the waterfall. The same day she'd prayed for him. The same day she'd first began to love him.

She glanced down at the order of service listed on the bulletin.

Today's sermon was entitled, "Finding Freedom," and the scripture reference listed below it was John 8:36.

So if the Son sets you free, you will be free indeed.

That was the first verse Daniel had written on the list he'd given to her with her Bible. Her tears blurred the letters on the order of worship.

Maybe today she'd find what she'd been searching for all these years.

Freedom.

20

Ethne flipped on the blinker and slowed to pull into the clinic parking lot. "Thanks again for coming with me today." She smiled at Alicia.

"It's been way too long since we were able to do a delivery together." Alicia grinned back. "The whole reason we decided to close the showroom on Mondays was so we could both go on installations, but I can't remember the last time that actually happened."

"Me, neither."

The delivery truck slowed and followed them into the lot.

"Besides, I love you too much to let you do this alone."

"The apartment is so different. I think I'd have been OK. But thanks, anyway."

Ethne parked the car, and then while Alicia supervised the maneuvering of the delivery truck, she unlocked the front door and entered the new alarm code Daniel had texted her. The guys would have to navigate through the maze of furniture in the waiting room and then up the stairs in the back to his apartment. She scooted some of the chairs out of the way to give them as much room as possible.

Corey backed through the door carrying one end of the headboard from her old bedroom furniture. Nick had done a beautiful job of converting it from the original double bed to king-size. If she hadn't lived with the furniture a big portion of her life, she would have never been able to tell any modifications had been made.

As Alicia walked up beside her, Ethne grinned. "Nick's a woodworking genius."

"Oh, he's a genius at a lot of things." Alicia winked. "I'm not sure why it took me so long to see."

Ethne hugged her friend. "I'm happy for you two."

"Thanks. OK, let's get this done." Alicia led the way down the hall and up the stairway in the back.

The living room was neat as a pin. It looked just as it did when Ethne checked it out weeks ago. So different from twenty-five years earlier.

"Eth, you did a great job. Doesn't even look like the same place."

And that was a good thing.

The guys came down the stairs from the third floor and headed back out to get more pieces of the furniture.

"You ready?"

She followed Alicia up the stairs to the bedrooms. The headboard leaned against the longest wall in the larger room, the one that had been Vaughn's and Mother's. Daniel had painted the walls a soft slate and the trim white. A plastic-wrapped new king-size mattress leaned against the back wall, and the inflatable mattress he'd been sleeping on was rolled up in the corner. The shoeboxes that had been in the living area a few weeks ago now lined the wall adjacent to the door. An interesting and economical storage solution, but not for much longer. Once they got the dresser in place, he'd have plenty of drawer space.

"Your boyfriend's got a good eye. Love the paint color he chose for the walls."

Her boyfriend. *Her boyfriend.* Daniel was everything she could have possibly wanted but never allowed herself to dream about or believe existed. Sometimes, she feared she'd wake up to find it was all a dream. And he'd be gone.

Years ago, she escaped from Crescent Bluff, but rather than freeing her, leaving had imprisoned her. Each step she'd taken to separate herself from her past had only added another link to the chain that bound her. And with no destination to run to, she'd run in a circle, the chain of bitterness becoming shorter and tighter with each revolution. Until it squeezed her so she could barely breathe, much less move. Her quest for freedom became a crippling burden that held her captive all these years.

Until Daniel. And the waterfall. And God.

The words from yesterday's sermon rang in her heart. True freedom came not from doing, but from being. God invited her to be

His child. He wanted to adopt her out of her bondage and into His family, but she had to let Him. He wouldn't force His love upon her.

So, what would she do about it?

Alicia picked up the inflatable mattress and carried it into the walk-in closet. "Whoa. You have to see this, Eth."

Ethne followed the sound of her friend's voice into the closet. The enticing warmth of Daniel's cologne greeted her, and she resisted the urge to wrap herself in his clothes.

"Look behind you."

Ethne turned. Stacked shoeboxes lined the opposite wall.

"Apparently your boyfriend's quite the fashionista. Must be at least a hundred pairs of shoes here."

"I think he's probably been using the boxes for storage." Ethne lifted one of the lids to take a quick peek. Shoes. And another. More shoes. And another. Still more shoes.

She flipped through the pages of their story together. In the scores of times she'd seen him, been with him, she couldn't remember seeing him wear the same pair of shoes twice. But maybe he had. She hadn't really been looking at his feet that closely.

"Good thing Dr. Handsome makes enough money to support his habit." Alicia elbowed her and grinned.

Ethne's heart summoned images of a dark-haired boy with chocolate-kiss eyes going through dumpsters, searching for dinner…and cardboard to line his shoes.

She tugged the sleeve of her shirt down. While she'd never lacked any physical provision, she'd known the pain of emotional poverty, and she would do anything she could to help him carry this burden.

~*~

As Ethne stepped through the glass doors, a soft beep sounded. The waiting room to the Vaughn O'Connor Free Clinic was about half full. Josh sat in the corner to her left, clipboard in hand, speaking broken Spanish and helping a young woman with a baby complete some sort of form. Other church members along with volunteer nurses were scattered about serving water, offering magazines, or just providing encouragement.

Ethne glanced toward the counter at the back. Rebecca Porter was on the phone, and reacting to the beeping door, she looked toward Ethne. Her face flushed bright red.

Unforgiveness is a prison. As Daniel's words echoed deep within, the chain around Ethne's heart tightened. She wanted to forgive, to break free, but nothing she tried worked.

So if the Son sets you free, you will be free indeed.

"Ethne. What a pleasant surprise." Josh slipped an arm around her shoulders. "Daniel didn't mention you were coming by today."

"He didn't know. I wasn't sure how long the furniture installation would take, so I didn't mention it to him."

"Well, I'm glad you finished in time to drop by. But not as glad as Dr. Spenser will be, I'm sure." He chuckled.

She could do this. "So, put me to work, Preach."

"Rebecca's been supervising volunteers. Let's see what she needs." He tightened his hug as they walked forward.

Rebecca forced a smile. "Hi, Ethne." Her voice quivered. "Uh, I heard your business donated the waiting room furniture. That was kind of you. I'm sure Vaughn, I mean your daddy, would have been pleased."

"Ethne came to volunteer, and I told her you were the woman in charge." Josh nudged Ethne forward.

"That's nice. Do you have any medical training?"

Ethne shook her head.

"Are you OK running the desk? I could give you a two-minute tutorial, and then I can help Daniel—Dr. Spenser—with the patients."

Ethne nodded. Paperwork and people she was good at.

Five o'clock came quickly. Daniel had winked at her when their eyes met one time as he rushed between exam rooms.

The waiting room was empty, and most of the volunteers, Josh included, had left. Besides Daniel, only Ethne, Rebecca, and another nurse named Fran remained. The cry of a young baby pushed its way out from one of the exam rooms into the waiting area.

Fran locked the front door and then turned toward Ethne. "I have to go over some home care instructions with the patient in room two, and Rebecca's finishing up with the family in room one. Do you think you could help Dr. Spenser for a few minutes in room three? Sounds as if he may have his hands full." She laughed. "Rebecca or I will be in there as soon as possible."

Ethne nodded, walked to room three, and tapped on the door. "Come in," Daniel offered in a sing-song tone. She sat at the laptop at the small desk and waited for instructions. The baby had grown quiet as it sat in its mother's lap and played with an inflated purple latex glove-balloon. Daniel had the stethoscope to its chest, listening. As he removed the earpieces, the instrument dropped around his neck. Then he began softly singing something in Spanish to the toddler. All the while he was checking the baby, its arms and legs, hands and feet, trunk.

Daniel's hands moved slowly and gently just as they had the first time he'd touched her after that panic attack. Just as they had when he'd checked Mr. Adams' arm on the house call that same afternoon. Like then, today's movements were a beautiful dance of love, gentleness, and healing.

The memory of his caress and the shiver his whisper evoked as he'd apologized the other night awakened in her a deep hunger. She longed for those hands to be touching her in love and gentleness.

And, what would she do about it?

~*~

Daniel pulled his truck into the clinic parking lot and turned off the engine. He was tired...in a good kind of way. He'd seen twenty-seven patients today, and the ministry only promised to grow. Josh had already put feelers out to recruit an additional physician. Working six days a week was fine for now, but if everything went as Daniel hoped, it wouldn't be fine much longer.

As Ethne parked beside him, he jumped out of his truck. She cut the car engine but didn't get out. She was learning. He opened her car door and offered his hand.

"I can't wait to show you your bedroom." A blush crept across her face.

She was so cute when she was embarrassed. "I can't wait for you to show it to me."

"I'm glad Alicia was happy to ride back with the guys so I could stay here for the reveal."

"Not nearly as glad as I am." He pecked her on the cheek. "Remind me to thank her next time I see her."

"I don't think her decision was an entirely noble gesture. She and Nick have started dating, and I'm pretty sure that had something to do with her wanting to get back by dinner time."

"I'm happy for them, but even happier for me. With Nick off the market, that's one less competitor I have to worry about."

She giggled. "Yeah, you better be worried." She grasped his hand and led him up the stairs and onto the front porch. "Here we go."

They stepped into the dark waiting room. Nowhere he'd lived in the past few years had ever felt like home. No matter where he'd slept or where his stuff had been, the place he'd laid his head belonged to Uncle Sam. And home in Texas had always been Mom and Dad's house. Maybe if he'd been married and had a family, he would have felt different.

But sometime within the last couple of weeks everything had changed. For the first time in his life, he had a home that was his.

She turned toward him, straightened her cardigan, and stood tall. "First of all, Dr. Spenser, Resurrections would like to thank you for your repeat business."

He grinned and played along. "You're certainly welcome, Ms. O'Connor. Your company does a wonderful job. Excellent quality, at an affordable price. Along with personable customer service."

"We appreciate that, sir. I'll pass your information along to our warehouse supervisor. And our CEO." She winked. "Now, if you'll please follow me."

She led him down the hall to the back staircase. Her earlier reluctance to go upstairs was gone. She was healing.

They climbed the first flight and then walked through his living room and up the back stairs to the bedroom. She placed her hand on the doorknob and turned toward him. "Dr. Spenser, this room has been designed specifically with you in mind. If you like it, we hope you'll go online and leave us a five-star review, just as you did the last time."

"What if I want to give it more than five stars?"

"I'm sorry. Five is the most allowed. But I'm sure we could come up with another way for you to express your gratitude."

"You mean like buying you pizza or something?"

"Or something."

She leaned her head to the side and flashed those emerald eyes at him. Then she opened the door, stepped back, and motioned for him to enter.

The room was unbelievable. It could have been featured in an ad for any number of upscale design firms in Dallas. "Babe, this is…" he turned back and winked at her, "amazing."

The headboard and footboard, nightstands, the chest of drawers, and the dresser were all simple line furniture, almost Shaker in style. The pieces had to be antique. The imported stuff stores today sold couldn't touch this quality. They even found the bedding he'd stored in the closet and made the bed.

She nestled up against him and grasped his hand. "Do you really like it?"

He nodded. "I love it."

"I'm glad. This was my bedroom furniture when I was a child and before that my mother's. Nick modified the head and footboards to hold a king-size mattress." She leaned her head against his shoulder. "I wanted you to have it," she whispered.

He kissed the top of her head. "Thank you," he whispered back.

As he turned to hug her, the stack of shoe boxes came into view. She'd discovered his little secret. "I guess you're wondering about those."

She shook her head. "No." Her gaze was soft.

"I'm donating them to a local thrift store. And I'll get rid of some of the others in the closet soon. I've got a problem. I know it. Addiction's addiction whether it's drugs or shoes."

She placed her head on his shoulder.

He ran his fingers through the fiery waves he loved. "Trusting

God isn't a one-time thing, Ethne. I'm learning, but it's a daily challenge, and happens in stages and different forms. Sometimes it's like a thunderstorm, and other times a spring shower. But the outcome's always the same. Both get you soaking wet. One just takes longer than the other."

As she drew away, a soft smile warmed her face. "And still other times you run through the waterfall and plunge into the pool below."

He grinned back. "Yeah." Her gaze tugged at his heart. He loved her, and this was the last place they needed to be right now. "Babe, we should probably go."

She shook her head and then slipped her cardigan off, the pink sleeveless shirt exposing her arms. Trust. She was trusting her deepest pain and secrets to him.

He grasped her left hand and brought it upward. He placed his lips against the white web of scars on her arm. "I'm so sorry for this," he whispered. "I wish I could kiss them away."

"Everyone has scars, but not all of them are physical."

And some took years to fade, while others never would.

Her fingers loosened his tie and pulled it over his head.

"Ethne."

She began unbuttoning his shirt. He covered her hand with his and shook his head.

She nodded and planted little kisses on his neck. Little electric kisses. He fought to breathe. They really needed to leave. "Babe."

She inched away and then lifted his right hand and cradled her cheek in it. She whispered, "I watched you today with that little baby." Her lips caressed each finger and then the palm. She placed his hand low on her back.

Hunger swelled within him. "Ethne." Emotion cracked his voice.

"Shhhh." As she closed the millimeters between them, she took his left hand and again, kissed the fingers and then the palm. "Before you, I never knew a man's hands could be so beautiful. Such instruments of gentleness and love."

She entwined her fingers with his and began swaying to some imaginary melody. Her eyes enticed him, invited him. Welcomed him. Every muscle in his body tightened in response. He had let things go too far. From someplace deep inside, a moan sounded. A primal desire urged him to grant what she asked.

Surrendering would be the easiest thing. But not the right or the best thing. He moved both his hands high onto her back. He pulled her against his chest and rested his cheek on the top of her head. "Not yet, babe," he whispered. "I love you too much to betray your trust."

She drew away and cast a sideways glance at him. "What do you mean, you love me too much? Isn't this what people who love each other are supposed to do?"

As her body stiffened, he held her more firmly. "Yes. After they're married."

She raised her eyebrows. "Surely, you don't expect me to believe you're still a virgin, Daniel Spenser."

This was not the optimum time nor place to have this conversation. But... "In college. Savannah and I had planned—promised—to get married. We were committed to each other, and then..."

Tears lined her eyes, and she rested her head on his chest.

"I'm sorry, Ethne." He brushed the top of her head with his lips. "What I...we did was wrong. If I could've seen the future and known God was bringing you to me," he swayed her back and forth, "it would have been easy to wait. Can you forgive me?"

As she raised her face to his, a tear trickled down her cheek. "Neither one of us could predict the future."

"Remember that Bible verse I wrote on the clinic wall about God making everything beautiful in its time?"

She nodded.

"I also wrote it on the wall above the bed. Believe me, Ethne, God's gonna finish the work He started in His perfect timing. And I promise, it'll be worth the wait."

She leaned against his chest, and her words vibrated within him. "I've never been known for being patient. And you and God are making this really hard on me, Daniel Spenser."

He chuckled. "So, Ms. O'Connor, can I buy you some pizza instead?"

21

Nick stuck his head into Ethne's office. "Morning, Eth."

"Morning, yourself."

He shifted the cardboard banker's box in his hands onto one hip.

"Something on your mind?"

"I, uh, just wondered how Dr. Spenser liked the bedroom furniture."

"Loved it. You guys did a great job. I'll text you some of the pictures I took so you can see for yourself."

"Thanks." He nodded and continued to stand in the doorway.

"Anything else?"

"What?"

"Anything else on your mind?"

"I…" his face blazed bright red. "Where's Alicia? Is she sick?"

Ethne pressed her lips together to hide her grin. He had it bad. "She went to check Weatherford this morning, but she should be in around noon. Just in time for you two to go to lunch together…if you want, that is."

"Great. Thanks." He turned and stepped into the hall and then came back into her office. "I almost forgot." He held out the cardboard box. "The guys found this stuff in the credenza from your dad's house. It's been in the corner of my office for weeks now, and I just keep forgetting to give it to you."

"What is it?"

He shrugged. "Don't know. Didn't check. Figured it's not my stuff."

"Well, it's not mine, either."

"Uh…yeah, by default it is. I'll toss it if you want, though."

She stood and grasped the box. "No. I can throw it away. No need for you to do my dirty work."

"All righty, then. Have a good one." And he was gone.

Her phone dinged. Nine fifty-eight. Time to unlock the showroom door. She'd have to dump this stuff later. She shoved the box into the kneehole of her desk, stepped into the powder room to take one final check, and then headed out to, hopefully, greet some customers.

~*~

Ethne set the box on the coffee table in her living room. She should have tossed it into the dumpster at the store, but her curiosity conquered her common sense. Besides, she could throw the stuff into the garbage here at home just as easily as at work.

She stuck some vegetable enchiladas into the microwave and then headed to the bedroom to slip into a pair of shorts and an oversized T-shirt. The microwave beeped just as she started back down the hall toward the living room. Daniel had some sort of meeting about staffing the free clinic tonight, so they wouldn't talk until later.

She grabbed the no-longer-frozen dinner and snuggled back into the couch. She stared at the box on the table in front of her, and it stared back, the handhold on the side smiling at her, inviting her to open it.

No. She turned so she could no longer see the box. Nothing Vaughn stored in the credenza could possibly interest her. She'd take it straight to the trash as soon as she finished eating.

Her gaze wandered back. Now the box frowned at her, daring her to throw it away without opening it. No way would she let Vaughn's box defeat her. Two minutes was all it would take to glance through the contents, and then she'd dump it in the trash and be done forever.

She set the half-eaten enchiladas on the table and placed the box beside her on the couch. She took a deep breath, scooted the lid up, and laid it to the side. The antiseptic scent of Vaughn's house invaded her living room, burning her nose.

Several small gift boxes filled the top portion of the box. She lifted them out and placed them on the coffee table. Next came a tray filled with pens, paper clips, and other routine office supplies. She set that on the table next to the gift boxes.

Some books lined the bottom—a leather journal, or maybe some kind of ledger, and a scrapbook. She slipped her hands under them, drew them out of the box, and placed them on the couch beside her.

Taking a deep breath, she opened the leather volume. Written on the first page in Vaughn's handwriting was a Bible verse.

The Lord detests all the proud of heart. Be sure of this: They will not go unpunished. Proverbs 16:5

What a strange verse for him to write as an introduction. Some sort of warning or curse. His peculiar choice raised goose bumps on her arms. As her stomach began to churn, she slammed the book closed. She definitely should have thrown the box away at work.

The Bible Daniel gave her lay on the table at the end of the sofa. His words challenged her. *Unforgiveness is a prison.* She wanted to break free, but she didn't know if she could do what was necessary. Forgive Vaughn. The verse from Sunday's sermon resounded in her heart. *So if the Son sets you free, you will be free indeed.*

She forced herself to reach over and pick up the journal again. She whispered a prayer. "Set me free, Father. Please set me free." She opened the book again and turned to the second page. The date written at the top was the day she graduated from high school, the day she'd told him she was leaving forever. The last day she'd seen him. His words read:

> I've destroyed what should have been one of the greatest blessings of my life. Ethne is gone. I've driven her away, and I have no idea how to get her back. Today I have been punished, and I have no one to blame but myself. I've earned it.

Hands trembling, she leafed through the journal. Each page was headed with a date and bore his handwriting. Oftentimes, his words filled the page. Other times only phrases or short snippets marked a few lines.

He admitted his failings as a husband and father. His words of confession cried out for forgiveness or begged for vengeance.

Salty tears burned her eyes and trickled down her cheeks into the corners of her mouth. Grief and loss squeezed her chest until her heart ached and she struggled to breathe.

This…this confession was the only thing she'd wanted from him. But in life, he'd refused to give it to her.

She set the journal aside and picked up the album. When she opened it, a photo of her twelfth-grade self stared back at her. The next page held an image of her receiving her college diploma. The trickle of tears grew into a stream. He'd been at her graduation.

A few pages over, came an article from the *Crescent Bluff Gazette* about her and Alicia founding Resurrections. The picture showed them shaking hands with the real estate agents after they signed their first lease.

He'd recorded any award or honor she'd received. He even saved a copy of the article from the *Fort Worth Evening News* written when she'd received the Young Entrepreneur of the Year award the second year they were in business.

She'd seen enough. As the chain tightened around her heart, the prison bars closed in on one another. She slammed the album shut and dropped it back into the banker's box.

She turned to the coffee table and picked up the largest gift box. She opened it and slid back the tissue paper to uncover the picture frame she'd made him in sixth grade. She opened the next box and pulled out the keychain she'd given him after middle school church camp. She lifted the lid on the last box to reveal the clay pencil holder she'd sculpted for his birthday the year after Mother died. He'd kept all these things, but he had hidden them from her, never letting her know. Why, if for no other reason but to hurt her?

Burning rage consumed her. Shaking, she fought to breathe. This was just like Vaughn. Even from the grave, his cruelty continued to ruin her life. Why couldn't he have made himself apologize and ask for her forgiveness before he died, instead of asking only after it was too late—way too late—to repair their relationship?

She threw everything into the box and jammed the lid down. She was heading straight to the trash. She should never have opened the box in the first place. She'd prayed and asked for freedom, but she'd received only bondage. Unfair. This was so unfair.

And what would she do about it?

~*~

Ethne wound her car through the hill country south of Crescent Bluff. She hadn't paid close attention the day Daniel drove, but according to her GPS, this had to be the place. As the road narrowed and the pavement dissolved into sun-hardened dirt, the edge of the ravine appeared, lined against the horizon. She'd found it. His favorite place.

The Bible verse she read last night needled her until she had no choice but to come today.

It is for freedom that Christ has set us free. Stand firm, then, and do not let yourselves be burdened again by a yoke of slavery.

Daniel was right. In her quest for vengeance, she made herself a prisoner, a slave...a captive. And the freedom she'd sought all these years could be found in only one place.

With legs quivering like jelly, she backed down the side of the canyon wall until her feet lit on the path below. The same roaring she'd heard that day with Daniel grew louder with each step. She wanted to run toward the distant crashing before she lost her nerve and returned to the car, but the narrowness of the path prevented any movement other than careful plodding.

She'd lost her mind. She was crazy to come here, thinking, hoping by some ridiculous coincidence, the waterfall would bring her the same peace it brought Daniel. She turned to go back, but a Voice within her heart held her in place.

So if the Son sets you free, you will be free indeed.

All these years she'd been searching for freedom, seeking the one tool that could break the links of the chain around her soul. The image of Daniel sitting across from her that evening at Ricky's and his comment that everyone wants to find unconditional love filled her heart. Work, friends, parents, none of those could provide the acceptance and love she craved all these years. The love that could free her was found in only one place. And just as he'd said then, she'd been looking in the wrong places.

But no more.

She grasped saplings and clumps of grass and pulled herself along the path. The crashing of the water intensified with each step. She rounded the final bend. The waterfall appeared.

She climbed up the path and into the cave. She crept between the stone walls until she emerged onto the ledge behind the falls. The water had no curative power. Jumping broke no bonds. But it was an outward symbol of an inward decision to trust.

Hands shaking, she slipped off her shoes. She slid her phone and keys down inside them. Her heart pounded in her ears. Each beat shook her body. She inched toward the edge of the cave shelf. If she looked over the side, she wouldn't do it. Her eyes rested on her left forearm. Tears blurred the scars. Freedom. She wanted to be free. No longer a captive. Taking a deep breath, she closed her eyes and counted to three.

And then…she jumped.

Icy water bore down on her shoulders. Pushing, pushing, pushing, harder and harder. She slammed against the surface of the pool. The force jolted the air from her lungs. She slipped beneath the water.

Kicking her feet, flailing her arms, fighting to pull herself upward. All in vain. The power of the waterfall pinned her beneath the surface. Her lungs burned, fighting to hold on to their last whisper of breath. The more she fought, the deeper she sank. And the heavier the water grew.

Panic tore through her body. Trapped, she had no sense of direction. Up, down, sideways. All were the same.

She opened her eyes. Sunlight. She reached her hands toward it and pulled. Her muscles ached. She could fight no more. She stilled her legs, stretched out her arms, and leaned back. She submitted to the soothing cool.

The weight burdening her arms and legs disappeared, and she rose. The sunlight grew in intensity, warming away the chill. The water ebbed apart as she surfaced, her struggle over. The canyon breeze rushed across her face, carrying the sweetness of the Texas air.

Sunlight glistened through the droplets overhead, painting the face of the cascading water with a mosaic rainbow. The rainbow...the symbol of God's promise, of His faithfulness. And in surrender, she found her freedom.

~*~

Ethne parked beside the only other car in the deserted clinic lot. Even Daniel's truck was gone. Maybe he was making his weekly house calls. She pulled the Medusa tresses styled by the waterfall into an exploding ponytail and then walked up the steps to the entrance. If Daniel wasn't here, she could go upstairs and wait. The door chimed as she let herself in.

Daniel's receptionist, Sarah, waved from behind the desk as she continued a phone conversation. The lights were off, the waiting room empty.

Ethne dropped into one of the gray and black striped chairs, picked up a magazine, and thumbed through it.

"Thank you for waiting, Ms. O'Connor." Sarah stepped out from behind the counter.

"No problem. I was, uh, just in the area and thought I'd take a chance and see if Dan—Dr. Spenser—happened to be available. But it looks as if he's already begun his house calls."

"Oh, no ma'am."

Ma'am? Really? Ethne wasn't that much older than Sarah.

"He had some sort of emergency at his parents' house and had to go to Fort Worth. I just finished rescheduling the last of his appointments for today and tomorrow morning."

Ethne's breathing caught. "Emergency?" She kept her tone casual. Surely, if it had been something really important, he would have called or texted her. "I certainly hope it wasn't anything too major." She punctuated her fishing statement with a little laugh.

Sarah shook her head and offered her most polite *I-really-can't-say-any-more-to-you* smile. "He plans to be back by noon tomorrow.

Perhaps you'd like to leave a message?"

"No, thanks." Ethne stood. "I'll just drop by the house and see him." She responded with her most self-assured grin and then turned and walked out of the office.

Only one little problem. She had no idea where his parents lived. So, how exactly would she just drop by?

22

Daniel slapped peanut butter and jelly on some bread and tossed the sandwiches onto paper plates. He'd made it absolutely clear to Savannah that this was a one-time thing. He couldn't put his life and the wellness of his patients on hold every time her babysitter fell through.

But reality reminded him this was for a court date, not a shopping date. And, after today, it should be a moot point, anyway. As long as Will didn't contest or fight her for the boys. Losing them would devastate Savannah.

J-Squared walked into the kitchen. "Uncle Danny," Jeremy said.

Daniel cupped his ear, pretending not to hear, "What?"

"Uncle Danny," Jared echoed.

"What? I can't hear you."

"Danny!" both boys yelled in unison.

Close enough. "Yes?"

"What should we do with these?" They held out their wet swimming trunks and towels.

"Toss them on the floor in the laundry room. Your mom'll take care of it later." Daniel slung the paper plates onto the kitchen table. "PB&J all around. No complaints about the food or you'll have KP."

"KP?"

"Kitchen Patrol."

Both boys saluted.

"Danny, can we play soccer after lunch?" Jared asked.

"Soccer?" Daniel hadn't played in years.

"Yeah," Jeremy offered. "Mom said we should ask you to play with us because you were a really good soccer player in school."

Not good enough to date a cheerleader. But that changed once they'd left for college and he went into pre-med. And then it changed again when he'd decided to join the Air Force. And now, he was glad it had worked out this way. If he and Savannah had gotten married, he would have never known Ethne. Funny how God had everything under control, and Daniel was much better off than he would have been had things gone according to his original plans.

When Mom and Dad adopted him, they gave him a card, and every "Gotcha-Day" after that they celebrated by giving him another card. The sentiment might be different each year, but the Bible verse Dad wrote was always the same. Jeremiah 29:11

"For I know the plans I have for you," declares the LORD, "plans to prosper you and not to harm you, plans to give you hope and a future."

Over the years, when things got tough, when Daniel didn't understand what was going on in his life, he turned to this verse in his Bible. He wrote it on a card and stuck it in his wallet. He drew it on one of the waiting room walls in the clinic. He knew the same God Who brought him out of his past would lead him into his future.

"Can we please, Danny?" Jared's voice pulled him back into the present.

Daniel set his plate on the table and joined the boys. "I'm a little rusty, but we can practice some passing and dribbling. I'll even teach you a few feints you can use to trick opposing players. After you finish your lunch, that is."

~*~

"So, did you find anything good?" Alicia perched on the edge of a chair in Ethne's office.

Ethne hadn't been exactly honest about her plans for today. "Something really wonderful. But nothing we could sell."

Alicia wrinkled her forehead in confusion.

"I owe you an apology."

"OK..." The wrinkles deepened.

"I wasn't exactly honest with you."

"About...?"

"There wasn't a Tuesday Market today in Hillsboro."

"So, you found something someplace else?"

"Yes."

"But if we can't sell it, why are we keeping it? For custom orders?"

Ethne opened her mouth to speak, but no words came. Tears choked away her voice and the best she could do was shake her head.

"Eth, are you OK?" Alicia stood.

She managed a whisper. "Yes." Then she cleared her throat. "You were right a few weeks ago when you said I'd been missing too much work."

"Oh, that...I overreacted, and I'm sorry. It had been a busy few days, but now that we've added Amanda, we have more freedom for you to be out if you need. And you were right. How can we stay in business if no one looks for new inventory to sell?"

"But I wasn't working today. I needed a morning off, so I lied to you. I'm sorry."

Alicia waited patiently. She obviously knew more was coming. She'd always been able to read Ethne better than any other person she knew. "And...? So...?"

"You remember Daniel's waterfall?"

Alicia's eyes widened. "You didn't?"

Ethne nodded.

"Did he jump with you?"

She shook her head. "I wanted to do it alone. Just me...and...and God."

Alicia came around the desk and placed her hands on Ethne's shoulders. "That was a reckless thing to do."

The memory of Daniel's smile when she'd said similar words filled her mind. She shrugged her shoulders. "Maybe."

"What if you'd been injured or...or killed?"

"But I wasn't. And there was something so freeing, so cleansing, about the whole experience." Her heart raced. "I can't even begin to explain what happened. All I know is I was never alone. It was...spiritual."

"What did Daniel say?"

"I went by the office to tell him, but he's up here in Fort Worth. Some emergency at his parents' house."

"Emergency?"

"Yes, and his cute little receptionist wouldn't even hint at what it might be."

"Did you call him?"

She shook her head. "I want to tell him face to face."

"Well, you can still call him and tell him you're coming by. You don't have to tell him why."

"No. I want it to be a complete surprise."

Alicia hugged her. "Then go on to his house. We're not busy. I can cover."

"I would if I knew where his folks live. I never got the address."

"Ethne?" Alicia shooed her away from the computer. "Scoot."

She stood as Alicia took her chair.

"Dear technologically-challenged Ethne, this day and time, you can track down anyone anywhere on the Internet."

~*~

Daniel grabbed the orange cones from the shelf in the garage where they'd been since before he'd left for college. He hadn't played soccer barefoot in at least fifteen years. He probably hadn't even touched a ball in ten. But muscles have memories, and some skills are never forgotten. Rusty, for sure, but not lost.

Mom and Dad had insisted he sign up for soccer right after they'd adopted him. They wanted him to do something that would make him part of a team. As a form of self-preservation, he'd always been a loner. He learned at a young age that relationships were never permanent. People came in and out of his life, but no one ever stayed. Until Mom and Dad.

Being in the service had suited him. The players constantly rotated, and he was already used to making superficial, temporary relationships. But a couple of years ago, everything changed. And God placed in his heart a longing for something lasting that neither the Air Force nor medicine could provide. He wanted to put down permanent roots.

And God had answered his prayers in a way Daniel could have

never anticipated and only He could have orchestrated. His Heavenly Father led him to Crescent Bluff and brought him Ethne. More than he could have ever asked or imagined.

"Unc—Danny." Soccer ball in hand, Jared grinned at him. "You're taking forever."

"Sorry, buddy. Just getting some cones. You guys ready?"

He nodded. "Uh-huh. Jeremy says we can beat you."

"He does, does he? Well, we'll see about that."

~*~

Ethne followed the instructions spoken by the soothing female voice coming from her phone. If Alicia was right, Daniel's parents' house was less than ten minutes from hers, just a matter of crossing the brick boulevard that divided Arlington Heights from Westover Hills. The houses on the south side were like hers: brick bungalows built in the 1920s and 1930s. The houses to the north were mansions.

Maybe surprising him wasn't the best move. What if the address Alicia found wasn't right, and Ethne showed up unannounced at some stranger's house? She slowed and pulled the car over to the curb. She flipped on her emergency flashers and pressed in his number.

"Hello, this is Dr. Spenser. I'm currently out of town."

His voice birthed a longing hunger deep within her.

"If this is an emergency, hang up and dial 911. If not, please call the office and leave a message with the answering service."

She hung up. Surprise him she would. She selected "Resume" on her phone and continued following the polite woman's instructions. She wound through the old, narrow streets, snaking deeper into Westover Hills. After following a route that paralleled the country club golf course, she came to his street, or at least what, according to Alicia, was his street.

Slowing to a crawl, she scanned the house numbers. On her left a quaint rock chapel sat nestled back among some pine trees. A high, brick privacy fence broken only by a black iron entrance gate enclosed the yard of the house across the street, which—if the numbering sequence was consistent—should be his.

She crept past the gate to confirm the house number. Yes, this was the address. Her heart raced. She couldn't wait to tell him what she'd found at the waterfall this morning. How today's visit to his favorite place had freed her, too.

The narrow road offered no space to park. If she turned into the driveway to push the call button, she'd block the gate. And what if Alicia was wrong, and this wasn't his address? She'd park in the chapel lot and walk across the street to the entrance. She could peek through the iron gate to see if his truck was visible.

As she pulled into one of the spaces, peace flowed over her. Five years...one year...six months ago she would have never envisioned this journey. She could have never dreamed her life's path would cross Daniel's. That even when she wasn't looking, God would bring her such a special gift, and that for all these years when she'd insisted on going one direction, God was quietly, lovingly clearing another path for her to follow.

Father, thank You for bringing Daniel into my life. He's more than I could have ever imagined.

Taking a deep breath to stem the rising tears, she stepped out of her car, and she saw him, a portrait framed by the iron bars of the gate. His hair was tousled. He was shirtless and shoeless, wearing a pair of athletic shorts. He juggled a soccer ball back and forth with his feet and then kicked it across the grassy carpet out of sight.

So, the house was standing, and Daniel was running around kicking a soccer ball and laughing. At least the emergency that took him away from the office certainly didn't appear to be life-threatening. She waved and called his name, but a delivery truck passed between them. He didn't see or hear her.

Two young boys ran into the picture. Both had dark brown hair. One of them passed the ball back to him, and the other tackled Daniel's legs, knocking him to the ground.

She answered their laughter with a smile of her own. As she started to cross the street, a car pulled into the driveway of his house.

The driver pushed in the code, the gate slid open, and the car slipped through. Ethne wasn't a car person, but even she recognized the prancing horse logo. The owner definitely had some money.

As Ethne walked forward, she raised her hand and waved again.

Daniel waved back. No, he wasn't waving at her but at the driver of the car. The car stopped on the driveway, and a blonde woman stepped out. She walked to Daniel.

The scene before Ethne shifted into slow motion, like the climax of an action movie. The woman and Daniel laughed, and then he picked her up and swung her around. The two young boys joined the scene. The woman picked up one, and Daniel picked up the other.

"Mommy, Mommy, Daddy taught me how to dribble a ball."

Ethne froze. Her insides knotted, and her stomach began to heave. A lump filled her throat, as sorrow gripped her chest. She slipped to the side, out of sight, and sunk against the brick wall. She thought he was different. She pressed down the urge to throw up.

~*~

Daniel set Jeremy onto the driveway. "So, it's really over?"

"He didn't even contest it. Agreed to the terms we'd drawn up. My attorney said it's because he didn't want all the details to be made public."

Jared jumped down and ran off to join his brother. "I'm relieved but scared. My life's been on hold the past few months, and now I can finally move forward. I've got to get our stuff out of the house. Find somewhere to live."

Daniel placed his arm around her and drew her close. "I'm happy for you, Vanna." But more than that, he was happy for himself. He no longer had to sneak around. He could be completely open with Ethne...and with Vanna. "You can stay here as long as you need. Mom's not due back for another six months at least. And it'll help me out to have someone here to watch the house."

Tears shimmered in her eyes. "You're a wonderful man, Daniel Spenser. I should have never let you go."

He hadn't exactly chosen to leave. She pushed him away. But now he could see God's hand in it all. "No need rehashing what-ifs. You were right when you said you'd never be happy as an Air Force wife."

She turned and grasped his hands. "But you're not in the Air Force anymore."

He pulled loose from her and folded his arms over his chest. "We need to talk."

As she closed her eyes, a tear tracked down her cheek. "Oh, no."

~*~

Ethne's phone buzzed as it vibrated against the glass top of Alicia's end table. Alicia picked it up, read the display, and held it out. "It's him again."

"He can leave a message." Ethne grabbed the phone and placed it back on the table.

"I think you at least owe him the chance to explain." Alicia tossed Ethne the sheets as they began making the couch into a bed. "He just doesn't seem like the type of guy who'd do that."

"You know what they say about pictures and words." The image burned in her mind from this afternoon had to be worth at least ten thousand words. "Thanks again for letting me stay here tonight. I'm not ready to see him, and I'm sure he's camped outside my house as we speak."

The phone vibrated again. "I can't take any more of this. You're being ridiculous." Alicia picked it up and tapped the answer button. "Hello, Daniel. It's Alicia."

Ethne turned away and began cramming the sheets into the cracks around the sofa cushions.

"Yes. She's here. Something's, uh, come up, and she's spending the night with me."

Burning tears trickled from Ethne's eyes down her cheeks.

"Eth, he wants to speak with you," Alicia whispered.

She kept her back turned and shook her head.

"Daniel, she's in the middle of something, but I'll give her your message." Alicia slapped the phone onto the table. "He has some news he wants to share with you."

"Oh, I'll just bet he does."

23

Daniel pulled his car into the Resurrections parking lot. Sarah had done a great job rearranging his appointments, so he had a couple of hours before he had to be at the clinic for his first patient.

Last night, he'd broken a promise he'd made to himself and to his Father. He'd stayed at Mom and Dad's even though Savannah and the boys were there. He slept in the guest room, but he wouldn't do it again.

Even though nothing happened and he had nothing to hide, he needed to let Ethne know. He'd hate it if she somehow found out on her own.

Besides, something was up. She hadn't returned his calls, and that was so unlike her. He'd probably have assumed she hadn't gotten the phone calls if he hadn't spoken with Alicia himself. Ethne definitely got his message but for some reason hadn't called him back. Maybe she was tired…or sick…or who knew what else?

As he opened the main door, the chime sounded his arrival. The showroom was empty. He walked over to the desk and raised his hand to ring the bell on the counter when Alicia appeared from the back. She'd know if something was wrong.

"Daniel." She grabbed him in a hug. "It's so good to see you."

"You, too, Alicia." He stepped away and then took a deep breath. "Is, uh, Ethne here? I'm on my way back to Crescent Bluff, and I thought I'd take a chance and see if she had a few minutes."

Alicia stepped behind the counter and glanced at the computer screen. A grin covered her face. "Yes, she sure does."

She picked up the phone and dialed. "Ethne, your ten o'clock is here." She winked at Daniel. "Yes, it was kind of last minute, and I didn't have a chance to get it on the schedule." She listened and then continued, "No, he asked specifically for you."

She hung up the phone. "She'll be right out. Why don't you go have a seat at that dining setting in the corner?" She gestured to the table and chairs where he and Ethne sat when they had their first planning meeting months ago.

He'd surprised Ethne then, and he was getting ready to repeat that today. "Thanks."

He turned to walk toward the corner, and Alicia grasped his arm. "I'm so glad you came, Daniel."

As if he hadn't already figured it out, her eyes telegraphed concern. Something was definitely up.

He walked to the far corner and sat down behind the hutch. Nerves made his right knee jump up and down. He wiped his sweaty palms on his pant legs, closed his eyes, and whispered a quick prayer. *Trusting You, Father. Bless our words.*

She stepped around the corner, copper hair billowing over her shoulders, right hand extended. A professional smile lit her face. "Hello, I'm—"

He stood. "Hi."

The smile disappeared. She bit her bottom lip and then drew up to her full height. "Daniel. This is certainly a surprise. I wasn't aware we had a meeting scheduled."

"Ah, I wondered if you'd listened to my message, but apparently not, since I mentioned I'd drop by this morning on my way back to the clinic."

She avoided his gaze. "I've been pretty busy." She glanced at her watch. "In fact, I've got another consultation in a few minutes."

He trained his gaze on her face and kept his voice gentle. "Alicia didn't mention it."

"I forgot to tell her about it."

He grasped her hands. "Ethne, it's me. What's up, babe?"

She closed her eyes for a couple of seconds and then withdrew her hands. She looked down at their feet. "I've been thinking about…life."

"Life."

She nodded. "Several employees have let me know I've been irresponsible with my time."

"Irresponsible?" He kept his tone even, calm, non-defensive.

"Yes, I've been spending too much time away from work, and it's impacting the business negatively. I'll have to stay here in Fort Worth more than I have been."

"Certainly understandable. But you're still closed on Sundays and Mondays, right?"

"The showrooms are closed, but I have paperwork to do. Inventory adjustments, budgeting, marketing, things like that. We're often so busy during the week, I have to do that stuff at home. And then, of course, we have installations on Mondays."

"Yes, I remember." He reached out and grasped her hand again. "You guys did my bedroom on a Monday."

Her cheeks flushed bright red. "Daniel, I don't know how I ever thought I could manage my business and any kind of dating relationship. Especially a long-distance one." As the flow of the words stopped, she removed her hand from his. She lifted her gaze and stared right into his eyes. "I'm sorry."

That two-word sentence was the first truthful thing she'd said. "Hey, babe. You want to tell me what's really going on?"

"Really. That's what's really going on." Her eyes teared up. "And I truly am sorry."

"Ethne, whatever this is, we can work it out."

She shook her head and then glanced at her watch. "I've got to get ready for my next appointment. Bye, Daniel." She disappeared around the hutch.

He was a pretty good judge of people, and very little of this conversation rang true. Her lack of candor said much more than her words. But then again, his experience with women was limited. He walked out to the middle of the showroom and turned toward the back. Alicia's face reflected the confusion he felt. "Daniel?"

He raised a couple of fingers to his forehead in a relaxed salute, turned, and then walked out the door.

Three things he knew. The woman he loved didn't want him. The woman he didn't love did. And all he could do was trust that God had this under control.

~*~

Ethne's knees shook as she lowered herself into her desk chair. Her ability to make it all the way across the showroom and down the hall to her office without her legs giving way was almost miraculous. She folded her arms on her desktop and cradled her head on them.

Soft raps sounded on her office door. She took a deep breath and sat up straight. "Come in."

Alicia stepped in and closed the office door behind her.

"Shouldn't one of us be out in the showroom in case a customer comes in?"

"Amanda just got here. I told her to buzz if she needs help." Alicia dropped into one of the chairs facing the desk. "So? What did he say?"

"About?"

"Eth…what was the whole reason you were trying to track him down yesterday? The waterfall. What did he say about the waterfall?"

"I didn't tell him."

"You're kidding, right?"

Ethne shook her head. "I decided not to." In less than twenty-four hours, her whole life had changed. The waterfall seemed like a lifetime ago.

"OK, then. What about the other thing? The woman and the two boys?"

"I didn't bring that up, either."

"Well, you talked about something serious. I saw the look on his face when he left."

Tears burned her eyes, and a knot filled her throat. "We broke up."

"I can't believe he'd break up with you just like that."

She shook her head and pushed a whisper out. "I broke up with him."

Alicia stood and walked over to the desk. She placed her hands on Ethne's shoulders and leaned her cheek against Ethne's head. "Oh, Eth. I wish you hadn't done that. You should've given him a chance to explain. I'm sure there's some logical and plausible explanation."

Ethne pulled away. "You're right. There is. He's not the man he pretended to be, the man he made me believe he was. He's just like Vaughn." She stood. "I watched my mother suffer and die from a broken heart because Vaughn not only cheated on her but lied to her about it when she knew it was true." Tears dampened her cheeks. "And I'm not putting Daniel…or me…in a situation where he'd have to lie to me or the other woman, because he's cheating on one of us."

"You're making assumptions without all the facts."

"Facts? My entire life has been one example after another of a man's incapability to honor his promises. I've got years of proof."

Alicia slumped back into her chair and focused her gaze on some point over Ethne's right shoulder.

"Not only is this the best decision for me personally but also for the business. As you pointed out, I've been stretched pretty thin these last few months trying to balance work and a dating relationship. It's not fair to the rest of you. Or Daniel. Or me."

"I told you, I overreacted when I said all that the other day." Alicia stood and stared right at Ethne. "Don't you blame any of this on us. None of us would have wanted this. We were happy for you." She walked to the door, opened it, and then turned back toward Ethne. "I only have one question."

"Yes?"

"Did you pray about this before you made your decision?" Not waiting for a reply, Alicia disappeared into the hall and closed the door behind her.

And the answer was…no. She hadn't prayed about this. This whole praying thing was new to her. Besides, should she have to pray about everything? God gave her a brain, and surely, He expected her to use it.

Last Sunday's sermon crept into her mind. The pastor referenced a passage in Matthew that said God cares for even the smallest of birds and the simplest of flowers. And just as they were important to Him and He cares for them, He cares for us…her…even more. Yes, she should have prayed about this.

She placed her head on her desk. *I'm sorry, Father.*

Her phone vibrated against the desktop. She really didn't want to talk with Daniel. She flipped the phone over and read the display. Josh. So, Daniel had already recruited the preacher to come to his defense.

She took a deep breath, and pressed the green button. "Hey, Josh."

"How's the best businesswoman in Fort Worth?"

"When I meet her, I'll ask and let you know."

He chuckled. "I'm sure you're busy, so I'll get right to the point."

Great. She took a deep breath and steeled herself.

"We're planning the formal dedication of the Vaughn O'Connor Free Clinic, and, since it's named after your dad, I wanted to invite you to come. I've already spoken with Sean, and he's committed once we set a date and work out the details."

She needed to think about this.

"If you'd rather not, I understand."

"No, no. I'll pray about it."

"That would be…great."

She could almost see his smile through the phone.

She'd spent most of her life holding a grudge against Vaughn. Building walls of protection around her heart, insulating, preserving her from the pain. And then Daniel shared his story at the waterfall. And Nick gave her the box. And she made the choice to trust her Father and jumped. But now, as she looked back, she could see her Father's hand in her life even when she'd ignored Him. She should have trusted Him more then. And she should trust Him more now.

"Unless I feel otherwise, I'll come. Sundays are the best days for me, but if another day of the week's better for everyone else, let me know, and I'll see what I can do."

"That's…wonderful, Ethne." Surprise tinged his voice, and she grinned. She loved getting a leg up on him. "I'll check with the rest of the committee and e-mail you when we have a firm date."

"Sounds good. Talk to you soon." She pressed the red button to end the call. So, Daniel hadn't contacted him. Josh definitely would have said something, if he had.

She didn't know whether to be relieved she hadn't had to defend her stance to Josh today or dread having to explain it the next time she saw him.

~*~

Ethne slipped into a pew about halfway back on the left side of the church. This was the third Sunday in a row she'd visited the little church on the boulevard. As soft guitar music filled the sanctuary, she opened the order of worship. Today's sermon was entitled "Who Are You?" The scripture reference was 1 John 3:1-2. She picked up the Bible Daniel gave her and turned to the table of contents. She flipped to the scripture and read over the verses.

See what great love the Father has lavished on us, that we should be called children of God! And that is what we are!

Daniel had pretty much said exactly these same words that day he took her to the waterfall. Her value did not come from who she was and what she did, but Whose she was and what He did. She was called a child of God. Earthly fathers may fail, but her Heavenly Father never would.

She didn't understand what was going on with Daniel. She'd envisioned and wanted them to share a future together. But maybe that wasn't to be. Maybe God's motives were not the same as hers. Perhaps he'd been brought into her life for one reason, and one reason alone. To lead her back to her Father. And if that was the purpose, it would have to be enough.

"Hello."

She looked up at the handsome blond man standing at the end of her pew. His blue eyes were striking, but fell short of the beauty of chocolate kisses.

"You've been here before, right?"

An old salesman's trick. It's all in the phrasing of the question. "Yes. This is my third Sunday."

"I knew I recognized you."

Oh, yes. Definitely sales.

"Welcome." He handed her a business card. "Andrew Duncan."

She grasped his offered hand. "Nice to meet you. Ethne O'Connor."

"Essie?"

"Ethne." She accentuated the "th" sound.

"Ethne," he repeated. "Beautiful and unique. Like its owner."

Oh, brother.

"A group of us are getting together for lunch after the service. We'd love to have you join us."

"What a kind invitation. Unfortunately, I need to work this afternoon."

"I'm sure you have to eat lunch." He winked.

"Yes, but mine will be a working one." Her smile dripped honey.

"I see. Maybe another time?"

She shrugged her shoulders. "Maybe."

Andrew walked down the aisle and sat a few rows in front of her. She probably could have been a little nicer, more encouraging. But that was the issue. The last thing she wanted to do was encourage him. She wasn't interested in dating.

She was interested in Daniel. She loved him, but after what she saw at his house the other day, she had to figure out some way to live her life without him.

24

Daniel pulled into the driveway of Mom and Dad's house. His last appointment had run long, so he was an hour or so later than they'd originally planned. He hadn't even taken the time to clean up and change clothes. It wasn't as if this was a date, anyway. Just two old friends getting together for a celebratory dinner. Celebratory on Vanna's part, anyway. He hadn't had much to celebrate lately.

"Sorry I'm late." His voice echoed through the mudroom and into the kitchen.

"Danny!" J-squared yelled and ran into the kitchen. They attached themselves to his legs.

"Hey, guys. Where's your mom?"

"Here."

He turned toward the voice behind him. Before him stood the beautiful cheerleader every guy in high school had wanted to date. Vanna posed, framed by the kitchen doorway, wearing a slim cut black dress and silver strappy heels.

He must have misunderstood about dinner tonight. "Hey, sorry. My last appointment ran long. I hope I haven't made you late."

Her cheeks pinked as a slight smile warmed her face. She slowly shook her head. "No problem. I made lasagna. It keeps great."

"Well, go on, then. The boys and I'll be fine."

"Go where? We're having dinner here."

"But your clothes… You're all dressed up."

She bit her bottom lip and shrugged her shoulders. "I bought this for my cousin's wedding next month. Thought I'd give it a test run while I could still return it if it didn't work out. What do you think? Should I keep it?"

He smiled. "It's beautiful. Perfect for a wedding."

A smile warmed her face. "OK, guys, give Danny a hug and then head on to bed, as we discussed."

"But what about dinner?" Daniel asked, bending down to hug the boys.

"They had hot dogs a couple of hours ago."

"G'night, Danny," Jeremy said.

"'Night," Jared echoed.

"Sleep tight, guys." Daniel gave them a thumbs-up, and they headed down the hall toward his old bedroom. "Well, that was uneventful."

"I must confess. Some bribery in the form of ice cream tomorrow was involved." She grasped his hand and led him toward the dining room. The table was set with Mom's china and crystal. She lit the candelabra and dimmed the lights. "Have a seat, Dr. Spenser, while I get our dinner."

Some old 70's music—Dad's favorite—played over the speakers. Vanna walked in carrying a tray that held two plates filled with salad, lasagna, and bread. "I found some of your dad's old CDs. I hope you don't mind that I'm playing them."

He shook his head. He didn't mind, and Dad wouldn't have minded, either. But still, the memories churned his stomach.

She sat beside him and then reached out and grasped his hand.

His first impulse was to pull away, but then…

"Would you mind asking the blessing?"

He breathed easier. "My pleasure." He bowed his head, "Father, thank You for this food, and this friend. I ask Your blessing on both. Amen." He took a bite. "Vanna, this is amazing."

"It's my mom's recipe. It takes hours to make. But it's worth it."

"You've turned into quite the cook. But you shouldn't have gone to that much trouble for me."

"I wanted to, Danny. You've helped us so much over these past few weeks and months. I don't know what we would have done without you."

The music changed, and she laid down her fork. "Oh, my goodness!"

One of those old line-dance songs played.

"I haven't danced this since our prom."

He didn't remember Dad ever playing that.

She stood and offered her hand. "Come on. Let's give it a try. See if we can remember the steps."

"It's probably been at least college since I've done it."

"It'll be fun. Please, Danny?"

"OK. One dance if you promise I can eat some more as soon as it's over."

"You betcha." She grasped his hand and pulled him out into the entrance hall. Mom had always said this foyer was big enough to waltz in. Looked as if she was right.

"One, two, three, four." And she was off.

The steps came back easier than he figured they would.

"Grapevine right," she prompted.

He hadn't seen her this relaxed and happy since she'd moved in here. His feet got tangled up on the next turn, and she burst out laughing.

He chuckled in response. "Are you making fun of me? Remember, I was always the science geek, not the athlete. Mr. Uncoordinated, that's me."

"That's not true, Daniel Spenser. You were quite the soccer player. You were just an even better student."

He got back in step and stayed in sync with her until the song ended. "OK. Dinnertime."

As the song changed again, she grasped his hand. "Do you remember this old love song?"

He remembered. The theme of their prom.

She took his other hand. "We danced to it."

He remembered that, too. "Yeah, Will wasn't too happy about that, if I recall."

She grinned and held out her hand. "For old time's sake?"

"Vanna, it's been a long day."

"Please. Just this one song, then we can finish dinner."

"That's what you said a few minutes ago."

"Please, Dr. Spenser?"

He drew her close. "Just one more. And that's it."

She snuggled up against him, resting her head on his shoulder.

She was wearing the same citrus scent she wore all through college. A lump formed in his throat, and he closed his eyes and let years of memories and pain rush back over him. He had loved her. In some ways, he still did. If she hadn't said "no," they might now be where she and Will were. Divorced, angry, wounded. As much as it hurt that night the end of their senior year, her refusal may have saved him additional pain. And now…everything was different.

"Danny," she whispered, her warm breath tickling his ear and sending electric chills to the soles of his feet. "I've loved you all these years. I never stopped. I was selfish. I thought Will would be able to give me a better life than an Air Force doctor." She sniffed. "Please forgive me. I was wrong."

"Vanna, we're past all that." He brushed a kiss against the top of her head. "Friends?"

"Oh, Danny." She turned her face up toward him and offered her lips. "No."

Taking advantage of her would be easy, but wrong. She wasn't the one his heart yearned for. But Ethne had rejected him. They were no longer dating. And while his heart might still be committed to her, his mind told him reality didn't match his desires.

Vanna nestled her head down onto his shoulder and tightened her embrace. Maybe this was God's way of showing him another plan, of leading him down another path. Maybe they were getting a chance to fix what they'd messed up years ago.

As she raised her face to his, he drew back. Silver tears shimmered in her eyes. "I love you, Danny."

"Vanna, I don't know if I can get there."

"However long it takes, I'll wait. I lost you once, and I don't intend to let it happen again."

~*~

The thunderstorm had blown up out of nowhere. Gripping the steering wheel, Daniel pulled hard against the buffeting of the wind in a battle to keep the truck on the road. He slowed to a crawl. The streetlights were out and any road signs had been knocked down by the force of the gale. He crept along, careful not to overrun the wash of his headlights on the serpentine road ahead. He glanced to his right. Vanna slept, her head against the passenger window.

A tree crashed across the road behind them, shifting his pulse into overdrive. Two seconds earlier, and the truck would have been crushed. They would have been crushed. Pulling off onto the shoulder in this weather would be disastrous. He had no choice but to creep forward.

Vanna rustled, and he turned toward her again. His mother's face sported her toothless meth grin. "Yeah, you just thought you was better than me. Looks like you're in a fine pickle. Where you goin' now, Mr. High-and-Mighty?"

Daniel jerked up, fighting off the sheet that bound his sweat-soaked body to the bed. Heart pounding, he stumbled onto the guest room floor. He shouldn't have stayed again last night. Nothing happened, but it was only because of his resolve, and he didn't know how much longer he could stand strong.

He pulled his clothes on and headed toward the kitchen. He'd leave Vanna a note.

~*~

The pounding on the clinic door alternating with the pulsing of the doorbell jerked Daniel awake. He glanced at his phone. He'd only been asleep for about two hours and his mind was detached, floating somewhere above his body. The knocking boomed again, followed by the ringing of the bell. Whoever it was needed him.

He jerked on a pair of jeans and a T-shirt, slipped on some tennis shoes, and headed downstairs. When he reached the waiting room, he answered the pounding. "Coming, I'm coming." He looked through the peep hole.

Josh stood there, disheveled and unshaven.

Daniel threw open the door. "Josh? What's up?"

"Thank God you're here. When I couldn't reach you on your phone, and then couldn't get you here, I was about to give up."

Daniel glanced at his phone. He'd set it on silent last night during dinner and then forgotten to take it off. The screen read *6 missed calls. 3 new messages.* "Sorry. Come in." He stepped back from the doorway. "I'm thinking this isn't a social call."

"Let's sit down, Daniel." Josh dropped into one of the waiting room chairs and motioned for Daniel to follow suit.

He sat across from Josh. "Shoot."

"I got a call from the US Embassy in Beijing. They've been trying to get ahold of you."

"The Embassy?" Daniel's heart thudded against his ribcage. "And?" He pushed the word past the lump in his throat.

"It's your mom. She's missing."

"Missing?"

"You know that recent earthquake in Kathmandu?"

He nodded. "But that's Nepal. She's in China."

Josh placed a hand on Daniel's shoulder. "She and some of the other teachers from her school had gone to Kathmandu on a humanitarian trip. They were there assisting a relief agency when a second quake struck. All remaining communication has been knocked out, and no one knows about her group. The embassy is staying on top of it, and they'll let us know as soon as they have any updates."

Daniel ran a hand through his hair. He'd lost Dad. He'd lost Ethne. And the thought of losing Mom, too... He opened the list of missed calls on his phone. One was from the mission organization Mom was serving with. One was from the U.S. Government. And the rest were from Josh or Vanna. So while he and Vanna were dancing, eating, joking around, Mom was, at best, lost somewhere. He swallowed back the fear. "You'll let me know if you hear any updates? And I'll let you know if I do."

"Deal." Josh glanced at his watch. "How about a cup of coffee at The Perks? It's after five, so they're open. I could use the caffeine, and you sure as crud look as though you could."

He needed a lot more than caffeine.

"We can spend some time praying for your mom and the other workers."

"Thanks, Josh. I'd like that."

~*~

"One double espresso." Josh slid into the seat across from him.
"Thanks."

"So, I'd like to pray for you and your mom. Is there anything else on your heart? Anything else you want to add to the church prayer list? How's the practice?"

Daniel blew across the top of the mug. "The practice is going good."

"Well, that can be a praise." Josh dumped sugar into his coffee. "Anything else, then?"

With Mom missing, praying for his current love life seemed trivial. But he served a big God, a God Who loved him and was interested in the largest and the smallest details of his life. Sharing his failures had never been easy. "I, uh… It's…" He took a deep breath. "Ethne and I broke up."

Josh slid his coffee aside. "Sorry to hear that."

"Yeah. I was, too. Sure didn't see it coming."

Josh shook his head. "Can't say I'm completely surprised, though." He gazed at the tabletop as he sipped his coffee. Then he looked up at Daniel, his laser stare conveying an unspoken message. "You remember what happened that night at the clinic."

He'd never forget the feeling of uselessness that had overcome him. His inability to provide the comfort she needed. "Yes."

"Then you can understand how she might have some trust issues."

He nodded. He completely understood. It had taken him years to trust Mom and Dad. He wanted to, but his life experience trained him to do otherwise.

"Especially with men."

"I totally get that. But it's made me wonder if God's trying to tell me something. If it's His way of getting me off the wrong path and onto the right one. Maybe I've been following my own heart and haven't been listening as I should."

"Daniel, that's a conversation I have with myself almost every day of my life. And then I remember life's all about God and His grace. Not me and my shortcomings. Most of my problems arise when I get so tied up in life I forget that. I just have to remember to ask and trust. And that assurance is all any of us needs."

Daniel's heart knew that, but his mind struggled with the inconsistencies between his desires and reality.

"I know one thing. God's got something great planned for your life." Josh winked. "Any other prayer requests?"

25

Ethne left the inn and walked across the town square toward Nacho Mama's. She hadn't eaten here since that evening months ago when Daniel had invited her and Sean to come talk after the funeral. She adjusted her cardigan to cover her scars and then walked into the restaurant.

Sean stood and motioned for her to join him at a corner table in the back. Ethne pointed to Sean as the hostess approached her and then headed toward the table. She pulled him into a hug. "Hey, baby brother. How've you been?"

Sean hugged her back. "Great." He gestured toward one side of the booth as he sat down across from her.

"So you said you had a surprise?"

"Not yet. Let's wait on everyone else."

"Everyone else?"

He grinned and then winked.

The basket of chips and salsa sat undisturbed in the middle of the table. Normally, he would have been chowing down. Something was up.

"Here's number three." He stood, hugged Liza, and brushed a kiss against her cheek. Then he sat after she slipped into the booth.

"Liza," Ethne said. "How are you?"

Her cheeks reddened. "Great."

Sean stood again. "And here's the last one."

Ethne glanced over her shoulder toward the entrance. Daniel was making his way toward their corner. A lump rose in her throat, and a knot filled her stomach. "You didn't mention Daniel was coming."

"I figured I didn't need to, that you two would talk."

Daniel stopped at the table. He wore khaki pants, a dress shirt, and a tie. She glanced at his feet. He wore the same brown shoes he'd worn the first day they'd met at the house.

Sean stood to shake hands. "Hey, man. Good to see you."

"Same here, Sean." He looked toward Liza. "Great to see you, too. How's that finger?"

She wiggled her forefinger in the air. "As good as new. You can hardly see where the stitches were."

"Glad to hear it."

His chocolate-kiss eyes found hers, and unwanted longing filled her. "Hi, Ethne."

"Daniel."

He glanced over his shoulder as if looking for something. Probably a chair.

Ethne scooted to the wall and patted the empty space beside her. "Have a seat."

"Thank you." He sat to the outside of the booth, careful to leave space between them, but the earthy warmth of his cologne spanned the void. The hours of the day had softened it until it was as much a part of him as his hair color or his smile. Her heart ached. She missed him, his closeness, his strength. But not enough to take him back. She could never share him with another woman.

Sean pushed the basket of chips aside and folded his hands on top of the table. As perspiration covered his forehead, he cleared his throat. "So, uh, Liza and I have a favor to ask you two."

Ethne's heart began to race. This couldn't really be happening.

"First of all, Ethne, I've asked Liza to marry me, and she's said yes. And," Sean continued, "since you're my older sister and our parents are gone, we'd like to ask your blessing."

Tears pooled in Ethne's eyes. "Oh, Sean, I'm so happy for you. Surprised, but happy. Yes…yes, you have my blessing."

He squeezed Liza's hand. "Plus, we'd like you two to be our maid of honor and best man."

Daniel stood and clapped Sean on the shoulder. "Congratulations, man. I'd be honored."

The other three turned toward Ethne, waiting. This was all so sudden, and to be paired with Daniel… But she couldn't turn them down. "Of course. As Daniel said, I'd be honored, too. Have you set a date?"

Liza snuggled up against Sean's shoulder. "Not yet, but it won't be until after football season is over."

Sean kissed her on top of the head. "Yeah, wouldn't be fair to my new bride to start our life together with her being a football widow."

"Wise man," Daniel laughed. "Just let me know when you get the date set."

Sean pulled the basket of chips to the center of the table. "Time to eat. And it's my treat."

~*~

Ethne strolled across the square toward the inn. The sun had set, and the first stars were beginning to slip through the evening sky. In the canopy of trees overhead, the cicadas grated in full voice.

So her baby brother was getting married. She would have never thought what began as some sort of macho game a few months ago would have ended up changing his life. She was happy for him. Being an attendant with Daniel would not be easy, but Sean was all the family she had left, and for him, she'd do almost anything.

"Hey, Ethne, wait up."

She could keep moving, pretending she hadn't heard. The cicadas were loud enough to cover his words this evening. But then, there was no need to be mean. She stopped and turned back toward Daniel.

He caught up with her and jammed his hands into his front pockets. He looked like a little boy asking his mom if he could stay up past his bedtime on a school night. He gazed down at the ground and then back up into her eyes. "It's nice to see you. How are you?"

"Fine. Busy."

"That's good…I guess."

She shrugged her shoulders. "Been better. Been worse."

As she moved on, he matched his steps with hers. "I was surprised about Sean and Liza."

"Me, too. I'm happy for them, but it seems a little sudden."

He stopped and grasped her hand. "When it's right, it can happen fast."

"At first you know only what you see. What the other person wants you to see. To really get to know a person's heart takes time...and patience. But then, sometimes all the time in the world won't make it right."

She squeezed his hand, looked down at his feet and then back into his eyes. "Glad to see you're wearing a pair of shoes more than once." She withdrew her hand from his, and as tears burned her eyes, she turned away. "Good night, Daniel," she whispered.

As she strode off, he called after her, "See you tomorrow?"

All she could do was nod.

~*~

The Channel Eleven News truck was set up at one end of the parking lot when Ethne arrived. A stage had been constructed at the other end with rows of folding chairs for the attendees facing it. A wide blue ribbon spanned the two poles flanking the front door into the clinic. By what could only be the grace of God, clouds filled the sky, lowering the afternoon temperature at least ten degrees.

Ethne had checked the weather before she left the inn, and no rain was predicted. Only an overcast sky. This late summer day could not have been any more perfect for the dedication.

She slipped behind the ribbon and into the clinic waiting room. A table on the left held cookies and punch provided, Ethne was certain, by the medical missions group from the church.

Talking with one of the reporters, Josh sported his regular Sunday attire, khaki pants and a tieless, button-down collar shirt. The only time she'd seen him more dressed up was for weddings and funerals.

Daniel's outfit mimicked Josh's with the addition of a tie and a lab coat. He and Sean stood in the corner, coffee cups from a local fast-food restaurant in hand.

She took a deep breath and headed toward them.

About halfway there, Daniel's gaze found her. A glimmer of sadness mixed with longing crossed his face. She recognized the emotions because the same mixture of desire and regret filled her heart. But as quickly as it appeared, it left, replaced by his professional smile. He waved and motioned her over.

Sean set his coffee down on the table and ruffled through a stack of index cards. She had none. Her speech would be brief, but respectful. After reading over Vaughn's journal and studying the scrapbook he'd made, she'd come to one conclusion. She never really knew her father. Only isolated facets of the man he was. He was a complicated mixture of opposites. A healer and destroyer. Dedicated yet unfaithful. A material provider and an emotional thief. And she grew up seeing only one side of each of the pairs.

Repairing their relationship was impossible. The past was lost forever. All she could do was safeguard the future. And that's why she had to let Daniel go. She would never risk putting herself or any children she might have in the same circumstances she lived through.

Yet, deep inside, a still, small Voice promised to redeem the wasted years if she'd only allow it.

"Dr. Spenser," Josh called. He motioned for Daniel to join him with the reporter and cameraman.

Daniel smiled at Ethne and then headed toward Josh.

"I'm nervous," Sean lamented. "Where's your cards?"

Ethne tapped one of her temples. "Filed right up here. No need to be nervous. Just tell yourself it's a pregame motivational speech for the team."

"Gee, thanks for nothing."

She chuckled. "You'll do great, Sean. You're a charming man. Just be yourself."

As the television crew exited the clinic, Josh called, "OK, let's round up here in the middle to talk over the order of the program and have a quick prayer."

~*~

Sean stood up at the podium delivering his speech, and he must be doing a great job judging by the laughter and engaged expressions on the audience's faces, but Ethne had no idea what he was saying. Or what exactly she'd said, either. All she could do was stare at the attractive blonde and the two young boys who'd scooted into the back row in the middle of Josh's welcome speech.

She glanced across the stage at Daniel. He wore an unreadable, professional expression. As well as she knew him, or at least thought she did, she had no inkling what he was thinking.

The mayor spoke next and then offered the podium to Daniel. He talked about the path that led him to Crescent Bluff. How he obtained the practice and grew the dream their fathers had. "I'm honored to continue the tradition my father and Dr. O'Connor began years ago by serving this community."

The blonde woman beamed like a proud mother. But she definitely wasn't Daniel's mother.

After Josh offered a prayer of dedication, she, Sean, and Daniel—the children of the original founders of Crescent Bluff Primary Care—walked from the stage along with Josh and the mayor to cut the ribbon.

Standing in the center, Ethne held a large pair of ornamental shears. On her right stood Sean, on her left Daniel. As they discussed before the ceremony, Sean covered her right hand with his and Daniel covered her left. Daniel's touch was magnetic. The memory of his hands on hers the day she'd showed him his bedroom revived in her a desire she might never lose. She fought the impulse to bury her head in his shoulder. Maybe if the two of them could escape, everything would be OK. Tears blurred the scissors. But that was fine. The audience would think the tears resulted from her memories of Vaughn.

As they leaned in close together and clipped the blue ribbon, a cheer arose from the crowd. The mayor and Josh joined them, and cameras clicked.

Ethne's breakfast was long gone. As the people pressed around her, she fought to breathe. Her head began to swim. She needed to find a seat before she lost it. She shoved the sheers into Sean's hands. "I've gotta sit down." As her knees weakened and her field of vision began to close in, she headed toward the nearest chair in the parking lot. Her foot went into one of the potholes and she fell.

~*~

Daniel opened the door to the center exam room. "Lay her on the table."

Sean did as instructed. "Is she OK?"

Daniel felt for her pulse. "Seems so. For some reason, she fainted." He elevated her legs. Her left ankle was swollen. "Looks like a sprained or broken ankle."

Taps sounded on the door, and then it opened. Fran stuck her head in. "Need help, Daniel?"

"Appears to be a sprained ankle. I think we'll be OK. Go enjoy the open house."

"Holler if you need anything."

Daniel gave her a thumbs-up.

Sean dropped into the chair against the wall. "It all happened so fast, I didn't really see her go down. She handed me the scissors, and next thing I knew she was on the ground."

Daniel wet some paper towels and dabbed her forehead with them. "Ethne? Ethne, wake up."

Her eyes fluttered open. Her brow knit in confusion. Her gaze searched the room. "What happened?" she slurred.

Daniel glanced down at her feet. The ankle was even larger. "I'm pretty sure you turned your ankle."

She nodded. "Oh, yeah. I got really dizzy and needed to sit down. I didn't see the pothole."

"Are you nauseated now?"

She shook her head. "I skipped lunch, and with the heat and everybody so close, I couldn't breathe."

Daniel turned back to Sean. "Hey, man, would you go see if they have any juice or something for her to drink?"

Sean closed the door behind him.

Ethne tried to push herself up onto her elbows.

"Don't get up just yet. Lie flat for a little longer." The color had begun to return to her cheeks but wasn't fully back. "So, have you ever injured your ankle before?"

She shook her head.

"Do you remember what direction the ankle turned?"

"It all happened so fast. But I'm pretty sure…inward."

"Would you mind if I examined it?"

She shook her head again.

He moved to the foot of the table and sat on the stool. He slipped off her shoe and gently palpated the swollen tissue. "I'm going to test your range of motion. Let me know if it gets too uncomfortable." As he began to manipulate the ankle, he glanced up at her face. It was screwed into a grimace, but she hadn't made a sound. "Sorry." He wanted to hold her close and kiss away the pain. Let her know how much he loved and missed her.

He gently placed her ankle back on the exam table and scooted the stool up by her head. "Do you want the good news or the bad news first?"

"The good news."

That he loved her still and always would? She probably wouldn't consider that good news. "I'm ninety-nine percent sure your ankle's only sprained and not broken. We can do an X-ray to confirm it if you'd like."

She shook her head. "And the bad news?"

"Channel Eleven got the whole thing on video."

"Oh, great…"

"But look at it this way, could be free advertising for your business."

Her gaze locked onto his, and a smile warmed her face.

His heart pounded in his ears. He grasped her hand. "Ethne, I—"

Sean pushed the door open. "They had some apple juice."

A glimmer of disappointment flashed in her eyes, and she looked toward her brother. "Thanks, Sean."

Daniel raised the head of the table. "Let me get that ankle bandaged up while you enjoy your sugary beverage."

Even though he took his time, the bandaging was finished more quickly than he might have wished. "How's that juice?"

"Good."

"Want some more?"

She shook her head.

"OK, when you get home, remember this: RICE."

"Rice?"

"RICE. Rest, Ice, Compression, Elevation. You can also take whatever pain relievers or anti-inflammatories you have at home for the discomfort and swelling. If it's not better in a couple of days, call your PCP...or me. You might need to get an X-ray. Do you have any crutches?"

She shook her head.

"I have some she can borrow," Sean offered. "From an old knee injury in college."

"Spoken like a true jock," Daniel said. "Now we just need to get someone to drive you home."

"Daniel, it's my left foot. I can still drive."

"No. Doctor's orders. No driving for at least twenty-four hours. And then no driving for longer than fifteen minutes at a time. That ought to be long enough to get you back and forth between home, work, and the grocery store. But that's it for a few days."

"You mean I can't go to work tomorrow?"

"I mean I'm recommending you stay off it and elevate it for at least a day."

"I'll be fine. Just help me out to the car."

Daniel ignored her command. "Sean, if you'll run home and get the crutches, I'll wait here with Ethne."

"Back in a few." Sean slipped out the door.

"You're being ridiculous, Daniel."

"Prudent is not ridiculous. It's for your own safety." He was not backing down.

"Whatever."

Whatever. If only he could fix whatever. Or change whatever. Or knew whatever the real reason was she no longer wanted him.

"Can I help you out to the waiting area, or would you like me to get Fran or Josh?"

"As I said, you're being ridiculous."

She held out her arms to him, and he moved beside the table to help her stand. He placed an arm around her waist and slowly guided her up onto her good foot. The soft scent of lavender, clean and pure, swelled over him. They were still together in the exam room, but he was no longer the doctor and she was no longer the patient. "Ethne, I—"

"Don't, Daniel. Please don't say something you...or I...might regret."

He nodded and looked into her face. Tears glistened in her eyes.

"I guess my ankle's a little more sore than I realized."

She was mourning just as he was. He could say so much, but she wasn't in the place to listen. "Confirmation of the wisdom of my orders not to drive."

In silence, they hobbled to the door and out of the room into the waiting area. Small clusters of people stood or sat enjoying the refreshments. Contemporary Christian music played in the background. Small groups walked in and out of the other two exam rooms.

"Danny." J-squared came running over.

"Hi, guys. This is my friend, Ms. O'Connor. Be careful, now. Her ankle's hurt." Daniel helped her sit. "Ethne, this is Jeremy and Jared."

"Wow," Jeremy said. "Cool bandage. Did Danny do that?"

"Yes. He's an excellent doctor," Ethne replied.

"Yeah," Jared said. "That's what Mommy says."

Savannah joined them, "Boys, don't bother Ms. O'Connor."

If he'd known Savannah and the boys were coming, he would have made sure to talk with Ethne. To explain. But true to Savannah's pattern, she'd just shown up. No warning, no explanation. "Ethne, this is an old friend of mine, Savannah Ross. Savannah, this is Ethne O'Connor."

~*~

Ethne lay in the backseat of Josh's car. He'd tuned the radio to some oldies rock station when they'd left the clinic. She'd excused herself as being tired and then played possum since they got on the road. She loved Josh, but he never had a problem asking probing questions. And tonight, she wasn't in the mood to try to deflect them. Questions about Daniel, and her...and Savannah.

So, Savannah was the blonde who'd driven up that day Ethne tried to find Daniel's house to tell him about her experience at the waterfall. She was Daniel's first love. And the boys...they called Daniel "Daddy."

In his bedroom that afternoon when she'd thrown herself at him, he made it sound as if he and Savannah had only been together in college. But judging by the age of the boys, that was a lie. They'd obviously had a long-term relationship. It may have been on again and off again. But it wasn't as "over" as Daniel made it sound.

Josh's phone rang through the car speaker.

"Josh Lewis."

"It's Daniel."

He was following them to Fort Worth in Ethne's car.

"Hey."

"I just got a call from the Embassy in Beijing."

Why would Daniel be getting a phone call from Beijing?

"Hold on." Josh paused a moment. "OK. Go ahead."

He must have taken the phone off speaker, because she could no longer hear Daniel's voice.

"Oh, man. I'm so sorry."

Ethne's heart began to race. His mother. It had to be something to do with Daniel's mother.

"Yeah, we'll talk about it on the way back home. I really am sorry. Praying for you."

As Josh changed the channel, the music on the radio transitioned from rock to contemporary Christian. She knew him. He was praying right now, so she waited.

After a couple of minutes, she sat up. "Josh. Sorry to bother you."

"Hey, girl, did you have a nice nap? How's that ankle?"

"What's going on with Daniel?"

26

The line was almost as long as it had been for Vaughn's memorial service, a sign of the love Crescent Bluff had for their new doctor. Ethne leaned close to Alicia. "Thanks for coming with me today. I didn't think I could make it by myself."

"What are good friends for, if you can't use them every now and then?" Alicia hugged her. "Seriously, I would never have let you come alone."

Daniel and Ethne had exchanged places. Today he stood flanked by Josh and Savannah, and Ethne took his spot near the end of the line. The memorial service for his mother had been moving. Josh and Daniel's family pastor did a wonderful job of helping the attendees who hadn't known Grace Spenser feel as if she was a sweet friend by the end of the service.

Three more people ahead of her. A lump rose in her throat, and her heart began to race. What if he didn't want to talk with her? What if he wouldn't? She shouldn't have come. She stepped back and whispered, "Alicia, I think I made a mistake."

"What do you mean?"

"Coming today. He's not going to want to see me. He's with Savannah."

Alicia leaned close. "People don't seek comfort where they hope they'll find it. They seek it where they know they will. What other choice did you give him?"

None. She'd offered him no other choice. But in many ways, he'd made his decision and chosen long before she entered his life.

The line crept forward and her turn came. Savannah took her hand, leaned forward, and placed a cheek against hers. "Thank you for coming. It will mean a lot to Danny."

The people speaking with Daniel moved on, and Ethne was next.

She took a deep breath and stepped forward. She held out her hand. "I hope you don't mind that I came."

He ignored her hand and drew her close. "I hoped you would. Thank you." His coarse whisper warmed her ear.

She leaned her head against his chest. "I'm sorry, Daniel. So sorry." And she was. Sorry for the loss of his mother, but also sorry for their loss of each other.

He hugged her tight and then drew away. Sadness shimmered in his eyes. "Thanks, again. I understand how hard it must have been for you to come."

As she drew away and moved toward Josh, Daniel grasped her hand and drew her back. "Hey."

She wanted him to say he loved her and he'd been wrong and made a mistake. That he didn't love Savannah and never had. But that would be one more lie to add to his collection.

"How's your ankle?"

"Fine. You're a good doctor."

~*~

The office was closed for the memorial service today. Daniel unlocked the front door and quickly pushed in the code to silence the alarm. He held the door open wider so Vanna could join him.

"Danny, oh, my goodness. Look at all the flowers."

Some of his patients and the other businesses in town had been overly generous with flower arrangements and cards. The place looked like a florist shop. They sure made him feel loved and appreciated. "Wait 'til you see the food upstairs from all the church ladies. I won't have to cook 'til Thanksgiving if I play my cards right."

He'd been in Crescent Bluff less than six months, but it was home. He loved it here, and over the past few weeks he'd begun to understand that maybe God had brought him here not for Ethne as he'd originally thought, but for the people…and for him. He'd never felt this settled and this much at home.

He and Vanna climbed up the stairs to his apartment. Even though the two of them were officially dating again, this was the first time she'd seen the place. He always came up to Fort Worth. It was just easier with the boys.

"Wow. So Ethne did all this, huh?"

"Yes. She's talented way beyond her realization."

"That's for sure. These rooms look like something out of a decorating magazine."

His heart ached. "I know. I've told her that several times."

She wandered into the kitchen and opened the refrigerator. "You need to get this food into the freezer if you want it to last. When will you redo the kitchen?"

"The kitchen? Why?"

"It's so outdated. I'd definitely knock out a couple of walls and put in an island. Install marble counter tops."

Yeah, she would. He shrugged. "I'm fine with it the way it is."

"You're probably right. It's not worth investing all that money into a place where you won't be living permanently."

"Who says I won't be here long term? Not forever, sure. But I like the town. The people. The size of my practice is perfect. Just what I always envisioned."

"Well, I just figured… What about the house in Fort Worth?"

"I haven't decided what I'll do with my folks' house. Nothing for a while. It's too soon. But don't worry. You and the boys can stay there until I get it figured out."

"I just assumed you'd be moving back up there once you get everything straightened out and sold down here."

He'd forgotten how demanding and pushy she could be. "What if I decide to sell the Fort Worth house and stay down here?"

She laughed. "You're kidding, right? You wouldn't dare give up that fabulous house in Westover Hills."

He hadn't decided. "It's just a house. Make yourself at home while I change really quick."

She dropped onto the couch as he scaled the stairs to the bedroom. He walked into the closet and flipped on the light. He slipped off his black tasseled loafers and set them on the shoe rack in his closet. He was down to about twenty pair and still culling them out.

Too bad relationships couldn't be as easy as buying shoes. But then, maybe that's why they were so special. People were irreplaceable. He took off his dress shirt and socks and dropped them into the hamper. He exchanged his dress pants for a pair of shorts, and then stepped out of the closet to get a T-shirt.

She was sitting on the bed.

He jumped. "Vanna, what are you doing up here? I'm getting dressed."

"You're dressed enough." She winked. "And don't be so weird. I've seen you in your swimming trunks at the house. Not much different than this. Plus, I've even seen you in a lot less, if you remember." She giggled.

He remembered, but he wished he didn't.

"And I must say, the Air Force and the years have been very good to you, Danny Spenser. Very, very good."

He pulled a T-shirt out of the dresser, jerked it down over his head, and jammed his arms into the sleeves. No longing filled him as it had that afternoon with Ethne. Nothing about this situation held any appeal for him. "Let me grab some shoes, and I'll be ready to go."

"You're so cute when you're embarrassed."

He went back into the closet and sat on the bench. If this was God's plan to make everything beautiful, he could learn to accept it, but it wouldn't be easy. And it certainly wasn't what he'd imagined a few weeks ago.

He slipped on a pair of hiking sandals and then stepped back into the bedroom. She'd found the gift bag. The gift he'd bought but never given to Ethne—would never be able to give her. He'd kept it for far too long. He should have tossed it when she tossed their relationship, but he couldn't.

Savannah was replacing the cover on the box that had been inside. Her eyes glimmered and her cheeks glowed red.

"What are you doing, Savannah?"

"Something I obviously shouldn't be." She slipped the box back into the bag. "I just saw the bag and assumed..."

"I've had it a while. I couldn't exactly return it."

"This isn't working, is it?"

"What isn't working?"

"You and me."

"I'm trying, Vanna. I am trying. I just need more time."

She slipped her hand in his. "I'll give you as much time as you need."

He squeezed her hand and then grabbed the gift bag. He'd stick it in the truck until he decided what to do with it. "Ready to go?"

~*~

Ethne leaned her head against the passenger window. "Thanks for driving today."

"Glad to do it," Alicia replied. "It was hard, wasn't it?"

"Hard?"

"Yeah, seeing Daniel so sad."

"Yes." Seeing him so sad and not being able to comfort him, to help bear his sorrow. Tears burned her eyes as she stared toward the blazing orange sky painted by the sun kissing the horizon. As Daniel had said, a reflection of the beautiful heart of his Father, now her Father.

"He doesn't love her, you know."

"What?"

"That Savannah woman. He doesn't love her."

"I don't know that, and I don't know how you can think you do."

"Oh, I know. All I have to do is see his eyes when he looks at you. She may have been the one standing next to him, but you're the one he wanted it to be."

"Well, as Grandmother O'Connor used to say, 'You can't have your cake and eat it, too.' He's chosen, and maybe he's made a mistake. I don't know. But one mistake doesn't need to birth another."

The glow in the western sky deepened to rich maroon. One of the verses Daniel had written on the list in her Bible resounded within her heart.

For I know the plans I have for you…plans to prosper you and not to harm you, plans to give you hope and a future.

A few years ago, she would have said it was ridiculous to believe that the omnipotent God who planned and cared for the tiniest detail of creation loved and cared for her so much He had a plan for her future long before she was born. Long before she even acknowledged Him. And when she'd been afraid or in pain, He'd hurt right along with her.

But now she knew it was not impossible. Deep in her heart, a Voice reassured her everything in her life would be used for her benefit. She only needed to allow it.

The stars in the sky overhead winked at her. Maybe Daniel's Dad had been right and God was just showing off.

27

The color of Sean's face fluctuated between ghostly white and sickly gray. Daniel's first impulse was to have him lie on the ground in the garden behind the little chapel and prop his feet up on some of the small boulders that edged the walkways.

"I don't think I'm gonna make it," Sean said. He dropped onto one of the benches.

Josh slapped him on the knee. "Sure you will. It's first down and goal, and you're inside the one."

"What if I trip and get tackled?"

"Daniel and I aren't gonna let that happen, are we?"

Daniel placed a hand on Sean's shoulder. "I got your back, man. I'll make sure you get into the end zone."

Liza and Sean hadn't been able to wait even a month to get married since they first announced their intentions, much less until after football season. But they were adults. No reason to wait as far as Daniel could see. So, the five of them were gathering in the prayer garden behind the old chapel for an impromptu wedding.

Sean took a deep breath. "OK. Let's do it."

Josh led them to the gazebo and picked up an acoustic guitar. He began playing that "Canon" song all of Daniel's buddies had used for their weddings.

The door on the back of the chapel opened and out stepped Liza and Ethne. The bride was in a short, white dress, and the maid of honor wore a full length, baby blue, gauzy gown. The wind ruffled her copper hair as the loose curls bounced below her shoulders. The maid of honor wasn't supposed to outshine the bride, but she did. Not on purpose. She had no control over her beauty.

Liza carried three white roses, and Ethne carried a pink one. That was all the grocery store had when Daniel went by after work. Not much, but every bride needed a bouquet.

Liza looped her arm through Sean's, and they turned to face Josh. Ethne and Daniel stood behind them, a little to the sides. But not too far. Daniel still wasn't convinced Sean wouldn't pass out. He wanted to stay close enough to break the fall, if necessary.

Josh began reading the "Love" chapter from Corinthians.

Daniel's gaze drifted from the pastor to the woman he still loved. He was trying with Vanna, but it wasn't working. He couldn't see how it ever would. How he'd ever love her as much as he loved Ethne. What was that old adage? "Fake it 'til you make it." He'd been doing a lot of faking these past few weeks in hopes his attempts would become truth. But they hadn't yet. If he knew what the issue was with Ethne, he could fix it.

"Sean," Josh said, "repeat after me. 'I, Sean, take you, Lisa'…"

I, Daniel, take you, Ethne…

~*~

Ethne's gaze found Daniel's. Despite the evening breeze, heat scalded her cheeks. The longing that filled his eyes resonated within her soul. But she could do nothing to satisfy the yearning that consumed them both.

Josh turned to Liza. "Liza, repeat after me. 'I, Liza, take you, Sean…'"

I, Ethne, take you, Daniel…

Ethne laced her fingers together around the stem of the rose to keep from reaching over and taking his hand. She wanted to tell him she still loved him. But her love wouldn't change reality. What happened had happened no matter how she felt about him or he felt about her. And he hadn't been honest with her. A relationship built on deceit would never stand.

Being married to Daniel could never be God's perfect plan for her. Her entire life had been tainted by Vaughn's infidelity. And this mess needed to stop with her. The last thing she wanted was for a daughter of hers to discover in twenty years she had half-siblings she'd never known about.

"By the authority vested in me by the State of Texas…"

Tears filled her eyes. Her baby brother was married.

"You may kiss your bride."

Sean cradled Liza's face in his wide-receiver hands and bent down. He placed his lips on hers.

Ethne burned with the memory of Daniel's lips against hers. Her heart ached for his touch.

Josh cleared his throat, and Mr. and Mrs. O'Connor drew apart. "I have only one more thing to say." He winked and then lifted both hands straight in the air. "Touchdown."

~*~

Daniel offered his hand to Sean. "Told you I had your back. Congratulations."

Josh picked up his guitar again. "Every couple needs a first dance." He began playing and singing.

Sean turned back to his new bride and bowed. "May I have this dance, Mrs. O'Connor?" Liza snuggled up against him in response.

Ethne sat on one of the benches, and Daniel moved to stand behind her. He leaned down and whispered, "I'm happy for them."

"Me, too. I can't believe my little brother really is a man. A fine man, I might add."

Josh transitioned to another song.

Sean came and took Ethne's hand, and then Liza grasped his. "Can the bride ask the best man to dance?"

"My pleasure." They moved farther out into the garden. "I had no idea Josh was so talented."

Liza nodded. "Sean said he used to play in a band before he went into the ministry."

Daniel could see that.

Sean tapped him on the shoulder. "Sorry, dude. I'm missing my bride."

Daniel bowed. "Thanks for the dance, Liza."

As Sean gathered Liza to him, he called over his shoulder, "Hey, man. Don't leave my sister hanging."

Ethne's cheeks turned crimson. "I'm sorry, Daniel. He shouldn't have said that."

"It would be my pleasure to finish this dance with you." He held his hand out, but she didn't move. "Don't make Sean think I didn't follow his instructions."

She shrugged her shoulders and then closed the space between them. He drew her close and began moving in time to the music. The wind swirled through the jasmine covering the gazebo, its sweet scent mixing with the soft, powdery fragrance of her perfume. Memories of her nearness that afternoon in his bedroom flowed over him.

He tightened his embrace and rested his cheek against her head. She had to be able to feel his heart pounding. "Ethne, I'm sorry. I should have—'

She drew away. "You're quite the dancer, Dr. Spenser. I had no idea."

"Ethne, I—"

"Have you had lessons?"

He may as well be dancing and talking with a complete stranger right now. Not the woman he loved. "Dad wanted me to play soccer, but Mom said only if I took cotillion, too."

"Really? I had no idea people still did that."

"Mom always said every gentleman should know how to dance well enough not to embarrass his date, his family, or himself." He stopped and drew away. "Am I embarrassing you?"

Her eyes searched his. "No."

"Mission accomplished."

"Your mom would be proud of you. For that reason and for many others."

A knot swelled within his chest. He struggled to breathe. He dropped her hand. "Excuse me."

He was on the verge of losing it. He made a beeline around to the front of the chapel and climbed into his truck. It was all too much. He'd lost Dad, Mom, Ethne. He didn't love Vanna, but right now she was the only person he had left.

Ethne came running around the corner of the building before he could get the truck started. She rapped on his door. He took a deep breath, blew out through his mouth, and then opened the door.

Her eyes glistened. "Daniel, I'm so sorry. How insensitive of me."

He shook his head. If he tried to say anything, it would be all over.

"Please forgive me." Tears spilled from her eyes and striped her cheeks. Then she whispered, "Please?"

All he could do was nod. He closed the door and started the engine. He backed out of the parking lot. He wanted to go to the waterfall, but it would be too dark by the time he got there. He'd drive wherever the truck led him until he could go no farther.

28

Where the Spirit of the Lord is, there is freedom. 2 Corinthians 3:17

Ethne glanced at the clock on her desk phone. She had a few minutes before the store opened. She pulled her cell out of her purse to call him.

The day after Sean's wedding, Ethne called Daniel three times and left messages. He'd looked so sad when he drove away after the ceremony, and she needed to know he was OK. But her calls went to voice mail, and he never replied.

The following few days afterward, she called once each morning. When his voice mail answered, she hung up. He'd see her number in his call log and know she called. And exactly how many times.

And she knew how many times he'd chosen to ignore her. She'd hurt him, but he'd hurt her, too. Neither was innocent.

She changed her mind and dropped her phone back into her purse.

A verse from today's devotion had haunted her since she read it this morning.

Where the Spirit of the Lord is, there is freedom.

Hadn't she prayed and asked for freedom? And hadn't her Father granted it to her? Yes. He was Freedom.

But she had returned His gift. The prison bars had started creeping upward, and the links to the chain were beginning to interlock with each other once again.

Unforgiveness is a prison.

Daniel's words rang as loudly in her soul as if he'd spoken them here in her office right this minute, and regret squeezed her heart. She'd believed she had offered and accepted forgiveness, but all she'd done was exchange one bondage for another. She'd vacated one prison cell only to move down the hall into another. She was not free.

Her Father had offered her His Spirit of freedom, but instead of accepting it with empty hands, she put conditions on it. She had tamped it down and covered it over with fear and hurt until His perfect gift was no longer visible.

And now she needed to know if her Father would once again meet her in her prison cell and lead her out of captivity into freedom.

She set her office phone to "Do not disturb," rested her head on her desk, and prayed.

~*~

Ethne's cell phone rang. Maybe Daniel was calling her back. She pulled it out of her purse. "Hello."

"Sorry to bother you, Eth." Alicia said in a hushed tone. "A customer is asking for you."

"I don't have any appointments today."

"I know, but I really think you should meet with this client."

"Who is it?"

"Trust me. Just grab a legal pad and come out."

Ethne slipped on her jacket and stepped out onto the showroom floor.

Alicia nodded toward the back corner that served as the conference area. She smiled and held up a "you-can-do-it" fist.

Ethne checked her left sleeve to make sure it covered the scars. She stood tall and walked around the hutch to the table.

Savannah stood. "Hello, Ethne. Thanks for seeing me without an appointment."

A lead weight plummeted to the bottom of her stomach. "Is everything... Is Daniel OK?"

"Not really. Physically he's fine, but emotionally? No."

"I'm sorry." She motioned for Savannah to sit and then followed suit. "I'm not sure what I can do to help."

"I don't know how much Danny told you about our history."

More than she wished. "I know you dated in college. I know he asked you to marry him, and that you turned him down." And she knew more that she wouldn't say.

Tears filled Savannah's eyes. "The biggest mistake I ever made."

"Everybody makes mistakes and has regrets. But at least you have the boys. And I'm sure they like having their father around."

"Their father? He's not around. That jerk ran off with his secretary."

Daniel and Sarah? Ethne wanted to throw up. While she was falling in love with him, throwing herself at him, he was stringing along at least two other women. He'd played her, but she'd been too stupid and naïve to see any of it, because he was really good at it. Really good, just as Vaughn had been. "I never would have thought Daniel—"

"Danny? What about Danny?"

"Their father."

"Danny's not their father. Believe me. If he was, I wouldn't be in this mess. Danny would never do to us what Will has done."

"But I heard the boys call him..." Danny. They all called him Danny, and in her surprise and confusion she'd heard...

Regret crushed her chest until she struggled to breathe. She'd made a terrible mistake. She should have trusted the quiet Voice deep in her heart. She should have listened to Alicia and talked with Daniel. Then none of this would have happened.

She thought she was building a wall of protection around her heart, but it was a wall of separation. Her stubbornness and self-preservation had won the battle but destroyed at least two lives. "Oh, Savannah, I've made a terrible mistake."

Savannah nodded. "I know. That's why I came. I tried to get Danny back, but his heart was already taken. There's no reason for you to end up like me when a wonderful man loves you." She reached down and picked up a gift bag from the floor. She slid it across the table to Ethne. "I stole this out of his truck, but he really bought it for you."

No gift tag hung from the handle. "How do you know it's for me?"

"I assumed it was for me, so I opened it. I'm really sorry. Now it's your turn."

The gift bag was mint green. Soft pink, lavender, and yellow flowers covered the tissue paper protruding from the top. She drew out the tissue and set it aside on the table. Then she reached into the bag and slid out the gift box. She recognized it. The top was navy blue and the bottom gold foil just like a box Daniel sent her weeks ago. She shook her head and slipped the box back into the bag. "This isn't for me. He already gave me a Bible like this."

Savannah grasped Ethne's hand and stopped her from reaching for the tissue. "Just open it, please."

Ethne pulled the box out of the bag again and slowly lifted the lid. This time the now familiar warm smell of leather combined with the earthiness of his cologne and brought tears to her eyes. Daniel had also held this Bible. She set the lid aside and slowly folded back the protective tissue.

The bottom corner of the cover bore a name in gold. Just as hers at home did. But the letters spelled out a different name.

Savannah rested a hand on hers. "Mistakes have broken enough lives. It's time to let God put a few back together."

~*~

The crispness of the breeze confirmed winter lingered around the corner. The temperature was at least ten degrees cooler than it had been the first time she came here. Today she wore long sleeves for warmth, not to cover her secret scars. They no longer needed to be hidden.

She maneuvered across the rough stone floor and through the narrow passageway. She turned left and stood at the entrance to the ledge. Daniel sat on the far end, knees to his chest, arms around his legs, chin resting on his knees. His gaze was fixed outward, on some point beyond the waterfall.

She looked at the man but saw the child. Here sat the little boy who'd been a mistake, unwanted, cast aside, orphaned. And now he was alone once again. But not unwanted. She loved and wanted him more than he could ever know, more than her words could ever express.

"Daniel?"

He made no move. The roaring of the waterfall, though less intense inside here than outside, still drowned out her voice.

She made her way to him and rested a hand on his shoulder. He startled and turned toward her. His face reddened.

"I'm sorry. I called your name, but the noise of the falls was too loud for you to hear me."

He turned away and stared back through the shifting window of water toward the canyon outside. "No problem."

"Mind if I join you?"

He shook his head.

She slipped off her backpack and sat beside him. "I came here by myself one day."

He nodded.

"I jumped."

His gaze found hers for the first time. "You should have called me. I would have come with you, you know."

"I needed to jump alone. Just me and God."

He nodded. "I get it." He reached over and squeezed her hand. "I'm happy for you."

She entwined her fingers with his and drew his hand into her lap. He let it stay.

He faced the shimmering curtain again. "Help me understand what happened, Ethne. I thought I was open about my feelings for you. That I let you know I loved you. And I thought you felt the same."

"Daniel—"

"Was it something I did? Or didn't do? In the bedroom that day, was that the reason?"

"No, Daniel, no. I watched my father, and it taught me men wanted only one thing from a woman. But you...you showed me all men aren't like my father. When you refused, it proved you valued me as a whole person."

"'Worth far more than rubies.'"

"What?"

"Nothing."

"Your refusal that day only made me love you more. More than I ever thought I could love anyone."

He drew his hand away, and his gaze left hers and returned to the waterfall. "Somehow, I didn't get that message."

"I know, and it's my fault." Tears burned her eyes. Her voice faded to a whisper. "After I jumped, I went by the office to tell you. But Sarah said you had an emergency and had gone to Fort Worth. So, I decided to drive to your parents' house and surprise you."

"You never showed up."

"Yes, I did, but… Oh, Daniel, I've made a terrible mistake. And I need to ask your forgiveness."

"You don't have an exclusive on mistakes." His voice was flat.

"I saw you through the gate, playing soccer with two little boys."

"Jeremy and Jared. So?"

"I heard them call you 'Daddy.'"

"They've never called me that." His tone was sharp. "Uncle, but never Daddy. They have a father, and it's not me."

"I know that now. They called you Danny, but my ears heard Daddy."

He jumped up and strode toward the back wall. He pressed his forehead against the rock. "So, two little letters have ruined our lives? You should have said something to me."

She moved to stand behind him. "I know that now, but then I… Other than Josh, you're the first man I've believed I could trust, and when I thought you betrayed me and lied to me, that you were no different from my father, I withdrew back into my cell of self-protection."

"It hurts to know you didn't trust me."

"The last thing I ever want to do is hurt you. I'm so sorry. Please forgive me."

He turned to face her. His eyes glistened. "I've been sitting here praying for direction. Asking God to take away my feelings for you. And then you show up. What am I supposed to think about that?"

"That your prayer was answered? But maybe not in the way you thought it would be."

He leaned back against the cave wall and stared toward the water.

She turned and picked up her backpack. She unzipped it, withdrew the gift bag, and held it out to him.

"What are you doing with this? How did you get it?"

"Savannah brought it by the store."

"Savannah? No wonder I couldn't find it."

"Open it for me."

He shook his head.

"A person I love and admire once told me unforgiveness is a prison. It took me a while to understand, but now I know it's true. And then that same person asked me a question."

"'And what will you do about it?'" He remembered.

"Yes." She withdrew the box from the bag and held it out to him. "So, what will you do?"

The intensity from his eyes reached deep into her heart. He moved his gaze from her eyes to the box, and then back. She understood the battle within him. She'd been fighting the same one for months now. Could he trust her enough to reveal his deepest hopes and dreams to her? To invite her to be a part of them?

Slowly, he traced the edges of the box with his fingertips. Then he grasped the sides of the lid and inched it upward. He set it down on the stone slab beneath their feet. As his fingers brushed against the tissue cover, her tears blurred the image before her. Drawing the paper back, he unveiled the cover of the Bible. The gold letters in the bottom corner spelled out *Ethne Spenser*.

"Yes," she whispered.

"What?"

"Yes. I want that to be my Bible. I want that to be my name. I want to spend the rest of my life married to you. You, Daniel Spenser, are the man I never thought existed, and God brought you to me."

He took the box from her and set it on the ledge beside them. Then he drew her against him. She wrapped her arms around his waist and leaned into his embrace. The beating of his heart shook her entire being.

His hands cupped her face, and as he rested his forehead against hers, his chocolate-kiss eyes melted her heart. Peace flowed through her, and she drew away. She reached up and stroked his cheek with the back of her hand. She traced his lips with her fingertips. "I love you, Daniel Spenser," she whispered.

He grasped her left hand and drew her arm upward. He placed delicate, healing kisses on the scars checkering her forearm. "I'm sorry you had to experience this, my love."

She withdrew her arm and reached her hands around his waist once more. She leaned her head against his chest. She could stay in the warmth of his embrace forever.

He fingered her curls and loosened the ponytail until her hair fell in ringlets over her shoulders. He grasped handfuls of curls and kissed them. Then he smoothed her hair back from her face and put his fingertips under her chin. He drew her face upward. Searching and hungry, her lips met his. As he deepened the kiss, his yearning fueled hers.

They had to stop.

He drew away first and rested his forehead against hers. His gaze pierced deep to the core of her being. "What are you doing for the rest of the day?" he whispered.

"I know what I want to do."

"Me, too. But…" He straightened and pulled his phone out of his pocket. As he tapped in a number, he winked. "Hey, Josh. I wonder if you'd have some time later today when Ethne and I could drop by. We need to talk with you about something." He laughed out loud. "Maybe. See you then."

"What's so funny?"

"He wanted to know if the three of us would be taking a road trip to Oklahoma."

That made no sense. "Oklahoma? What's so funny about that?"

"No waiting period."

"I love you, Daniel."

He brushed his lips against her hair. "I love you more."

She grasped his hand and turned toward the falls. "Jump with me."

"I think I just did."

29

Ethne waddled over to unlock the door. The Crescent Bluff branch of Resurrections celebrated its first anniversary last week. She hadn't been sure Mary Grace would postpone her arrival long enough for Ethne to make it through the festivities, but she had.

As she headed back to the counter, the front door chimed. She turned. The man she loved, the father of her soon-coming daughter, smiled at her. "Good morning, Mrs. Spenser."

"Good morning, Dr. Spenser. Why aren't you with your patients?"

"I had to make a special delivery before you make yours." He winked and drew a velvet box out of his pocket and held it out to her.

She lifted the lid to reveal a necklace bearing a ruby heart pendant. "Oh, Daniel. It's beautiful."

"I never thought you could be more beautiful than the day we met, but you are." He stepped behind her and clasped it around her neck. "'A wife of noble character who can find? She is worth far more than rubies.'" His whisper sent delicious shivers through every inch of her body.

Liza came out from the back. "Daniel, would you please convince your wife to go home and get off her feet? I've got everything under control."

He held his hands up in surrender. "I've been trying to do that for the last month with no success. But keep it up. Maybe you'll have a better outcome."

Ethne grasped her husband's hand and led him to the front door. "Remember when you told me that if I would just wait for God's perfect timing, I'd have lots of wonderful things to tell about our relationship?"

He nodded and kissed her cheek. "Yep. And, was I right?"

She leaned forward and whispered, "I'm thinking of writing a book. Or if things keep going the way they are, maybe a whole library full."

The night is nearly over; the day is almost here. So let us put aside the deeds of darkness and put on the armor of light. ~ Romans 13: 12

When we have been abused in some way, we often suffer long-term negative emotions. We feel unworthy of love, but our hearts cry out for tranquility. Instinctually, we know that we are not at fault and often we want revenge, or at least a form of justice that sees our abuser suffering a similar fate. We want the abuser to pay for their sins. But God wants us to be free to love and have joy. Extending forgiveness without justice is extremely hard. God promises that one day, He'll visit justice upon those who do evil, and we have to leave our vengeance in His hands.

In **No Longer a Captive**, the protagonist has taken drastic measures to ensure she will never again be abused and that she never becomes an abuser. But her lifestyle isn't moving her towards the love and happiness God intends for all of us. Coming home, she faces the worst time of her life, and finds that all is not as it seems.

Have you ever been wronged by someone and found it difficult to forgive? The worse the offense, the harder it is to forgive, it seems, but it's important to remember that forgiveness isn't weakness. It's actually strength. And, forgiveness doesn't benefit the offender, it benefits you. It removes a stone from around your neck that keeps you trapped in a pit of ill feelings, anger, hatred and bitterness. When you forgive, those negative emotions vanish—if not immediately, then with time—and you are freed from recrimination and feelings of unworthiness. God loves you as you are. He will comfort you and He will see justice is served for you.

LORD, HELP ME TO FORGIVE OTHERS WHO HURT ME, AND TO SHOW HOW MUCH YOU VALUE AND LOVE ALL OF US. IN JESUS' NAME I PRAY, AMEN.

Thank you

We appreciate you reading this White Rose Publishing title. For other inspirational stories, please visit our on-line bookstore at www.pelicanbookgroup.com.

For questions or more information, contact us at customer@pelicanbookgroup.com.

White Rose Publishing
Where Faith is the Cornerstone of Love™
an imprint of Pelican Book Group
www.PelicanBookGroup.com

Connect with Us
www.facebook.com/Pelicanbookgroup
www.twitter.com/pelicanbookgrp

To receive news and specials, subscribe to our bulletin
http://pelink.us/bulletin

May God's glory shine through
this inspirational work of fiction.

AMDG

You Can Help!

At Pelican Book Group it is our mission to entertain readers with fiction that uplifts the Gospel. It is our privilege to spend time with you awhile as you read our stories.

We believe you can help us to bring Christ into the lives of people across the globe. And you don't have to open your wallet or even leave your house!

Here are 3 simple things you can do to help us bring illuminating fiction™ to people everywhere.

1) If you enjoyed this book, write a positive review. Post it at online retailers and websites where readers gather. And share your review with us at reviews@pelicanbookgroup.com (this does give us permission to reprint your review in whole or in part.)

2) If you enjoyed this book, recommend it to a friend in person, at a book club or on social media.

3) If you have suggestions on how we can improve or expand our selection, let us know. We value your opinion. Use the contact form on our web site or e-mail us at customer@pelicanbookgroup.com

God Can Help!

Are you in need? The Almighty can do great things for you. Holy is His Name! He has mercy in every generation. He can lift up the lowly and accomplish all things. Reach out today.

Do not fear: I am with you; do not be anxious: I am your God. I will strengthen you, I will help you, I will uphold you with my victorious right hand.

~Isaiah 41:10 (NAB)

We pray daily, and we especially pray for everyone connected to Pelican Book Group—that includes you! If you have a specific need, we welcome the opportunity to pray for you. Share your needs or praise reports at http://pelink.us/pray4us

Free eBook Offer

We're looking for booklovers like you to partner with us! Join our team of influencers today and periodically receive free eBooks!

For more information
Visit http://pelicanbookgroup.com/booklovers

How About Free Audiobooks?

We're looking for audiobook lovers, too! Partner with us as an audiobook lover and periodically receive free audiobooks!

For more information
Visit http://pelicanbookgroup.com/booklovers/freeaudio.html

or e-mail
booklovers@pelicanbookgroup.com